MAKING TIME

Visit us at www.boldstrokesbooks.com

By the Author

Dreams of Bali

Magic of the Heart

First Love

Making Time

MAKING TIME

by

C.J. Harte

2014

Credits
Editor: Cindy Cresap
Production Design: Susan Ramundo
Cover Design By Sheri (graphicartist2020@hotmail.com)

Acknowledgments

Although writing can be solitary, this book wouldn't exist if it weren't for the efforts of many people. Thank you to Gail, who reads first drafts and always gives positive feedback. Thank you, Cindy Cresap, my hard-working editor, who takes my good intentions and helps me shape a novel into a fantastic manuscript. To my many friends who give me moral support and provide chicken soup when I get sick—thank you for keeping me going. I want to thank Radclyffe for encouraging so many of us. She is not only a great writer, but an inspiration.

Dedication

Mary Harris, December 22, 1952–February 14, 2014.
She was my first lover, my dearest friend, and my biggest
fan. Thank you for making time for me.

PART ONE
FINDING TIME

CHAPTER ONE

Huge mansions dotted the landscape. They oozed wealth and exclusivity. Mia Daniels once again felt like an intruder. She had once been plopped down in the largest and most ostentatious of estates and then banished, permanently. Very little seemed to have changed. She was still an outsider, a fake. The memory of a certain evening fifteen years ago still elicited an intense visceral reaction. Every mile that brought her closer to that destination increased her level of discomfort. Bile rose in her throat.

Mia slammed her hand against the steering wheel and pulled the car over to the side of the road. The engine was running, but the car wasn't moving. And neither was she. Natalie's whispered words danced in circles in her head. *You need to let go. Let me love you. You need to let go. Let me love you. You need to let go before you can love me.*

Mia was stuck. She desperately wanted to turn around and go back to her safe life. That life no longer existed. If she moved forward, she had to let go of memories and shattered dreams. That didn't seem safe, either.

"This is getting me nowhere." She wiped a tear, then turned up the radio. The day was too nice to be drowning in such morose thoughts. Her entire adult life was spent stuck in the past. She pushed her sunglasses up on her nose and resumed driving. She knew all too well the fragility of life. She was determined now to grasp it and live it. And not keep making the same mistakes. To do so meant moving forward. She put her foot down on the accelerator.

The top on the rental convertible was down, and the breeze, blowing through her recently cropped hair, reminded her that she was alive. She could choose to heal. She brushed her hand through her hair and began to hum. The breeze felt like a caress as it gently passed through her hair. The sun covering her face and arms was warm and healing. It was time.

All too soon, she was turning into a well-manicured drive. Thick grass stopped exactly at the edge of the blacktop. Not one blade even leaned in the wrong direction. The tree limbs were trimmed and hung at least ten feet above the road. She briefly wondered if even nature bent itself to the demands of the dwellers. An eight-foot tall wall separated the residents from the less worthy. Mia had finally arrived at the one place she had carefully avoided all her adult life. Stanton Estate.

Large wrought iron gates guarded the entrance. Mia drove up and gave her name. The guard, like his surroundings, was formidable and cold. His condescending expression failed to dissuade her. She carefully hid a smile when he found her name on the approved list. The gates opening not only allowed Mia to drive in but to face her ghosts.

Her father's promotion to chief financial officer had been her entrance into this magical world. Her family moved from their small apartment in the city to one of the large homes nearby, available only to Stanton's highest level executives. Mia was ten and had been in awe. Glittering parties, people all dressed up, the music and dancing. How often she had watched and pretended.

One person, however, always captured her attention. One person occupied her thoughts and dreams. One person aroused such intense emotions that teenaged Mia wandered around in a happy fog imagining herself in love and loved. Until the day her world came crashing down. Mia sighed. *Stop! You can't keep doing this.*

Huge, heavy double doors guarded the entrance to the inner sanctum of the main dwelling. Large, imposing columns rose up to intimidate anyone approaching the front. Mia shivered and stopped short of the entrance just as the front door was opening. Jeremy Stanton was one of her oldest and closest friends. Only their friendship would entice her to visit the Stanton estate. That and knowing no one else would be there.

"Welcome to my humble home," Jeremy said. He pulled her into a huge hug as soon as she was out of the car. He grabbed her luggage and led her in.

"Jeremy, you live in a mansion." Mia snickered. "I live in a two-bedroom apartment in the Parisian arrondissement nearest work, and I think functional would be an accurate description, although I prefer quaint. This…." Mia waved her hand to encompass the grand staircase, the expensive chandeliers, the original priceless artwork, and the custom furniture. "This opulence is overwhelming. I feel as if I should be buying a tour ticket only I'm afraid I'd be told I'm not deserving."

"Mia, I can't change my family. My parents…"

"Please, you don't need to justify your family, your surroundings. I've never felt comfortable here."

"Well, then, I'll take you to one of the quaint cottages if you prefer."

Mia laughed. "Even those are rather intimidating."

"Exactly what my grandfather intended."

"Looking back, I'm glad my dad got transferred to Europe. After he quit working for your family, he began enjoying life."

"Dad and Teri haven't learned that yet. How are your parents?"

"They're off to Wales for the holidays." Mia followed Jeremy into one of the guest cottages. She wasn't ready to discuss her parents, even with such a close friend. She still needed to come to terms with the changes in her life. "This is ten times the size of my Paris apartment. The color and decorations are…I think bleak austere would be an appropriate description."

"No one ever accused my family of being gauche."

"I've been in monasteries more ornate." She wanted to ask about Teri, but the question stuck in her throat. Just as the memories of that evening often did. Instead, she walked around the cottage, opening windows, touching objects. *It would do for tonight.*

"My parents wanted everyone to know where the money and power was."

"It's in the manse, not the cottages. Expensive sculptures, art originals, custom white wool carpets, and the crystal glass. All verboten to anyone under the age of eighteen."

"Verboten to all but the chosen. And we used to sneak in." Jeremy paused and turned a light switch on and off. "Teri is well."

"Oh?" Mia prayed she wasn't that transparent. "I guess that's good." Her heart was beating much too fast for her head's contentment.

"She's still single and a heart breaker. Work's her lover, mistress, and only friend, but I'm not her keeper."

"Too much information."

"She's my sister and I wish she'd get a life. She wishes I'd show more of her work ethic. We seem to get along less and less."

"I'm sorry."

Jeremy set the bag on a small table against the wall. "Mia, I love my sister, and you're my best friend. I may not always like what she does or how she treats people, but she's my sister. I know she hasn't always been nice to you."

Mia's eyes widened. "Nice? Nice! Jeremy, I was fifteen years old. She called me a selfish, self-centered liar. The next thing I know, we're all being shipped off to Europe. My whole family was being punished."

"Mia, your father's transfer was a business decision. It had nothing to do with you."

"Right! My dad's moving us to Oregon and then he suddenly discovers all the arrangements, including housing, have been made for us to move to Europe. And that was only five days after Teri's tirade." She shook her head. "Jer, I don't want to talk about this. We've hashed and rehashed this whole episode, and I'm done with it."

Jeremy smiled. "About damn time."

Mia hugged him. "Maybe, but I haven't forgotten, or forgiven. I'm just movin' on." *Or at least, trying to.* She looked around. Unpleasant memories niggled at the corners of what little peace she had. She pushed them down—as far down as she could without wiping out brain cells.

"If it makes you feel any better, she treats everyone that way. At least she's supposed to be out of town for the next several days. You, however, I probably won't see again unless I go to Europe."

"It's your turn," Mia reminded him. "I've met you in San Francisco, Atlanta, and Miami. You've met me in Rome once. Besides, I may be moving back to the States. So you'll have no excuses then."

She opened her luggage and began hanging her few items. "Let me change and you can take me on the grand tour. Surely there have been some changes to the manor." Her voice was mocking, but her smile was warm.

Twenty minutes later, they were strolling along the river. Mia wrapped her hand around Jeremy's arm. "I used to love walking along here."

"Not like the Seine?"

Mia smiled, recalling the many times she had walked from the Sorbonne to the Latin Quarter and then along the river to the Ile de Cite. "No! There is definitely something wonderful about that river." She paused and looked around. "Don't get me wrong. I can't imagine living anywhere else. This place and this river remind of my young, naïve days. B.T."

"Before Teri?"

She nodded. "It was a time of innocence and make-believe." She looked at Jeremy. "I'm sounding jaded, and I'm not even close to forty. Sorry."

Mia leaned against Jeremy and rubbed his arm. "How are things going with you and Elaine? I really like her." She sat on the grass under a large oak tree and stretched her legs.

"I want to ask her to marry me. I'm tired of us living apart. I just haven't found the right moment."

She leaned against the tree and relived her own regrets. "There's never the right time, Jeremy. You've got to make the time." A large boat pulling up to the nearby dock served as a healthy distraction. "You're perfect for each other, but…" Mia paused, trying her best to maintain a serious expression. "I can't imagine Elaine getting really excited with you getting down on one knee without a ring."

Jeremy grinned. "Don't worry. I plan on having flowers, a wonderful dinner, and the ring."

"When are you going to tell your family?" Jeremy grimaced. Mia laughed. "You have to tell them."

"I will. I'm going to ask Elaine to marry me first. I want to make sure she says yes."

"You, idiot. She's madly in love with you."

Jeremy blushed. "I hope so." He was silent for so long Mia wondered what he was thinking. "Mia, I'm so sorry about Nat." Mia shrugged. "Maybe you'll find someone, too."

"Maybe," Mia said. "Maybe," she said again with more optimism in her voice. "I've sabotaged too many relationships and I'm done with that. Nat changed that. She made me realize life is too precious. Now I have Michel, and I want to get my life together for him. I need to get it together."

Jeremy turned and stared at the boat at the dock. "Oh, shit. Mia, I'm so sorry. Teri is here. She was supposed to be heading for California."

Mia stood and dusted the grass off her pants. "This was a bad idea. I think I should go." *Run is what I should do. I can't believe my worst nightmare is happening.*

"Mia, don't go. Maybe she just forgot something."

This was ridiculous. The fight-flight battle was in full swing. Mia was fifteen and being called a conniving liar. At the same time, she recognized she was no longer the heartbroken teenager. If she was truly determined to move on with her life, then she had to face her nemesis. That meant dealing with Teri. If Jeremy and Brenna were to be her friends, she would also have to deal with the rest of their family. "I'll gird my loins and grit my teeth. My dentist won't be happy, but I'm a good gritter."

Jeremy rolled his eyes. "I've missed you. Come on. Might as well get it over."

"Why do you continue to work for her?"

"I don't. I work for the family business."

"Come on, Jer. Isn't Teri C.O.O. now? Not bad for someone who's thirty-eight."

"She is, but Dad's still C.E.O. and chair of the board. You, dear friend, are only thirty-two and cultural attaché at our French embassy."

"The correct term is cultural affairs officer. I'm the assistant CAO in the Paris office. Bottom line, it's a government job, Jeremy, and fortunately, one I enjoy. Not that glamorous but I get to meet some amazing people."

Any response was halted by Teri's shouts. "Jeremy, come grab the ropes and tie the boat."

It was a command. Mia couldn't ever remember Teri asking for anything, or anyone. Teri's voice boomed across the dock and trilled down Mia's spine. *After all these years. Remember, you're letting go of the past.*

Mia walked over with Jeremy and helped anchor the boat to the dock. It was a task she hadn't done in years, but muscle memory kicked in. They unloaded whatever Teri handed them onto the dock. Hopefully, she wouldn't be noticed. Or remembered.

CHAPTER TWO

It wasn't until the boat was unloaded that Teri even acknowledged the presence of a third person. As long as people did what she said, she didn't care who it was. No, that wasn't true. She wasn't too thrilled with Jeremy out walking with the staff. She would have a chat with him later. Being a Stanton entailed certain responsibilities and behavior. *When the hell is he going to grow up and start accepting his role in the family and the business?*

Teri turned toward the female and carefully scrutinized her brother's companion. She looked familiar. The blond-haired beauty was attractive. Curved hips set off by the khaki pants. The powder blue top had a V-neck that showed enough of well-formed breasts that Teri declared them delicious. Ice-blue eyes stared back at her.

Teri started to walk away. It had been years since she had seen eyes that color. The only person she knew with those color eyes was....

"Mia Daniels?" Teri turned and stared at her.

"Hello, Teri." Mia's expression was grim.

"Well, you've certainly…grown up." Her gaze slowly moved down and then back up until she was again staring into the remarkable bright eyes. The unexpected pleasure of seeing Mia stunned her. She quickly closed that door. *What the hell is she doing here now?* Teri had sent Mia away once. Was she going to have to do it again?

Mia folded her arms across her chest and stared back.

"What're you doing here?" Teri asked.

"I invited her," Jeremy said.

"Why?" Teri asked.

"Why do I have to explain?"

Teri glared at him. She definitely needed to have another chat with him. *As if it would do any good.* "You don't. Nice to see you, Mia. Are you staying long?"

"No. Are you?" Mia looked pained, as if she regretted the comment. Teri doubted it.

"Touché." Teri ran her eyes over Mia one more time. Her appraisal was thorough and dispassionate. Mia may be an attractive woman, but she didn't belong here. Teri had business to conduct, and she didn't need any distractions. Certainly not from someone so impudent. "You, however, are at my home. I have a right to be here any time I want." She stared into the bright blue eyes. There was a brief flare and then calm returned.

"You're right. This is your home. I thought I was an invited guest, obviously not yours." Mia stood erect, refusing to look away.

"You're my guest." Jeremy was next to her.

"You certainly have…" Teri paused, looking for the right word, "changed."

"I hope so. I would be boring if I hadn't." Mia returned her stare.

Teri leaned forward. Her face was inches away from Mia. "Change just for change isn't always good. Change for a purpose, for a business improvement, can be worthwhile."

Mia shook her head. "You haven't changed much."

"What does that mean?" Teri's voice was no longer calm. She struggled to suppress the first rush of anger.

"You still have an answer for everything. Right or wrong doesn't matter."

Teri stepped back and glared at Mia. She wondered if Mia was intentionally baiting her. "You've grown up. Physically. Your behavior hasn't changed." She turned and quickly walked up to the back of the house. She had too much to do today to deal with this now. *Why the hell did she have to show up now? And how will I get rid of her this time?*

She quickly pushed the thought down to the bottom of her list. She had more important concerns. And they were all related to her current business venture. *Maybe I can just send her to a hotel in the city. A suite at the Ritz. That may impress her.*

"Jeremy, our parents will be arriving shortly. The Miltons are coming for dinner. Mr. and Mrs. Milton and their daughter, Pamela. I want this evening perfect. Don't know why they're in New York, but we need to find out. Understand?"

Teri didn't wait for an answer. She walked quickly to the back of the house.

CHAPTER THREE

A nd you haven't changed," Mia whispered. *Still ordering people around. Don't give a damn about anyone but yourself.*

"I'm sorry, Mia," Jeremy said.

She gently touched his arm. "No, I'm the one who should apologize. I've had more than one girlfriend tell me I use my sarcasm to push people away. It's true. I need to stop that." Mia couldn't believe how easily she turned on Teri.

Mia had put Teri up on a pedestal, and when that pedestal blew apart, Mia was devastated. Now she was focusing all the years of pent up anger and frustration at the source. "I know it's ridiculous to let something that happened when I was a teenager ruin relationships, but every time someone got close, I kept waiting for some bad thing to happen. If it didn't, then I created the problem. I wonder what would've happened if Nat hadn't died?" She wrapped her arms tightly around herself. "This has got to stop."

"I think you two would still be together. She was strong and madly in love with you."

"Maybe." *It's time. Teri Stanton has to go.* "I can catch up with you later."

❖

There would be no way to avoid Teri now. Mia lay on the bed and considered her options. If she weren't so damned tired she would have just packed up her car and left. She had a hotel room in New York City. It might still be the best, and safest, choice. Her quest for a quiet, simple visit had become complicated.

If she didn't need Brenna and Jeremy's help right now, she would be gone. She felt the tears come unbidden. She didn't belong here. This wasn't her world.

❖

Mia jumped out of the car just as her father was pulling to a stop. "Mia Daniels! Stop where you are and wait." Her father's voice brooked no nonsense. She shoved her hands into the pockets of her pants. Jeremy was waiting for her, and somewhere out there was Teri. *Teri. Beautiful, sophisticated Teri. Some day she will walk up to me and ask me to dance.* Mia's eyes were closed. She began to sway. She could feel Teri's arms around her.

"Earth to Mia." Her brother hissed at her. "Dreaming of kissing Teri again?" He made kissing noises and danced around her.

"Shut up."

"You two behave tonight. And stay together." Her mother's frequent reminders only made her more determined to get away from her brother. As soon as she could, she slipped away. Unlike her brother, she had few friends.

Mia had trouble finding her friends in the large crowd. The Stanton's Fourth of July barbecue was one of the few affairs that included all the children of many of the executives. Her family's house was half a mile down the road. Her parents often brought her to most of these events knowing that, when she tired, she could walk home. Mia rarely left. She was too enchanted by the Stanton's oldest. Teri was everything she wasn't: beautiful, graceful, elegant, outgoing. And she always had some beautiful female on her arm. *If only it could be me! One day I will be all dressed up and she will ask me to dance. She will put her arms around me and we will....*

"Hey, lezzie, looking for some of this?" One of her male classmates grabbed his crotch and reached for her.

Mia pushed him away and walked quickly into the crowd. She had been caught by a female classmate drawing hearts with her name and Teri's inside. Within an hour, word had spread throughout the school. She was tormented mercilessly after that. She quickly learned all the names. Dyke, butch, cunt, lesbian, lezzie, muff diver. The words were all foreign to Mia. And hurtful. She didn't even know if she was gay. At fifteen, all she knew was that she was madly in love with one person. Teri Stanton. Someone who didn't know she existed. *Maybe someday, when I'm older.*

She walked faster. Her detractors struggling to keep up. A hand reached out and grabbed her.

❖

A knock on the door brought her back to the present. "Come in." She sat up and wiped the tears. *Well, I'm older and noticed.* She could at least pretend to put on a good face.

Jeremy came in and sat on the bed. "I'm so sorry. I didn't know anything about this. If you can survive this evening, then, in the morning, we can both run away. Brenna is on her way back from Brazil. I'll ask her to meet us in Maine at our family place there."

"Jeremy, you're a good man. That's unnecessary."

"Listen, I'd rather be in Maine. The weather will be much nicer and we can have the place to ourselves. It's my favorite place to hide from my family."

"Don't they know that you go there?"

"Of course. Still, I'm usually the only one who goes there, and I go up as often as I can. They think of it as the hinterlands. Bren has a condo in South Beach she uses when she wants to run away."

"What does your family say when the two of you disappear?"

"You don't want to know. What do you say?"

Jeremy was a loyal and caring friend, almost from the moment they met. As teens, they had been nearly inseparable. They studied together, took piano together, and their mutual interests meant they spent much of their free time together. And they included Bren in as many things as they could. Mia always felt welcomed around the two of them.

"Your family apparently has made plans for you for the entire weekend. I can go back to the city, then you can catch up with me when you get free."

"Mia, I made plans with you. My sister and parents are perfectly able to entertain their business friends. I'm just an accessory. Besides, I told Bren I'd take care of you until she got back. I know how important this visit is."

She kissed him on the cheek. "You're a dear, dear friend. Your family would be unforgiving with you disappearing. Besides, these are dress-up affairs, and I didn't even bring anything to wear for a formal dinner, much less any parties." She sat up. "I'm going to go."

"Then I'm going with you," Jeremy said.

"Going where?" Teri asked. She leaned against the door, looked around, and then stepped inside. "The door was open. Hope I didn't interrupt anything."

There was something disingenuous about Teri's last statement. Mia had no doubt that interrupting was exactly Teri's objective. "We're just talking. How are you, Teri?"

"Fine. You?"

Mia almost smiled. Teri appeared thrown off. "Do you need something?"

"I wanted to remind Jeremy of his responsibilities. Entertain Pamela Milton. See what she says. I want to make sure they were forthcoming when we were doing due diligence."

"Yes, boss." Mia saw the muscles in his jaw tense. Jeremy's heart was not in Stanton Enterprises.

"Jeremy, I want this deal closed by the end of our fourth quarter. Use your Stanton charm. Pick her brains."

"Teri, you've known I was taking this time off for over two months. I'm not changing my plans."

"And you know how important this deal is to the family." She stared at Mia. "I'm sure Mia understands business comes first."

Mia refused to be pulled into this argument. If it were anyone other than Teri Stanton, she would easily and graciously offer to reschedule. In this case, she crossed her arms over her chest and silently stared back.

"Teri, no."

"This is non-negotiable. Milton Senior will be sitting between me and Father. Be prompt. We're having dinner at eight." Teri stopped. She looked from Jeremy to Mia and back. Her eyebrow shot up, and a strange expression spread across her face. Mia didn't think it boded anything good.

Teri turned back to Mia. "Are you joining us for dinner?"

Mia was nonplussed. The invitation was out of character and unexpected. Mia was suddenly vigilant. "No, I don't think so. I'm tired and I didn't bring anything to wear. Besides, I plan on driving back to New York shortly. Thank you, though."

"I can arrange to have someone bring some things out for you to look at if you want."

"Why?" Mia shook her head wondering what Teri was up to.

"You're still as blunt as usual, I see."

"And, as usual, you didn't answer my question."

One corner of Teri's mouth turned up. It was almost a smile. "You've gotten bolder. You wouldn't have questioned me once upon a time."

"I'm not afraid of you anymore, and once upon a time, you wouldn't have dared invite me."

Teri stood at the door. She appeared lost in thought, as if she was reappraising the situation. Mia wondered what Teri was thinking but was unable to discern any hint from the flat affect.

Finally, Mia broke the silence. "That's a nice offer. I've been up almost twenty-four hours. I'll pass."

"Join us for dinner. As my guest."

Mia stared, unsure she had heard correctly. "Why?"

"Why not?"

Another question and no answer. Mia remembered her vow to work on being pleasant. "Are you sure my presence is acceptable?"

"Why wouldn't it be?"

"Well, I don't own any companies so there isn't a business reason for you to invite me. I certainly don't have any money to invest. I come from a working class background and didn't get my undergraduate degree from Harvard. I have to wonder why Teri Stanton would invite me!"

"Are you always this difficult? Is it that hard to believe that I'd invite you for dinner?"

"Yes. And you didn't invite me. You commanded me."

Teri clenched her jaw and glared. She finally forced a smile, but it didn't move higher than her lips. "Ms. Daniels, would you join us for dinner? It would make Jeremy happy, and we have inconvenienced your plans. Now, I'm fairly sure *that* is an invitation."

Mia wanted to laugh. She could tell it was taking every ounce of Teri's reserve to make that offer.

Teri's request was as unwelcome as the manner in which it was offered. *What was the point of asking me to stay? Is she trying to figure out another way to humiliate me?* Mia didn't trust the invitation, but she was determined to be pleasant even if it killed her. And it just might. "Thank you, Ms. Stanton. That is a generous invitation." She tilted her head to one side and placed her hand on a hip. It was definitely a challenge being thrown out. "Unfortunately, I don't have anything appropriate to wear. So I'm going to have to politely decline."

"If you can meet me in the study in thirty minutes, I'll have the dressmaker there." Her cell phone ringing drew her attention. Picking up her cell, Teri turned and quickly walked out without even a backward glance.

"What was that all about?" Jeremy asked.

"I have no idea." She stared at the empty doorway. "Did she just ask me to join her for dinner? Or am I hallucinating?"

"Trust me. I'm as surprised as you are."

"Maybe she wants me to see how well the Miltons' daughter fits in and I don't."

"She's not that bad, Mia. Milton owns a high-tech company that my father and Teri are considering taking over. This is all about business."

"So are you supposed to be the pimp and woo the young daughter to convince the father this is an ideal match?"

Jeremy stood and glared. "I'll ignore that only because you're my friend and I know you're tired."

"From what you've told me, you've never been happy working in the family business."

"It's complicated. At least right now I'm spending more time on the West Coast and Elaine is there. I wouldn't mind running the business out there."

"Then do it. Time is short."

Jeremy sat closer. "How are your mother and father really?"

"She's a trouper. Trying to keep us all cheered. I think the heart attack scared her as much as it did us." Mia became serious. She had to swallow to keep the emotions down. "My parents are spending the summer traveling. They don't want to waste time. And they're enjoying the time with Michel. It's put a strain on my dad, however. He's losing weight." Tears threatened, but she brushed them away before they could fall. "My brother and I are trying to find a way to get them back here so…." She choked.

"I'm sorry I didn't fly over."

"Don't, Jer. You were there when Natalie died. My parents are grateful for your thoughtfulness in arranging an accessible place for them to live. Now they're having a wonderful summer." Mia leaned her head against his shoulder. She just wanted to go to sleep and wake up someplace else. "I definitely have jet lag. Maybe the real reason Teri invited me is to see if I fall asleep during the soup and drown."

"There are times when she's quite reasonable."

"I bet it's when she's asleep." She looked at her watch. "We better get over to the manse and see what the mistress wants."

"One of the things I love about you is that your tongue's as sharp as your mind, but you don't use it to hurt."

"That isn't always true. I'm working hard to be a better person. One not afraid to let someone get close. One deserving of the kind of love Natalie offered. And I want to be a good mother and role model."

"You will be. You have no idea how much I admire you and want to be strong like you."

"Stop." She grabbed his arm. "Come on. Let's go." The short walk across the lawn was pleasant, and she was enjoying Jeremy's company. When she reached the door, one of the staff grabbed her and insisted that Ms. Stanton was waiting in the library with the dressmaker. Mia sighed. As soon as dinner was over, she'd excuse herself and get some sleep. She just needed to survive—she looked at her watch—oh, shit, another nine hours.

Chapter Four

Teri stared out the open French doors, totally unaware of what, if anything, she was looking at. She finished off her Scotch and placed the empty glass on the coffee table. She knew she should be meeting the Miltons. It would only be minutes before someone came looking for her.

Mia Daniels had disrupted her equanimity. She was distracting, impudent, challenging. And lovely. It was almost like she was seeing her for the first time. Everything about Mia breathed life. She chatted easily with the dressmaker, and the two carried on conversations about clothing and dresses for almost twenty minutes while she just stood and watched. She was so at ease in her own body that Teri could barely take her eyes off Mia. Had Mia been a stranger in a lesbian bar, Teri would have wanted to take her to bed. It had been years since she had felt that strong an urge.

She wasn't a stranger, however. She was her brother's guest. Still, Teri was well aware that her own behavior was inappropriate. She was in the middle of a major acquisition, and nothing should distract her from business. No matter how she tried to rein it in, Teri had trouble controlling her thoughts. Worse, there was no way for her to control the physical reactions she was having. She had even bought a dress for that damn woman.

Teri had been on the cell phone while Mia was trying on dresses. When she saw Mia in the ice-blue evening dress, Teri forgot to whom she was talking. She hung up in the middle of the conversation. The only thing on her mind was Mia. The dress fit

Mia's curves perfectly. The back was cut in a vee that dipped almost to her waist. Thin straps showed off gorgeous shoulders and arms. Teri was mesmerized. She ached with longing.

Teri insisted that Mia have the dress. She didn't want anyone else to wear it.

Mia protested, saying she had plenty of dresses and couldn't afford this one. Teri was adamant. Mia continued to argue.

"I'm going to pay for the damn dress." She couldn't believe Mia wasn't more grateful. "I invited you and I want you to have it. I'll make sure it's in your room in an hour. As soon as the alterations are done. So don't worry about it."

"That's very generous. I cannot accept such an expensive gift."

"It's nothing compared to the inconvenience we've caused. I insist."

"I insist that you not pay for it, and I cannot afford it."

Teri felt the anger surging through her. How dare she refuse the offer? "It's my money and I can spend it however I want. I want you to have that dress."

Mia just stomped out.

"What the hell is the matter with her?"

As angry as she was with Mia, Teri was even angrier with herself. She was surprised by her own erratic behavior and singular lack of control. In a relatively short time, she had been rude to Mia, invited her to dinner, and then bought a damn dress for her. This aberrant behavior would stop. She had more important business—the merger.

She picked up her glass and poured a shot of Chivas neat and then sipped it. She liked the warm, full-bodied feeling as it slid down her throat. The same kind of feeling Mia was causing. Teri put the glass down.

She had always liked Mia. Mia was bright with a sharp sense of humor. She excelled at whatever she did. Teri saw her younger self in Mia and admired her determination.

If only she hadn't been hanging around so much with her little brother. Teri slapped her hand against the wall. No, why hadn't she stood up to her parents? Teri had a choice, but she did what was expected. What was convenient. She had chosen the path regardless of the consequences to others. *Or to me. Damn!* Teri's thoughts flew back in time. It was her twenty-second birthday.

❖

"Damn it, Theresa. Jeremy is over there with that girl again." Teri's father was angry.

"They're friends, Father." Teri grabbed a bottle of chilled champagne. She had a beautiful woman waiting for her on the yacht. She didn't have time to worry about Mia talking to her brother.

"I don't want him mixing with the staff," her mother said.

Teri couldn't believe what she was hearing, even from her mother. This was the twenty-first century, and her mother was lost in the nineteenth. "Her father is the chief financial officer for our business. We were the ones who insisted he move his family closer. Besides, Mia is one of the best students at Echolls Academy."

"Who's Mia?"

Teri was clenching her jaw so tight it was beginning to hurt. After the last conversation she had with her date, Teri acknowledged other parts of her body were beginning to hurt. She desperately needed to fuck her brains out tonight, and this conversation was not helping her get there. The image of a certain redhead lying naked waiting for her flashed in front of her. *Why the hell am I having this inane conversation with my parents?* "Mia is the girl with Jeremy, Mother." All Teri wanted was to get out of this room and have a little fun.

Teri looked out at the mix of Stanton Enterprises employees, their families, and guests. Jeremy was holding Mia's hand and walking out to the dock. Teri's younger sister, Bren, was sitting out there with a couple of other teenagers. *Why am I stuck with this job?* She turned and looked at her parents. "Mia's father is a high-ranking member of our company." *I've got a hot woman waiting for me and I'm playing nursemaid.*

"Her father is nobody. Her mother is nobody. They are both from someplace in Indiana. Or someplace like that."

"They're from Minnesota."

"No respectable family comes from Minnesota." Her mother was on a roll. "They're not from the first families. My great-great-great-grandfather was one of the first families of Boston. I don't want Jeremy or Brenna hanging around with the wrong kind of people."

What are the *right* kinds of people? Teri was getting angrier and angrier. Not at her parents. Not at her date. At Mia Daniels. "Mother, we're planning on her father moving to vice president of operations in our western area. The family will be gone soon."

"I don't care who or what he is or how smart she is. She isn't from one of the proper families. She's not suitable for Jeremy to be seen with." Her mother's voice was clear and determined.

"What the hell is a proper family, Mother? Mia is Jeremy's friend. We're not talking about marriage." Teri shook her head. How was she going to one day run the company with one foot in an earlier century? Her interest in sex was beginning to wane. She put the bottle back down in the ice.

"Theresa, you were brought up to know the difference. You went to all the right schools, met all the right people. If we don't carefully choose Jeremy's friends, who knows what kind of decisions he will make. You obviously have no plans to provide grandchildren with the Stanton name. Jeremy, then, must be pushed in the right direction." Her mother's voice was calm and cold. Almost as if she were assessing the daily menu.

Teri was angry now. Her parents accepted her sexual orientation but only because she had dated acceptable females. Daughters of proper families. Still, they were disappointed that she had no plans to marry and produce offspring.

"What do you expect me to do?" Teri sighed. She knew what was coming. No matter how much she might disagree, she knew she would do what was asked. *Why did I waste my time on my education?*

"Take care of it," her father answered. "If you're going to lead this company one day, you need to learn how to do that."

Since joining the family business a year ago, Teri had heard that phrase too many times. She poured a quick shot of Scotch and downed it. She would do whatever was asked. Each time she did, she lost a little of her soul. Was this the way her life was going to be? She downed another shot of Scotch. *Might as well get it over.* She would need the sex afterward. It was the only way to release the tension and frustration. First, she needed to get rid of Mia Daniels, permanently and quickly.

She called the vice president of Human Resources. Then she went to make sure Brenna and Jeremy would be left alone by that damn Daniels kid.

❖

Teri looked at her watch then wondered why that particular memory reared its ugly head. It happened fifteen years ago. Mia was just fifteen. It wasn't that important. Just the first of many "take care of its" since joining the family business.

She closed her eyes and took a deep breath. She was lying to herself. That incident did matter. She got Tom Daniels and his family transferred to Europe and had lost the one person in the company who had been a caring mentor. The relationship with her brother and sister began to change. And Teri felt like a shit. She took her anger out on a damn, unsuspecting fifteen-year-old. She had lost a big chunk of her soul that night. Today, she wondered if there was any left.

This emotional aberration was pointless. All that mattered was how she behaved from this point on. *That* she had control over. The past didn't matter. It was easier to do business. She exited the library reaffirming the importance of the merger.

"I've been looking for you." Teri's mother grabbed her as soon as she walked into the large dining room. "Who is this person with Jeremy? What is she doing here? Who is her family? We don't know anything about her."

"Mother, Mia is an old friend of Jeremy's. They had plans for the weekend and we interrupted them. It was only polite that we invite her to dinner."

"There's nothing going on between them, I hope. We don't know her family."

"We do, Mother. Her father is Thomas Daniels. He used to work for us."

"Hired help!" Her mother's voice seemed to increase an octave.

"Mother, please try to remain calm. Mia's father was once one of our chief executives. There are no royalty or serfs in the U.S. Now, let me go talk with the Miltons before they think we're being rude." Her mother's comments were only echoes of her own thoughts, yet hearing them out loud made her uncomfortable.

"Ah, Theresa," her father said, "Milton's son has just arrived and will also join us tonight. Can you please make sure another place is set at the table on the other side of you? I want to keep control of the conversation. I'm not sure why the son is here, but something may be up. The daughter is in charge of marketing, but they've never said anything about the son. You need to find out what's going on. Tell the staff to put him on your right and Milton between us."

"Not a problem." Teri readily agreed. She couldn't remember the last time she hadn't. She looked around the room. No Mia. For that matter, no Jeremy. *Where the hell are they now?* She was angry with Jeremy. *He knows he's expected to be here when the guests arrive.*

She walked into the kitchen and arranged for an extra plate then checked on the food. Her cell phone rang and interrupted her inspection. She recognized the number and quickly answered. "Did you find out anything?" She didn't listen for the complete answer. "I don't care how difficult it is, get the damn information." She shut the phone off. Tomorrow, she would fire him. Information Technology people were plentiful.

Teri walked into the dining room and stopped. Mia was standing on the far side of the room. Her blond hair was a mass of curls framing an elegant face and neck. She was wearing a simple navy blue suit. There was an unassuming elegance about her, even in the unadorned outfit.

Why didn't she wear the blue gown? Teri's anger shifted. *Is she intentionally defying me?*

Mia smiled. Teri forgot everything but Mia. The suit appeared to be tailored for Mia's soft, well-developed curves. The only jewelry was the watch and the gold necklace Teri had seen earlier. She was breathtaking. Nothing anorexic about Mia. Even in that goddamned suit.

Her laughter, faint from across the room, sent a delightful chill through Teri's body. She rubbed her arms to reduce the tingling. It didn't work. Mia glowed. Teri wanted to bask in that light, that laughter. She wondered who had Mia's rapt attention. Milton's daughter, Pamela! They were laughing and whispering like old friends. Teri couldn't help herself. She walked over. As she approached, she realized they were speaking in French.

"Pamela, I see you've met our guest."

Silence. The laughter and conversation stopped immediately.

"Did I interrupt anything?"

"No," Mia said. "Pam discovered I spoke French and asked if we could converse in it so that she could practice."

Pam? How the hell did she get so friendly? I've only heard her addressed as Pamela. She turned toward Pamela Milton. "I hope you're enjoying your French lesson."

"Absolutment." Pamela winked at Mia. "It's amazing how much comes back when talking to someone who speaks it so well." She raised her glass of champagne. "To a good teacher."

There was something sexual and predatory in the way Pamela spoke and looked at Mia. Teri had picked up or flirted with enough women to recognize it. In this situation, it irritated the hell out of her. What the hell was going on?

CHAPTER FIVE

Mia hid her grin behind a sip of champagne. Teri's grim expression and Pam's double entendres were certainly making dinner interesting. If she had been less tired, she would have looked forward to the rest of the evening. This was definitely not starting out as a typical event at the Stantons. Of that she was sure.

Mia noticed Teri's clothing for the evening: tailored black silk trousers with a subtle satin stripe down the side of each leg and white silk shirt with very thin, barely noticeable blue pinstripes and French cuffs. Her earrings were diamond and sapphires that shimmered in the light and offered great contrast to her dark hair. Although Teri was nearly six feet tall, she still had on heels that add another two to three inches. Towering was the word that came to mind. Impressive was another. In black and white, she was sophisticated and imposing. Mia could fall in love with her again. She stopped that line of thought. She had more important concerns in her life right now.

"Why do you get to wear the pants and I have to get dressed?" She lifted one eyebrow and gave Teri the same kind of appraising look she had been given earlier.

"I'm the boss. No one cares what I wear."

"You're wrong. They would definitely care if you didn't wear anything." Mia turned and walked over to Jeremy who led her to her seat.

"Interesting woman." Pamela Milton's words had definite sexual overtones.

Mia grinned. Definitely not a typical Stanton evening. She was less pleased when she discovered that Pam had followed her over to the table and sat beside her.

Mia was determined, however, to maintain her composure in spite of Pamela Milton. Pam tried to dominate conversation, even casually draping her arm around the back of Mia's chair. Mia turned in her chair, leaning away from Pam and toward Jeremy. She quickly engaged in conversation with Pam's brother and other dinner guests.

This evening won't be over soon enough.

❖

As soon as dinner was finished and the group adjourned to the parlor, Mia excused herself. She could barely keep her eyes open, much less maintain any semblance of conversation.

"I'll escort you," Jeremy offered.

"You are such a gentleman," Mia whispered as he wrapped his coat around her.

"The evening air can be chilly, and I doubt if that suit, although it looks lovely on you, will keep you very warm."

"Want to come in for a few minutes?" Mia asked.

"Just a short time. Thank you for keeping Pamela Milton busy. I'm not sure I would know how to handle her."

Mia laughed. "I don't think you have anything to worry about with her."

"Is she engaged?"

Mia laughed. "Oh, she's engaged, but not the kind of engaged you mean."

"Okay, you've got my attention." He sat next to Mia.

"Pam Milton's more interested in engaging a female. Ten seconds after I met her she asked me how long I was staying and if I wanted to have dinner with her."

Jeremy's eyes grew wide. "She's a lesbian?"

"Well, let's say she has a definite interest in females. She asked me if I wanted to take a walk in the garden."

"No." Jeremy struggled with holding his laughter. "Do her parents know?"

"No. That was why she wanted to walk in the garden. She assured me she was very discrete. I think she said she needed to protect the family name. How gallant! She did assure me, however, that it would be well worth my time. And that she was quite—I think the word she used—versatile." Mia was now laughing and struggling to speak. "Of course, she said it didn't matter if I was involved with you or your sister. She just wanted me with no strings attached."

"She propositioned you right there in front of her parents and my parents? That's too much. What did you say?"

"I politely thanked her for her offer and reassured her that I would need to take a rain check. I had been traveling nearly twenty-four hours and was quite tired. She then tried to convince me that she could help me relax and not even mess a hair on my head."

Jeremy was convulsing with laughter. "This is too much. My mother with her uptight friends and attitude is encouraging me to be nice to Pamela while she is playing footsie with you."

Mia wiped the tears from her eyes. "The real kicker was that she was actually playing footsie with me during dinner. When it started, I nearly spit my water across the table at her brother. I'm too embarrassed to even mention what she was whispering to me in French."

"Stop!" Jeremy was laughing so hard he was having trouble talking.

"I think I showed amazing restraint. I will admit the entertainment enabled me to stay awake during dinner." Mia took a couple of deep breaths. Her sides hurt from too much laughter. "I politely told her we had made plans and that I would only be in the U.S. for the weekend. A white lie, but it was effective. However, that was when she started pushing for the walk in the garden. Walking was not what she had in mind. I, for one, was not about to ruin this suit. I have my priorities."

"Stop. You don't give a rat's ass about clothes."

"True." Mia sighed and leaned back on her hands. "Good thing I wasn't wearing the dress you sister bought for me. Pam may have been more insistent and the dress would have been ruined. I want to return it to Teri in good condition."

"My sister paid for a dress for you? Well, that's news!"

"Jeremy, why are you looking at me like that?"

"I don't know of any woman my sister has bought clothes for. You must be special."

"Get outta here. I'm sure Teri wanted to make sure I wouldn't embarrass anyone. I felt the dress was much too expensive for me to wear one time and possibly ruin. And there is no way I would accept anything that expensive, or personal, from her. Speaking of Teri, you better get back before you're missed. Your sister is probably sending out a SWAT team. I'm going to shower and get some sleep." She kissed him on the cheek.

"In the morning, we'll plan our escape. I found out from Teri that the Miltons only called yesterday morning and informed her that they will be in town for the next couple of days. So let's slink away before more of these activities are foisted upon us."

"Yes, sir, Captain, sir." She offered a sharp salute and took a deep breath. "Let's talk about it in the morning I've already had too much excitement for one day. I'm usually up early." He nodded and left.

Once she was alone, she continued to chuckle about the events of the evening. If only Teri and her mother knew. Mia loved the absurdity. *Theater of the absurd. Oh, God, I need to get some sleep. I'm getting punchy.*

As she got ready for bed, she remembered the last time she had been to a party at the Stantons. The events of the evening were permanently etched in her long-term memory. A scar on her heart.

❖

Mia was grateful Jeremy had found her. She took his hand and they began to walk toward the dock and Bren.

"Mia, I'm so sorry I didn't see you sooner. Those guys are just a bunch of bullies. I want to kick them all into Long Island Sound."

She wiped a tear away. "Jer, it's not your fault. I should've known I couldn't trust Priscilla. As soon as she saw Teri's name on my notebook, she told me she was going to tell everybody unless I did whatever she told me. I refused, and you know what a gossip she is."

Mia had barely reached the dock and Bren, when she heard a familiar voice call her by name. *She knows my name!* Mia felt her heart racing.

"Mia, I need to talk to you. Brenna, Jeremy, you need to go back to the house."

"I'm staying with Mia," Brenna said as she stood close to Mia.

"You are going. Now. Mia, you come with me."

Mia nodded at her friends and then followed behind Teri. Her heart was pounding. She wondered if Teri would kiss her. She hoped so. Although she wasn't sure what she was expected to do. Jeremy had once kissed her, but they both decided it was like kissing a sibling.

She was so lost in thought she ran into Teri's back when Teri stopped abruptly. "Sorry." She shoved her hands in her pockets and then quickly pulled them out. Her mother kept reminding her to stand up straight, stop wiggling her hands, and walk, not run. Once again, she had acted like an idiot. Teri could never like someone who was such a klutz.

"Mia, I want you to leave my brother and sister alone."

Huh?

"You had half a dozen boys following you around a few minutes ago, and you acted like you didn't even notice. Then my brother comes along and you're holding hands and acting like a queen with him part of your entourage. It's obvious you don't care about him. Bren and Jeremy are impressionable. You're using them."

"I don't understand." Mia was hurting. Teri couldn't be saying these things. *She's finally talking to me, but not this way!*

"Don't play dumb, Mia, because you're not. I've seen the way you treat the kids around you. I've also watched you lead Jeremy around. You're just hoping to catch a rich boyfriend. All you think about is yourself and what you can do to get ahead. Well, not with my family."

"That's not true!"

Teri leaned closer. "Are you calling me a liar?"

"N-n-no, but I'm…" Mia

"You're what? Self-centered? Manipulative?" Teri grabbed her arm. "You leave my family alone!" Each word was spit out like arrows loaded into a bow and released, one after another, until Mia was sure there was nothing left of her heart.

She pulled free and strode around to the front of the house. Once out of sight of prying eyes, she ran to the wall, climbed it, and ran home as fast as possible. She flew up the stairs to her bedroom. All the anger, disappointment, and hurt oozed out in every tear until her pillow was soaked and her heart empty.

"I'll never love anyone again!"

Seeing Teri had brought back so many memories. Mia never wanted to be fifteen again. She had closed off her heart. Until Nat.

How stupid to allow something like that to ruin my life! It was just one event and I've let it color everything. Mia had read the research on bullying. The impact of bullying could last for decades. It was not reassuring. *Not anymore.* Mia crawled into bed, determined tomorrow would be a better day. Too many changes were occurring in her life, and she needed stability. And she had finally learned about love, the unconditional kind. She would never settle for less in the future.

Chapter Six

Teri looked at her watch. Jeremy had been gone nearly twenty minutes. *Where the hell is he? It's about time he started caring about the business. I'm getting tired of paying his bills and he keeps disappearing.*

With each passing minute, her anger was growing and her ability to concentrate decreasing. *If that—*

She stopped. Mia wasn't *that person.* She was Mia Daniels. She had spent much of the evening defending Mia to her parents, and now she was ready to denigrate her worse than her mother had.

She needed to shove all this back in her dead file. Mia Daniels was a distraction, one she would not tolerate. She would give her brother two more minutes and then go looking for him.

Teri had just decided to find him when Jeremy walked back in. His face was mottled and he was grinning from ear to ear. What the hell were they doing? Anger and jealously reared their demanding heads.

"What took you so long?" she hissed at her brother.

"I wasn't gone that long."

"Long enough for everyone to notice."

"I don't think Father cares how long I'm gone as long as his glass is kept full. Mother's too busy making sure the Miltons know our family tree."

"Don't you dare talk about our parents like that! You know how hard they've worked to make sure we have the kind of life we have."

Jeremy stared for several seconds before responding. "They worked hard, if they really worked, to have the kind of life they want. If this is the kind of life you want, then have at it. It's never been the one I want. Now excuse me, I'm going to talk with Pamela Milton and her brother. I'll make sure to support your lifestyle." Jeremy started to walk away. "By the way, that was a lovely dress you bought Mia."

Teri gritted her teeth. Her brother's sarcasm was growing. She feared Mia would only make the problem worse.

She walked over to the bar and switched her champagne for Scotch. This was too many times in the same day that she had allowed emotions to interfere with business. No, Mia interfering with business.

She would get through the evening and then have a chat with her brother. He needed to realize this was serious business and Mia was a distraction that could be put off until another day.

She walked to where her parents were standing and joined their conversation with the senior Milton. Out of the corner of her eye, she noticed Pamela Milton walking around as if she were looking for someone. Teri's level of irritation shot up another notch. She looked at the clock. She would get everyone to retire in the next twenty minutes if she had to drag everyone out of there herself.

Teri stood next to her father. "We should call it a night. We have an early meeting."

"Yes, you're right. I'll take care of this." Teri watched her father as he announced the evening was over. He had relegated so much of the day-to-day operations to her she was surprised he hadn't told her to handle it. For fifteen years, anytime something unpleasant came up, she was told to take care of it. How long had it been since she had even questioned his orders? Too long, she decided, but she was not ready to stop. *One day, this will be my company and then I can run it the way I want.*

❖

Teri had managed four hours of sleep. She grabbed a small bottle of juice out of the refrigerator and walked back into the study. This was her home office, the one truly sacrosanct place where interruptions were not allowed. Her laptop, a few working files, and her notepads were carefully aligned on the desk. She turned on her computer and started to sit. As she briefly looked out the window, she noticed a light on in Mia's cottage. It was only five in the morning. *Maybe something's wrong.*

Teri knew she was being irrational. The thought of seeing Mia, however, put a bounce in her step. Her well-worn mantra came rushing back. *Don't think. Do!*

Chapter Seven

Mia sat on the terrace watching the sun come up. She was on her second cup of coffee and enjoying the quiet of the morning. This was one of her favorite times. There was something healing and life giving about sunrises. She cherished each and every one. She was at peace.

The brilliance of this sunrise was matched only by the fresh breezes coming off the water. She leaned back and let the gentle winds fluff her hair. She stretched. Any residual tension slid from her body and into the ground.

She had slept soundly for about six hours and then became restless. After thirty minutes, she got up, made coffee, drank some juice, talked with Michel and her parents, and then came outside. Now that the sun was up, she was whole again. She decided to shower and pack her clothes. Staying here would be uncomfortable and complicate her life more than it already was.

"Good morning. I didn't think anyone else would be up this early."

Mia groaned. Teri! There went the morning. And the peace. "Good morning."

"The coffee smells good."

Mia stared up at Teri. She was dressed in a dove-gray, fitted cotton shirt and black linen trousers. Dressed for work. Teri's dark eyes and hair were even darker with the color choices. Mia sighed. Teri was too damned attractive for her own good. She felt the nascent desire building. She couldn't allow this. She wouldn't allow it. "The coffee pot is inside. I just made it. Help yourself." Mia remained seated. She was trying to hang on to the good feelings she had felt before Teri arrived.

Teri sat down. "Nice morning."

Mia suspected that ordinary conversations were not something Teri often, or ever, indulged in. Teri set the cup down and then picked it up again and then looked around everywhere at except at Mia.

"Nice morning," Teri again said, a little more loudly.

Mia just nodded and hid her grin. *Speaking louder won't necessarily start a conversation. Wonder when was the last time you talked with someone instead of to someone?*

"Any plans for the day?"

Mia shook her head.

Teri's frustration was not easily disguised. Her sighing was getting louder. She began to slowly spin her coffee cup. "We're heading into New York for lunch. You can come with us after breakfast or have our driver pick you up later. This is an invitation."

Mia shook her head. Teri's idea of an invitation still sounded like a command. "Teri, why?"

"Why what?"

"Why did you invite me to stay for dinner and why are you inviting me to have lunch with you?"

"You're Jeremy's guest." Teri's expression was blank.

"But Jeremy wasn't the one who asked me to stay for dinner or to have lunch today. You did."

"Isn't that the polite thing to do?"

"When did you care about what was the polite or right thing to do? I'm not adding to your global empire. I don't work for you. You have nothing to gain from my presence."

Mia saw a brief flash of anger that was just as quickly gone. Teri's face was unreadable again. "I have a question. Why didn't you wear the blue dress?"

"It was a generous gift, but I don't accept such personal and expensive gifts from strangers."

"First, I'm not a stranger." Teri's countenance was one of indifference, but her voice betrayed her. Irritation was clearly evident. "Second, I invited you to dinner and felt it was the least I could do."

"Were you afraid I would embarrass you if I wore something of my own?"

Even the calm was beginning to fade from Teri's face. "You said you didn't have dinner clothes. I wanted you to feel comfortable at dinner. Is that a problem?"

"No." *No need to be so abrupt, Mia.* "Thank you. I didn't realize it was that important to you."

"It's not. It was the least we could do to compensate for the inconvenience."

"Thank you." Mia didn't want to argue. *We? Inconvenience!* Mia shook her head. *What the hell am I doing here?*

"Are you joining us for lunch?" Teri's request was still a demand. "Or you can come into the city with us in the next hour, if you prefer."

Mia watched the transformation in awe. Teri went from glaring to uncaring in such a short timeframe. She couldn't believe Teri, or anyone, was capable of such emotional transitions. "Thank you, but I'll decline. I still have jet lag."

"Then get some rest."

Another command. *Get me coffee. Get me the contract. Get some rest. Is it even possible for her to have a normal conversation?* "I will." Mia smiled, offering a pleasant facade. "Thank you for the offer. Have a good day." *I can be nice. I can be nice.*

Teri stood and left her cup on the table. "I have work to do before breakfast."

She was gone almost as quickly as she had appeared. No good-byes, no "see you laters." Mia relaxed. Now she could enjoy the time and the sunrise by herself. She stretched her legs out, leaned back in the chair, and sipped her coffee. She let her mind wander wherever it wanted to go. To the halcyon days with Nat and Michel. To her youthful, exuberant days as a student in Paris. Even to the hours of concern with her mother's heart attack. Anywhere. Except to thoughts of Teri. She wanted the feeling of calm to return. She needed the equanimity as a constant.

Around eight thirty, she decided to take a walk before breakfast. She barely made it to the Sound when she noticed a female coming from the direction of the house. *Pam! So much for a quiet walk.* She turned and walked back toward the main house, meeting Pam halfway.

"Good morning, Pam. Didn't know you were an early riser."

"Au contraire. I'm generally at the office by six thirty. My most productive times are early in the morning." She leaned close to Mia's ear. "For work. That's because I save my personal productivity for nights."

Mia could feel the warm breath on her neck. It caused a mild stirring, but the desire to laugh was greater. She had to hand it to the woman. She was undaunted. If she was half that good at work, Mia had no doubt that Pamela Milton ran successful marketing campaigns. And like Teri, Pam rarely had people say no to her. The best course was to ignore the flirting.

"You and Teri Stanton will get along great then. She's been working since before sunrise. She's probably somewhere in the big house."

"I'm not interested in what the Stantons are doing except when it's related to the merger of our two companies. Right now, I'm more interested in a different type of merger."

Mia shook her head and walked faster. She briefly wondered if she had stepped into an alternate and perverse universe. "I think it's about time for breakfast." She nearly ran toward the back of the house with Pamela intent on catching her. For once, she hoped Teri would be nearby.

CHAPTER EIGHT

Teri watched Mia and Pamela Milton talking and again wondered what was so interesting. She leaned one hand on the doorsill and debated whether she should go out and join them. After all, the Miltons were *her* guests. She watched as Pamela Milton leaned close enough to Mia that Teri wondered if she was going to kiss her. Suddenly, Mia was moving at a rapid pace toward the house. Teri didn't know what was going on, but she needed to put an end to it.

"Teri, imagine seeing you twice in the same morning." Mia swallowed the grin. Her voice was light, pleasant, and friendly.

Teri was flummoxed. *What the hell is going on? Earlier, she was barely talking to me, and now she's acting like my best friend.*

"Ms. Milton, I believe, was just looking for you. She was saying that she was interested in talking business." Mia turned toward Pam and smiled. "I believe you wanted to discuss a merger."

Pamela Milton laughed. "Très astucieux." Teri wasn't sure what was said, but she didn't like Pamela's tone of voice.

Mia quickly disappeared into the kitchen.

Very few things surprised Teri anymore, but Mia was a conundrum. One she wanted to understand. She spoke, or at least knew some things, in two languages, started conversations with perfect strangers, and apparently got along with everyone. Was it possible she didn't really know Mia Daniels at all? What other surprises were there? Teri gritted her teeth. She hated surprises.

"Fascinating woman." Pamela finally turned toward Teri. "Are you up for discussing business, or shall we have breakfast first?"

Teri's body tensed. Whatever interest Pamela had in Mia was not related to business. What right did she have to care, as long as it didn't interfere with the merger? After all, Mia was a grown up. She could take care of herself. "Breakfast should be ready. Shall we go in?"

❖

"I've arranged a small party for this evening," Teri's mother announced. "Just a few people."

"A few hundred," Richard, Teri's father added, laughing.

Teri drank her coffee. She was amazed at how easily her mother could put a party together. But then that was her role. Just as she had a role. Her father had a role. Brenna, as the corporate lawyer, had a role. Everyone except Jeremy. He was once again missing. *Oh, he did run in and grab a plate, filled it with food, and then disappeared. Where the hell is he?*

"Is your brother joining us to discuss business?" Pamela asked.

"Probably. Any particular reason for asking?" Teri was getting annoyed with Pamela Milton.

"I guess someone must entertain your guest," Pamela said. Her tone of voice intimated the entertaining was very personal.

"What time are you going into the city?" Teri's mother asked.

"We're meeting with the merger specialists at ten," her father said. "Then we're having lunch at our club. We should be back by four. Plenty of time for your party."

"I thought everyone was going into the city," Pamela said.

"I have too much to do here," Mary Milton answered.

"And Jeremy?" Pamela asked.

"He'll be joining us," Teri said. She smiled, but it was forced. Very few things made her smile, and she rarely laughed. This morning, she was doing a slow burn.

Teri didn't know what was swirling through Pamela's brain matter. Something was going on, and she would get to the bottom of it. Her gut was telling her Pamela Milton wasn't completely focused on business.

❖

As soon as breakfast was done, Teri went looking for her brother. She would bet the merger she knew where he was. She started to knock on the door to Mia's cottage when she heard the voices coming from around back. She walked around and found Mia and Jeremy leaning together at the table on the deck looking at something. They were laughing and talking in an intimate tone.

"I can't believe you kept that," Mia said.

"How could I not keep that picture of you? You were so cute."

"You are perverse." She pinched his arm.

"Jeremy, you need to get ready for our meeting." Teri walked up to the patio. She had heard enough to know the conversation was personal. "Good morning, again." She nodded at Mia and then faced her brother. "Need to be ready in twenty minutes."

"I'm riding in with Mia. She has a couple of errands to run."

"You need to be on time."

"Don't worry," Mia said. "We're leaving in a few minutes. And I'm a good driver. I'll take good care of him."

Teri clenched her jaw and shoved her hands into her pants pockets. She glared at Mia, trying to determine if she was again being challenged.

"Teri, I know this merger's important to you. All these plans are ones you made at the last minute. They're not my plans. I'm going to spend as much of my free time with Mia. Is there a problem with that?"

"Yes, but it's obvious you're going to do what you want." Teri continued to stare, but Mia didn't flinch. Finally, she looked at her brother. "Just be on time." *Why was Mia so damn important?*

Teri walked quickly back to the house. Her irritability was growing. Part of it was from acknowledging that maybe there was something special about Mia.

❖

The day had been productive. Teri was pleased. The small orchestra was playing by the time Teri wandered into the garden. The weather was perfect, and several dozen people were already present. She had opted for a gray silk suit with mid-calf skirt, tuxedo style silk blouse, and her black heels. She had carefully crafted an image that was controlled power. It was an image she was safe with.

She grabbed a glass of champagne and walked up to the Miltons. Both her parents were already circulating through the crowd.

"Let me introduce you to some of our other guests." She led the foursome around introducing them to a various associates and business leaders. Mr. and Mrs. Milton started chatting with one of their California congressmen. After a few more minutes, she left the Milton siblings chatting with other guests and went to look for her brother. She had to admit he was impressive in the discussions earlier in the day. Jeremy had surprised her in how much he knew about the negotiations.

Teri placed her empty glass on a tray and grabbed another. She was about to wander back toward the Miltons when she noticed Jeremy and Mia coming from the directions of the guesthouse. Jeremy was elegant in his black tuxedo. Mia, however, was stunning in a simple, knee-length black cocktail dress. Teri stood mesmerized. The only person she could see was elegant, attractive Mia. The only thought filling her brain now was how much she wanted Mia.

Mia's laughter brought her back to her surroundings. For a brief second, Teri wanted to be the one escorting Mia, but she quickly shoved the impulse down. It was not related to business.

She waited until they were close. Teri grabbed another glass of champagne and handed it to Mia. "Good evening. I'm glad you decided to join us. The dress is lovely. Is it new?" What she really wanted to know was whether her brother bought it.

"No, I've had it for some time. One of my errands in the city was to pick up some things from my hotel and to check out."

"I didn't realize you were staying in the city." Teri's curiosity was piqued. Mia was staying at the Stantons but had a hotel room in New York City. That meant she was choosing to stay out here.

"Mmmm." Mia sipped her champagne.

God, she can be irritating.

"May I have this dance?" Jeremy asked. He removed the glass from Mia's hand and gave it to Teri. He quickly led her out to the dance floor.

Once again, Teri felt control slipping. Mia looked lovely and comfortable dancing with Jeremy. *This is insane.* No matter how she tried, she couldn't get the image of Mia far enough away or buried deep enough to ignore. *She's an excellent dancer. I didn't know that Jeremy could waltz, but Mia...Mia is exquisite.* Teri's pulse was racing.

"They make a lovely couple." Pamela's brother, Gary, had walked up without Teri noticing.

"They're good friends. Known each other a long time." *I need to pay more attention to business.* "So, Gary, what is your role in the company?" Before he could answer, Teri was distracted by her sister walking in and hugging Mia. *Is there no end to the influence she has in this family?*

CHAPTER NINE

D oes checking out mean you're leaving?" Jeremy asked.
"It means I don't want to stay around here. Your family
has demands on your time. I know how much this is creating tension
in your family."

"Mia, will you wait until I talk to you in the morning?" Bren
asked. "I hurried back to meet with you. Not the Miltons."

"Bren, you can't change your family. Teri is all business, and
the company's in the middle of a big merger. The Miltons will be
around for a couple of more days."

"Just promise me you'll wait until we talk. It will be early, I
promise."

"I promise, but only until noon."

"Thanks," Jeremy said. "Let me go make a couple of calls." He
kissed her cheek and ran toward the back of the house.

"Let me change clothes," Bren said. "I think I know what
Jeremy's up to, and it will give us time to talk. I've some good news.
Let me say hello to some of the guests first."

Mia felt elation creep in. She watched Bren walk away. Could
she have the news Mia was hoping for?

"Alone? Maybe I can provide some company?"

Pamela Milton! Mia took a deep breath and challenged herself
to be polite. "I'm fine, thank you."

"You're very fine." Pamela proceeded to whisper a rather
indelicate invitation in Mia's ear.

"I'm not interested."

"Pourqoui pas? You won't regret it." Pamela ran a finger slowly along her arm.

Oh, I will definitely regret it. "My only regret would be saying yes."

"I take that as a challenge. I promise no regrets."

"Yes, you've already said that."

Pamela ran her hand over Mia's back causing Mia to move farther away. No matter how much Mia moved away, Pamela followed.

"My French is not nearly as good as yours. When I get excited, I have trouble thinking in English."

Mia mentally rolled her eyes. She wasn't sure how much more of this game playing she could take.

"Pamela, your parents want you to meet someone." Somehow, Teri appeared and stepped in between them. Her voice seemed somewhat forced, as if she were struggling to be civil. "Let me introduce you." She pushed Pamela across the room before a word was spoken.

Mia offered a whispered thank you when Teri looked back briefly.

Teri just nodded.

"It's definitely time to get the hell out of Dodge," Mia said as she headed to the guesthouse.

Mia was accustomed to people who were more forthcoming. More honest. There were too many games being played, and she was not going to get caught in the middle.

Tonight, she was exhausted. Tomorrow, early, she would pack and drive back into the city. Hopefully, she would be able to say good-bye to Jeremy and spend some time with Bren.

CHAPTER TEN

It was nearly eight in the morning when Jeremy knocked on the door. "Glad you're packed. We're going to Maine."

"Jeremy, your family expects you to be here."

Jeremy's expression was determined. "No one asked me what I was doing. I'm not asking them. Bren has the helicopter standing by on the other side of the river and she's already packed."

"If you both leave, hell will break loose for both of you."

"I've spent most of my life doing what my family expects. I went to Harvard and hated business. I changed to archeology and disappointed my parents. I go to the office every day but rarely have anything to do. Bren handles all the legal. Teri does the rest. You and Elaine are my only real friends. If she'll have me, I'm going to marry Elaine, and I want you to be my best woman."

Mia chuckled. "You're certifiable. You just need to do something that *you* feel is worthwhile."

"You've made me realize that there is more to life than work and making money."

"You're a good man, Jeremy. Between the two of us, we make one perfect person. Or one screwed up one."

"You and I both know what your problem is."

"Yeah, I know. I'm working on trusting my gut. And learning to trust that I can be loved for me. My mom's illness and Nat's death reminded me of my own mortality and that I don't want to waste a minute of my life. There's so much more, Jeremy. God, if we could only have the knowledge and confidence at eighteen or twenty we do when we're older. But I'm getting there."

"Good. Now, let's get going. We've got everything planned, and we're on a tight schedule."

Mia laughed. "Are we escaping?"

"Absolutely."

Mia pulled the blue dress out of the closet and put it on the bed. "Let's go, then. I feel like a kid sneaking around on our parents."

Fifteen minutes later, the three of them were boarding the boat. The trip was fast. Mia was accustomed to the boats that took tourists and residents between the Greek Isles. They were water taxis compared to the luxury high-speed vessel the Stantons kept.

Once they crossed the river, a helicopter was waiting. Mia had never been in one and approached with caution. After they were airborne, however, she was fascinated at all they could see.

"This is incredible." Too soon, however, they were setting down at Long Island's MacArthur Airport. There a small private jet was waiting.

"Okay, this is too much. If you're trying to impress me, you've done it."

"This is a Gulfstream 650," Bren said. "The company bought it because of its speed and functioning. It can make international flights with no problem."

"This is where I'm leaving you two," Jeremy said. "I'm flying to San Francisco to ask Elaine to marry me. I'll call tomorrow and let you know what she said."

Mia was surprised he wasn't going to Maine, but she was happy for him. She hugged him good-bye and watched the limo drive him over to another waiting plane.

"Let's go," Bren said as she climbed aboard the Gulfstream.

Mia climbed aboard and was impressed with the large, comfortable leather interior. Lighting gave it a sense of space.

"It's gorgeous and comfortable. Like flying first class." Mia settled in her seat and looked out the large windows.

Once they were in the air, Mia looked at the large video screen showing the route they were flying. "We're flying up the coast." It had been so long since she had spent much time in New England. "I've missed this. My trips to the States have generally been business or family visits, or you and Jer."

"Jeremy loves this area. Me, I love the nightlife of South Beach. I've come up here a few times during the summer to spend time with my brother."

"Well, tell me. What news do you have?"

Bren grinned and opened her briefcase. "First, Michel. You have friends in the State Department. His passport should be ready in about ten days." She pulled out some documents. "Here's his citizenship papers."

Mia reached across and hugged Bren. "I can't tell you how much this means to me. Especially now."

Bren squeezed her hand. "I'm honored that you asked me for help. I know how hard the last couple of years have been."

"You and Jeremy have made the time passable." A lump of emotion lodged in Mia's throat and threatened to choke off any speech. She swallowed once, then twice until she was sure she could utter a syllable without falling apart. "Last year, when I began the adoption process, I was looking forward to starting a new chapter in my life. I didn't realize what a big difference it would also make to my family. Or how complicated."

Bren stroked her hand. "I'm glad I could help, at least with the adoption."

Mia smiled. "My parents are so excited about becoming grandparents. My brother's not in any hurry to have kids. When I told Mom and Dad, I was adopting Michel, you should've seen the look on their faces."

"I'm happy for all of you. I also have a good friend looking at property in northern Virginia. She assures me she can find a place in your budget. Now, let's celebrate a better year for us all."

Mia raised her glass of juice. "Hear! Hear!"

The conversation turned to hiking, museums, and sunrises. By the time they landed at Bangor International Airport, Mia was looking forward to an enjoyable vacation.

On the ground, a Mercedes GL class SUV was waiting. Mia tossed her bag in the back and climbed in front. The leather seats were so comfortable she could easily fall asleep. The car still had that new car smell and look.

"How did you arrange all this in such a short time?"

"My admin makes all my travel arrangements. She's accustomed to my having to leave on a moment's notice. The plane we flew in is usually reserved for Teri or my dad's use."

"And the Mercedes?"

"I generally opt for a Prius."

"Being a Stanton definitely has its privileges."

"And disappointments. Yes, it's easy to get whatever we want or need, but there's a cost for everything."

"Does Teri know that you would like to do more than legal work? Does she know you want to be C.O.O. one day?"

"Hell, no. My father and Teri expect Jeremy to step up."

"Bren, I'm so sorry. I'm glad I don't have to deal with those problems. I make good money, but I'm not even close to being able to afford this. Plus, I've tried to help my parents as much as I can."

"I envy you," Bren said. "Like Teri, I've become somewhat spoiled. Jeremy is the smart one. He knows what he wants. He just needs the courage to do it."

Mia needed to lighten the mood. "Come on. Let's explore this charming hideaway."

The next forty minutes were spent driving around Bar Harbor. Mia was excited about the historical character of the small town and the lovely cottages. The town was small but delightful. Bren had brushed up on the history and life of the area and provided running commentary.

"If you'll stop at a grocery store, I'll fix dinner."

"How do you find the time to cook?"

"It's something I enjoy. Tonight, I'll keep it simple." Shopping was quick and then they were back in the SUV.

Bren pulled up a long driveway and stopped behind a three-story, white, typical New England house that had to be at least a hundred years old.

"This isn't a cottage. This is huge. How many rooms does it have?"

"I've never counted, but there are eight or nine bedrooms, depending on whether you count the sleeping porch. My South Beach condo has five bedrooms and baths."

Mia grabbed groceries and clothes. "This is probably the biggest house around."

"My grandmother was born and lived in Maine until she married my grandfather. She came from a large family, and this house was where she grew up. She was determined to have a place in Maine. She generally spent every summer here. Teri, Jeremy, and I used to come up every summer until she passed away. I think that was when Teri started changing."

"How did she change?"

"She stopped laughing. Everything became serious. She was fourteen. Jeremy had just turned seven. I think Granny kept us all grounded. When she died, we lost our grounding. Mother thought Bar Harbor primitive and never came up. Dad came up and brought me along until I was ten. Jer continued to come up once he was old enough to drive."

They managed to unload the car in one trip, and Mia got a quick tour of the place. Bren showed her to a large bedroom that looked out on the water. She opened the windows. "I want this one, if it's okay."

"It's not like there aren't enough bedrooms that we could each sleep in a different one each night. Except that might make a lot of work for the housekeeper."

"Well, let's give her the night off and mess up the kitchen. Let me change and I'll get started fixing something to eat."

Mia changed into sweats and a well-worn T-shirt. She quickly put away all the groceries except what she needed for dinner.

"Can I help?"

"No, I've got everything. Sit and talk while I cook." Mia quickly mixed ingredients and had dinner cooked and on the table. Conversation was light. She enjoyed sharing wine and catching up on each other's lives.

Dinner over, Mia sat on the front porch and enjoyed the music of the frogs and crickets. She could feel her body relax. She put her head back. She hummed as she rocked, feeling the most relaxed since before her mother's heart attack. She watched the lights of a vehicle turn up the drive.

Wonder who's coming up here at this time of night?

The car stopped and the door opened. Mia stopped rocking. She had an answer.

"Brenna," she called, "you need to come out."

CHAPTER ELEVEN

Teri was furious but was determined to remain in control. "Hello." Her voice was barely civil. "Thought I might find you up here." She stretched her fingers. They were sore from being in tight balls for most of the trip. Teri had listened to fifteen minutes of harangue from her parents, snide comments from Pamela Milton, and then discovered the helicopter unavailable and the jet she had personally chosen still on its way back to New York. To make matters worse, the private investigator had called. Pamela Milton was well known in certain circles on the West Coast for her discreet affairs with attractive women.

Her thoughts were everywhere. Could Mia be a spy sent to disrupt the merger? Teri was reluctant to believe it, but she couldn't come up with another explanation. She had waited two hours for another helicopter, and that only added fuel to her fire. Checking Mia's room, she found the blue dress and nothing else. What else could she think? She would take care of this once and for all.

"Is Jeremy here?" She walked up the steps and could barely make out Mia sitting on the rocker in the fading twilight.

"No, he should be in California by now."

Teri was confused. She was sure Mia was not alone.

"Hi, Teri." Bren wiped her hands on the dish towel.

Brenna? Teri hadn't noticed her sister's absence. "Can I talk to you for a few minutes?"

"Why don't you two stay out here and I'll go in." Mia walked to the door. Teri was less than five feet away but refused to make eye contact. Mia shook her head. "We were just getting ready to have some dessert and coffee. Would you like to join us?"

Teri finally looked at Mia. Even in baggy sweats, she was attractive, although she was still a pain in the ass.

"I haven't had dinner."

The way Teri spoke it was obvious she didn't expect an answer. "No problem." She looked at Bren. "You two come on in when you're ready."

"What were you thinking?" Teri asked as soon as the door was closed, her voice controlled rage. "Everyone is talking about all of you being missing."

"I think you're overreacting."

"Trust me, the Miltons have noticed."

"Oh, come on." Brenna laughed.

"What's so damn funny?"

"Sorry, I don't think the Miltons' concerns are about business."

"You don't know that. The household is well aware that Mia was visiting, and now she's disappeared. And you. And Jeremy. What will the Miltons think?"

"Give me a break. You're one to talk."

Teri didn't like having her personal life thrown into her face. "You're to go to California in the morning. I need you to find out as much as you can. Now. Have Jeremy do a walk around. You sit down with their legal."

"Teri, this can wait. I haven't seen Mia in quite a while, and we only have these few days. She's come thousands of miles and we've made plans."

"You go tomorrow. You can talk to her any time."

"No. I've had these plans with Mia for some time, and I have no intention of letting her down. You go."

"This is not a negotiation. You're going and that's it. This is a very sensitive time. I'll stay here with Mia."

"You'll what? Teri, give me a break." Bren chuckled. "You never take time off. Mia is here for a vacation, to relax."

"Relaxation is greatly overrated. Whatever you planned, I can handle." Teri was not happy that Bren was being so adamant. This obstinacy was new. No doubt Mia was rubbing off on her, too.

"My point exactly. I'll go next week or you go tomorrow."

"*You* are going tomorrow. I've arranged your transportation and hotel. A corporate jet will be ready at ten and you will be on it."

Bren folded her arms across her chest. "I've never asked for anything from you or this business. I've made a commitment to Mia that's very important for us to finish together. California can wait a week or two."

Teri was losing her patience. What could be more important than the merger? After all, Mia wasn't family. "You're needed in California tomorrow, not next week. Is your only objection to going Mia being alone?" Bren nodded. "Then I assure you I will entertain Ms. Daniels until she leaves."

"Give me a break. Why would you want to spend time with my friend?"

"I need you on that plane in the morning."

"What is this really about?"

"It's about you going to California tomorrow."

"I don't believe you." Bren paced up and down, her arms flying in the air as she spoke. "You start off by complaining about what others may be thinking, and now you're telling me I'm the only one who can handle this situation. Oh, and you're going to take a vacation, go hiking. I'm not buying it. I've never been allowed to do anything but legal work."

"You're going to do legal work. Besides, how many times have you told me to get a life? Well, maybe it's time to start."

"With Mia?"

"Why not?"

"Why?"

Bren was beginning to sound like Mia. Teri was so damn frustrated. They were talking in circles. "You said you didn't want to leave her alone, and I need you to go to California in the morning."

"That's an excuse. Why me instead of you?"

"I need your legal expertise."

"Why would you want to stay here with her? She's perfectly capable of taking care of herself."

"Will you go to California if we leave her here by herself?"

"No."

"Then you go and I'll stay." Teri crossed her arms across her chest. As far as she was concerned, the issue was resolved. "I'm done talking."

"I need to talk with Mia."

"No, you don't. Just tell her that you're going to California and I'll entertain her."

"That's not the way this works. I don't tell people. I ask them. Besides, she might not want to stay if I'm not here."

"Why not?"

"Because she may not want to spend time with you!"

"Why?"

"Mia's right. You never answer questions but you sure can ask them. Mia thinks that you don't like her. And I agree with her."

It was said so matter-of-fact that she didn't have time to react. *What does any of this have to do with business?* "I don't believe that."

"You really don't understand, do you?"

"You said she was here to relax."

"She is. And that's something you don't know how to do. Or show any inclination to want to learn."

"How fucking hard can it be? I'll stay and do whatever is necessary to entertain your friend. I'm perfectly capable of attempting any task."

"Let me get this straight. You're going to take time off from work and New York and spend time with Mia in Maine? You're going hiking and eating boiled lobster with your hands?" Bren laughed. "This is too much. Let me talk to Mia and then I'll give you an answer."

"What's so damn funny? I'm not that incompetent."

"Give me ten minutes and then come in."

"This is ridiculous. I'll just tell her that is what we're doing."

"No. I'll talk to Mia first."

Chapter Twelve

I'm standing out there and wondering why the hell I'm out on the porch of a place my family owns. Where are the cooks and staff?" Teri was looking around the downstairs.

"Everyone has the night off." Mia kept her voice calm.

"Who's going to fix me something to eat? And why did you let them have the night off?"

"I suggested they have the night off." Mia stood in front of Teri. "We weren't expected and they had other plans. I'm perfectly capable of cooking."

Teri stared at Mia. "You cooked dinner?"

Mia took a deep breath. *Remain calm.* Bren's words had unnerved her. She had no doubt that, once again, Teri was trying to keep her from associating with Bren and Jeremy. "Yes." *This was going to be a long night.* Every minute was convincing her that doing anything with Teri Stanton was a bad idea. "If you sit down, I can have something hot in about fifteen minutes."

She returned the quiche to the oven. Mia set the table for Teri and added three dessert plates. She turned away and finished preparing dinner. In less than twenty-four hours, the visit had become a nightmare. She stared down at her hands. They weren't very steady. If she didn't agree to spend time with Teri, Bren would stay. If Bren stayed, Teri would probably make Bren's life miserable. If she did agree to spend time with Teri, Teri would probably make her life miserable. How many times had she wondered what it would be like to have a night with Teri? How many times had she dreamed about being noticed by Teri? *Well, guess what? Reality sucks.*

The timer went off. She needed to make a decision. Bren had been arguing with Teri the entire time she had been heating the quiche. She turned the oven off and set the quiche and the warm pie on the table. She pulled the ice cream from the freezer and slammed it on the table.

"Enough!" Mia looked at Teri. "I don't know what this is about, but you two are going to stop arguing. I'm an adult and capable of making my own decisions: what I do, whom I spend time with, and where and when I go." She put her hand over Bren's. Teri glared at both of them. "Go ahead and go out to San Francisco." Her smile was meant to reassure Bren that she would be fine. "You have everything here under control, and I can wait for the rest."

"Well, I guess that's settled." Teri picked up her fork and began to eat. "Make sure you pick up the analysis I prepared on the Miltons." She stopped and savored the quiche. "This is delicious."

"You seem surprised," Mia said. "Thank you. I assume that's a compliment. Now, if it's okay with you, I'll stay here tonight and then go to the airport in the morning. You will go back with your sister and take care of whatever business you need to. Now it's settled." Mia put pie and ice cream on a plate and took a bite. For the first time in her life, she was grateful that her father had been sent to Europe.

"Where are you going?" Teri asked.

"What difference does it make? As long as Bren goes to California, what I do is not your concern."

"You can stay at my place," Bren offered. "As for you, dear sister, you do not control my life outside of work."

"She can stay here and I will entertain her." Teri shoved the plate of ice cream away. "There's no need for her to stay at your place. You won't be there. You do work for me."

"Teri, I don't work for you. You can't tell me what I can or cannot do." Mia would have told Teri to leave if this had been her house. It wasn't.

CHAPTER THIRTEEN

Teri put the fork down. No one ever said no to her.

"No, it isn't settled. The agreement was that Bren would go to California and I would keep you busy this week."

"That was not my agreement. That was between you and your sister."

"What's the problem then?"

Bren started to answer, but Mia stopped her. "This is between Teri and me."

Bren nodded and grinned.

Mia gathered her thoughts. "Teri, I'm not a bargaining chip. You cannot negotiate what you want your family to do and use me for leverage. I can't imagine any reason you might want to take time away from your work to do something unrelated to work. And I'm sure you've never been hiking in your life."

Teri slammed her fork down. The slow burn was turning into a wild fire. "Are you daring me?"

Mia laughed. "Not hardly. Just a statement of fact. Teri, go back to whatever you were doing before you came up here. I'll leave tomorrow and you won't have to see me again."

There was something grating about Mia's words. She had pretty much told Teri to get lost, and no one did that.

"Believe it or not, I occasionally do things that have nothing to do with work. And I can't imagine hiking being that hard." She leaned back in her chair. "I'll negotiate with you, if that's what you want. My sister needs to go to California to do some legal work. That leaves me with some time on my hands. Why don't I show you around this area? If that's okay with you?"

Mia just glared.

"Do you have problems with that?" Teri asked.

"You really want to go hiking?"

"Yes."

"You really want to spend time walking around the shops looking at touristy kitsch and eating lobster by hand?"

"If that's what you want to do, yes."

"You want to spend time in the kitchen cooking or washing dishes?"

Teri looked at the sink and then at Bren. *She's kidding, isn't she? Call her bluff.* "Yes, but we have staff for that."

"I know you do. These are things I do every day and enjoy doing."

"O—kay." Teri was quickly trying to figure out if this was a test or did Mia really want to do all those things.

"Sorry," Mia said, "but I don't believe you. I have no doubt you work hard at what you do, but I'm sure you've never washed a dish or cleaned a floor." Mia didn't try to hide the smirk.

Mentally, Teri was already trying to figure out how to get out of this agreement.

"Teri, I'm fine. This is not something you would choose to do. Go home and go to work."

"Damn it!" Teri threw her napkin on the table and stood up. "I made a legitimate offer and you turned it down without even giving me a chance to prove I'm serious." This was supposed to be a done deal. She was being out-negotiated. "I'm staying and that's that." Teri was furious. Being calm around Mia was getting harder and harder. What was really pissing her off was that she was arguing to do things she had no real intention of ever doing.

Mia stood, her hands on her hips. "The only thing decided is inside your head."

"What the hell does that mean?"

Bren wedged herself between Mia and Teri. "Mia, what would you like to do?"

"I thought we had already agreed," Teri said.

"I'm asking Mia."

CHAPTER FOURTEEN

Mia was amused by Teri's reaction. She was also confused. Teri Stanton was so uptight Mia doubted she knew what the word relax meant. Her life was about work, winning, and money. Teri didn't give a rat's ass about anyone or anything that didn't increase her own stature or the company's wealth. Mia had no reason to think that Teri had any interest in actually spending time with her. Why then was Teri so insistent? *It must have to do with some perverse sense of winning a battle. Being the victor.* Mia had to bite her lip to keep from laughing. *Teri hiking?*

What did she want to do? Did she even want to deal with Teri? Would this be a different type of revenge? Dragging Teri's butt up a mountain at zero dark thirty in her expensive shoes and silk suit? Mia's smile widened. *Wonder how much hiking and sightseeing Teri can stand? Maybe this will be one way to get rid of Teri once and for all. Call her bluff.*

Mia stuck out her hand. "Done. You're my escort and my guest for the remainder of my visit. Now, how long do you have free?"

Teri's eyes got wide. "How long did you plan on playing tourists?"

"Seven to ten days," Bren answered. "Or more. Mia actually was planning on being around for at least two weeks."

"Shit!" Teri may have whispered, but Mia heard her, loud and clear.

"Well, Teri, do you have two weeks?"

"Don't worry. I can arrange the time." Teri gritted her teeth.

Mia was chuckling now. *This might be fun.* She didn't know, or care, what Teri's motivation was, but she had no doubt that Teri was not up to anything that didn't involve work. Her work.

"Fine. You arrange your schedule." Mia pulled Bren up.

"Fine. Where are you two going?"

"Bren and I have some business of our own to take care of." Mia followed Bren upstairs.

"What kind of work does she have with my sister?"

Teri made no effort to hide her muttering. Mia chuckled and pushed Bren. "Your sister is going to be miserable here."

"Not much I can do about it. Are you sure you want to go through with this?"

"No, but it's useless to argue. Tell me what's going on with the passport, where it's going to be sent, and who I contact in case you get detained."

"Mia, it's under control. It's coming to my apartment in the next few days. I'll give you my admin's phone number, just in case. I'll also give you the key to my place. I have an extra. I'll get back as quickly as I can." Bren put an arm around Mia. "We'll get this all taken care of, I promise."

Bren took out the extra key and gave it to Mia. "I'm so sorry."

I'm probably going to be very sorry. "I'll be fine."

CHAPTER FIFTEEN

Is this really necessary?" Teri was tired of trying on hiking boots. Besides, she really needed to answer some phone calls and text messages. Every time she pulled out her iPad or cell phone, Mia found another pair of boots to try.

"Your heels are lovely, but they would not be safe on uneven surfaces and I can't imagine you walking through mud and muck in those. They look expensive."

"They are."

"I bet," Mia mumbled. "We can leave now if you want to go hiking in those." Mia pointed at Teri's feet.

Teri's eyes became slits. "Are you determined to make my life difficult?"

"I'm serious."

"Isn't there any place to go hiking that has flat, dry land?"

Mia laughed. "Sure, Manhattan."

Teri glared and tried on another pair. "Okay, what about these boots?" She pointed to her feet. "They are comfortable and I like the fit and feel."

"Perfect. Now on to jeans and shirts."

Teri rolled her eyes. *What the hell have I agreed to?* "Let's go."

"What size and what type?"

"I don't know," Teri said. "Why waste money on something that I can't wear to work?"

"Okay, take two different sizes from the same style and see how they fit."

When Teri came out in the dark blue jeans, Mia looked uncomfortable. Teri looked in the mirror. She knew she had a good body, and the jeans certainly showed off her flat stomach.

"Those are perfect. Don't need to try the other ones. Now off to shirts." Mia turned and walked away.

Selecting shirts turned into a major task. "I don't own anything that's not black, white, or gray." Teri said. "It makes it easier to get dressed."

"Let's add a little color," Mia said.

Teri looked at different colors but ended up selecting a black-and-white check. When Mia rolled her eyes, Teri held it up and looked at it. "What's wrong with it? I tell you what. I'll pick one out for you, and you can pick one out for me. But I'm still getting this one."

Mia nodded. Teri pulled out a royal blue solid color shirt and brought it up to the counter. She laughed when she saw Mia had gotten the same color shirt but in Teri's size.

"Well, at least there's one thing we agree on." She held up both shirts.

❖

Teri grinned and Mia realized that she had never seen her smiling. Oh, she put on a smile when greeting people, but it never reached her eyes. And it rarely lasted. The ever-present flat affect, or the more ominous scowl, would quickly replace it. Teri was attractive when she smiled.

Teri pulled out her wallet and handed over her credit card.

"No, I'll pay for my stuff," Mia said.

"It's the least that I can do. Besides, all this costs less than the shoes I'm wearing now."

Mia looked at Teri's feet and back up.

Teri shifted her feet. She appeared uneasy. "I can afford good shoes. There's nothing wrong with that." It was nearly six. "How about if I buy dinner? You don't have to cook tonight."

"I enjoy cooking," Mia said. "It's relaxing for me."

"I understand, but I want to thank you for today. I can't remember ever relaxing and enjoying anything as much." Sarcasm oozed from every syllable.

"And I have swampland in Colorado for sale." Mia laughed and climbed in the car.

In spite of the sarcasm, Mia suspected a sliver of truth. It wasn't that Teri was always a bitch, she just expected people to do what she asked and that didn't require politeness.

"If that's what you want. I don't mind and it's not that late."

"Good. We can get something to eat and you can relax. You must be tired from all the traveling. And shopping." Teri held up her bags. "And I need to make a few calls."

Ah, this has little to do with saying thank you or being polite, but the need to take care of business. "Of course." Mia was irritated. She had almost let herself believe Teri could relax. "You have real work to do. There are quite a few good takeout places."

"It's not necessary to do takeout."

Mia needed to be by herself. Teri was always about work. Slipping into old behaviors or letting her guard down would only resurrect the pain and the memories. "There's a good steak house, but I'm tired. If you want to go out to eat, you can drop me off." How much longer would she have to put up with Teri?

"Takeout is fine, then. I thought after all this shopping you might enjoy going out to eat." Teri shook her head. "Women! What recommendations do you have?"

Mia's preferred method of handling conflict was to resort to data. It was safer. She mentioned the name of an Italian, a Thai, and American restaurant.

After a brief discussion of likes and dislikes, Teri picked up Thai and drove back in silence. Mia stared out the window, lost in thought.

Once back at the house, Mia took her pad Thai and a glass of wine up to the sleeping porch. She sat in one of the recliners and put her feet up. The river lapping at the edge of the property restored some composure. Teri was shoved into a box for bad memories. Mia put her wine glass on the floor and closed her eyes. She loved the night sounds. It was so relaxing.

CHAPTER SIXTEEN

Ineed those numbers! I can't believe I've only been out of the office one damn day and you still haven't run the analysis. Everything that the Miltons are into. I want it no later than tomorrow night. And I want a fax machine in our cottage in Maine tomorrow morning."

Teri slammed down the phone. She should be in New York at the office. She poured another Scotch. She paced around the room. Milton needed them. *And we need their core business.*

Teri sat back down in front of her laptop and sipped her drink. She needed to review her notes. There were no holes, she was sure of it, but she needed the complete analysis first. Fuck it! She turned off the computer and went looking for Mia.

Mia was sound asleep. Her head tilted to one side with a slight smile that gave her an almost rakish look. She seemed so relaxed, so calm. Teri couldn't help herself. She lightly pushed a strand of hair out of Mia's face. The soft blond hair felt like silk. She picked up the nearly full wine glass and set it on the small table by the chair. She then sat across from Mia and stared.

She's lovely. I can still see the remnants of the lanky teenager, but she's definitely turned into a beautiful woman. Her eyes are so distinctive when she's awake that it's easy to forget how marvelous the rest of her is. Teri wanted to touch the lightly tanned cheek. It had been so long since she had touched a woman in an intimate manner. *This is nonsense. I'm just tired.*

No matter how much she tried to justify the feeling, she couldn't completely dismiss it. Nor could she pull herself away from sitting and staring. She slid back in her seat and leaned her head back. She was able to carefully examine every part of Mia without qualm.

Nice. She felt a chill. Before she could question why, she stood and pulled a light blanket off one of the futons on the porch and then covered Mia. Her senses were filled with Mia's scent, her body heat, her nearness.

She sat back down. She needed the space. The closeness was unsettling. Teri wanted to touch her, to taste her, to pull her close. She wanted to forget about anything but being a part of Mia.

Taking a deep breath eased some of the desire. Teri sipped her drink and enjoyed the view. She couldn't remember ever just wanting to stare at a woman. *What is it about you that's so damn intriguing?*

Mia's neck was sore. She stretched. She had fallen asleep in an awkward position. When she looked around the room, she realized she was not alone. Teri was asleep in an Adirondack chair across from her. As she sat up, a blanket fell to the floor. Someone had covered her. *Teri? Who else?*

Mia returned the favor and covered Teri. She removed the empty drink glass from her hand and set it on the floor. "You surprise me," Mia whispered. Even in sleep, Teri didn't seem relaxed. Mia wondered when was the last time Teri did anything not related to work. When was the last time she really laughed? When was the last time she sat and enjoyed a sunrise? When was the last time she took a deep breath and was truly grateful for being alive?

The few times that she allowed a smile to slip out, Teri was beautiful. Her eyes sparkled. Her face relaxed. It was a fleeting smile, but Mia felt it deep within her. It was obvious that smiling, or joy, was not part of Teri's everyday world. *That's too bad.*

"Which one of the Teri Stantons will you be tomorrow?" She walked into her bedroom and hoped she could sleep soundly.

CHAPTER SEVENTEEN

Bright sunlight woke Teri from a sound sleep. She looked at her watch. She had slept for nearly six hours. Her neck was sore, her back tight, but she felt rejuvenated. Teri couldn't remember the last time she had slept that many hours. She looked around and realized she was alone. Sometime during the night, Mia had disappeared. Teri stood and stretched. She wondered where Mia was.

The rooms upstairs were empty, and Mia's bed was made. Heading downstairs proved to be more fruitful. She heard Mia humming as she walked into the kitchen. *Was this goddamn woman ever in a bad mood?*

Sunlight streamed in the kitchen and danced around Mia. She looked like a goddess with her fiery blond hair and sundrenched body. Her jeans fit her body like a glove. The loose hanging top swayed with every move. Her movements were both graceful and sensual. Teri watched, mesmerized. She couldn't remember ever being so hypnotized by a woman. A groan escaped before she could stop herself.

"Good morning," Mia said without turning around. "I didn't know if you ate breakfast, but I found a French bakery and got a fresh baguette and some locally made preserves. I also have bacon and sausage, eggs, yogurt. Coffee is already made."

Teri scanned the kitchen. It smelled heavenly. The last time she remembered it smelling like this was when her grandmother was still alive. Buried memories struggled to surface. "Something smells wonderful."

"I'm fixing an omelet. Peppers, green onions, mushrooms, and Emmentaler. Would you like one?"

How many times had her grandmother stood in this kitchen and cooked breakfast for her and Bren and Jeremy? How many times had she pinched Teri's cheek and told her to smile more? How many times had her grandmother hugged her and said that she loved her? How long had Teri sat alone at night and cried for her Nana?

Teri felt some emotion rising in her throat. She quickly pushed it back down. She was beginning to hurt. "Where's Mrs. Davis?"

"She had some grocery shopping to do so I told her I would fix breakfast."

Just who does the staff work for? "What can I do to help?" *Did I really just say that?* Teri was on unsure footing and needed some semblance of control.

"Pour your coffee and sit. Tell me what you want."

Mia still had her back to Teri. She was busy at the stove. Everything about her breathed life and strength. Mia seemed to belong wherever she was. No wonder her brother and sister liked her so much. She was an easy person to like.

"I'll have whatever you're having." Teri poured herself some coffee. Mia's hair was in disarray. She wanted to run her fingers through it. She wanted to feel those silken locks. Mia looked young and filled with all the hope and joy of youth. Teri had to remind herself that Mia was only six or seven years younger, her brother's age.

"How've you been? Jeremy said you have some type of government job." Teri needed to return her focus.

Mia put the food on the table and poured her own coffee with cream before answering. "I do work for the government. It fits well with my interests and helps me to enjoy living not far from my parents. I can fly there for the weekend." She cut some slices of baguette and put them on a plate. "I hope you enjoy the food. In Europe, eating is an important part of living and socializing. A meal is always to be enjoyed. Bon appétit!"

"Whenever I was in Europe, meals were associated with business."

"I don't doubt it. Americans are often known for being in a hurry and not wanting to waste time with dining and enjoying." Mia put butter and preserves on a slice of baguette. "Now, taste that." She put the slice on Teri's plate and then fixed a slice for herself. She leaned back and closed her eyes while she chewed. "These are locally grown berries, and you can almost taste the honey in them. The bread is crisp and fresh." She opened her eyes and looked at Teri. "Savor what you eat."

Teri took a bite of the omelet. She followed Mia's example and closed her eyes. Mia was right. If the taste was incredible, the texture was heavenly. It was a sensual, almost orgasmic experience. She couldn't ever remember enjoying food.

"This is amazing." She opened her eyes. "You *are* a good cook." She let the food melt in her mouth and then swallowed. *Who knew eating could be so amazing?*

"When my father was transferred to Europe, it was a real change for all of us. European food has some different ingredients, many much healthier. Living in Europe introduced us to another world, literally. Food, culture, lifestyle." Mia appeared to be lost in some memory.

Teri was surprised when Mia's father resigned within a year of being moved to London. And disappointed. More than once she had questioned moving him. His analytical skills were unmatched. It was old news, however, and not something she could, or would, do anything about it. The move seemed to be good for the Daniels family.

"So, do you take three martini lunches?"

Mia laughed. "That's so American. In France, I'm more likely to have a glass of wine with my meals. Sip, savor, and enjoy. Dining's a time to spend with friends, family, associates, or to meet new people."

"Is that what you do for work?"

"Sometimes." Mia's smile was a knowing one.

When breakfast was over, Mia asked if Teri wanted more coffee.

"What are our plans?"

"Well, I'm going to have another cup and sit on the front porch."

Sitting still was not something Teri did very well. "I'll grab my cup and make a few calls. I'll meet you on the porch in about an hour."

Teri watched Mia leave the room, and as she did, so did the peace Teri had been feeling. Work again occupied her thoughts and actions. Teri needed to be more guarded around Mia. She was allowing her emotions to go unchecked. That was not acceptable. Work was her second skin. She donned it without thinking. Now she was comfortable.

"Jeremy, where the hell have you been? I've called the hotel and you aren't even checked in." Teri paced around the room, her Bluetooth firmly attached to her ear as she studied the printouts. "What do you mean you aren't staying at the hotel? How the hell am I going to get reports to you?"

"Send them to the office. I don't work twenty-four seven like you."

"Fine. I'll fax it to you now. Be at the office before anyone else sees it."

"It's six in the morning. I'll be there by eight."

Teri ran her hands through her hair. Frustration was too mild a word for what she was feeling. "I don't want anyone reading those but you."

"I thought you were doing things with Mia."

"She's fine. Can we talk about business?"

"Teri, the deal was that if Bren came out here, you would entertain Mia. Is she still there?"

"Of course she is. We just finished breakfast." Teri took a deep breath and tried to calm herself. "Don't worry. I'll keep my end of the bargain. Just make sure you get this report before anyone else does." She pushed the off button on her Bluetooth. "Is everyone crazy? Is anyone working? What's so damn important about Mia?"

She put her papers away and went out to the front porch. "Fuck. Where is she now?" Teri wiped the raindrops off her clothes. "Well, I guess we aren't going shopping." Teri searched for Mia and found her sitting on the sleeping porch.

"Guess this isn't hiking weather?" she said.

"Not today. Tomorrow is supposed to be much nicer." Mia stared out at the rain. "I thought we would get up early and watch the sun come up on Cadillac Mountain."

"How far is that?"

"About an hour away?"

"About?"

"About."

"So what time does that mean we need to leave?"

"Around four thirty." She looked up at Teri. "That isn't too early, is it?'

Another day wasted. She would take her iPad. She stared down at Mia and was captivated by the blue eyes. She looked away. "Not a problem. I love wandering around in the dark." *Not.*

CHAPTER EIGHTEEN

*A*h, *the sarcastic Teri is back.* This was the Teri Mia preferred. This Teri was easier to deal with. She closed her eyes and listened to the rain. *Such a restful sound. If Teri wasn't around, I could really enjoy the solitude.*

"What do you want to do today?" Teri was again looking at her. Staring. It was disconcerting. Teri's facial expression was a blank, but her eyes were telling a different story. There was definitely conflict. Mia looked out at the rain. It was safer.

"We could drive to Orono or just drive along the river. Or we could just sit and listen to the rain. It's a great day for taking a nap."

"I have a few calls to make and some e-mails to check on. Why don't I take care of that, and maybe by then the rain will have stopped. We could go out for a drive." Teri turned and headed out of the room.

"Why are you here?"

Mia's question stopped her. Teri didn't bother to turn around. She was getting tired of the question. "We have a deal."

"I release you from the deal. Go home. Go to work. Isn't that what you want to do?"

Teri spun around. "It's what I have to do" Her volume was raised a notch. "Maybe government employees don't understand how important work is, but I—"

Mia stood. "You mean I don't understand how important *your* work is."

"That's not what I said."

"What government employees were you talking about then? There's only one in this room."

"You can't possibly understand how important my work is."

"What I do understand is that you're up by five every morning, making calls, writing e-mails, ordering people around. During the day, you're texting or talking. Every night, you're up until two or three doing the same thing. Every moment that we're not doing something else, you're working. Even the little time we *are* together your phone is glued to your ear."

Teri's expression was grim. "I do serious work. I have thousands of employees all over the world that depend on me to make sure they have a paycheck. My work supports my family, including your good friends, my brother and sister."

"Oh, yes. Your family's barely scraping by on the pittance they receive from your efforts."

"Damn it! I will not apologize for having money or for the real work I do. If it takes long hours to get the work done, then I do whatever it takes. If I have to spend weekends and nights to make sure things are done correctly then I do it. You may not understand that. Your job may allow you to leave work at five, but my job doesn't."

Mia wondered why the hell she was even trying to have a conversation with Teri. Teri had very strong opinions and wouldn't listen to anyone. She was overbearing and opinionated. Mia's calm was slipping. She struggled for control, but it was futile. She was allowing herself to be pulled into Vortex Teri in spite of her best intentions.

"How much money is enough?" Mia wasn't going quietly. "You're right. You have to work long hours, and my job doesn't require any brainwork. Go home, Teri, and take care of your work."

"Are you trying to pick a fight to get out of our agreement?"

"No, I'm just a lowly government employee. I don't understand about work," Mia said. She wanted out of this uncomfortable situation. "Be honest. Wouldn't you rather be working than here?"

Teri glared at Mia for several seconds. "One of the things I appreciate about you is your directness. It can sometimes be annoying. Yes, I would rather be at the office." Teri moved her shoulder length hair behind her ears. "We're in the middle of a major acquisition, and there are too many loose ends I need to attend to. However, I committed to entertaining you this week, and, by damn, I will."

Mia kept her mouth shut. She was tired of arguing. Tired of anger. Tired of the pain. Tired of the last year. She had promised a new start.

"No comment?" Teri asked.

"What do you want me to say?"

"Just a few minutes ago you had plenty to say."

Mia shook her head, feeling years of pent up anger demanding to be free. "It seems that no matter what I have to say you have an answer. I'm releasing you from your commitment. Again. Then we can each go our separate ways. You can go do your real work."

"I made a commitment and I plan on keeping it." Teri's voice was now booming.

"Fine! Go take care of your real work. I'll find something to do until then." Mia walked away. She would be damned if she would let Teri know how angry she was. Or how close she was to tears.

CHAPTER NINETEEN

Teri had trouble concentrating. Nearly two dozen e-mails and several voice messages were awaiting a response. Most dealt with the merger. One urgent call was from her financial group. A couple of e-mails were from their new office in Germany. Nothing she read, none of the messages she listened to made sense.

Instead, the encounter with Mia occupied her thoughts. If she wasn't arguing with Mia, she was enchanted by her. Or she was wondering where the hell Mia went. Teri didn't understand this aberrant behavior. There was nothing logical about this seeming obsession. Work had been her life for so long. These distractions were irrational and preventing her from doing what needed to be done.

"This is ridiculous. I've got work to do."

Teri looked down at her list of prioritized tasks. *Where to start?* She picked up her cell phone and again listened to the messages. She forwarded them to her visual voice mailbox. *At last, something is getting done. By focusing on one task at a time, one message at a time, I can return these calls and get these e-mails taken care of.* Teri nodded. This was easier, understandable. After three hours, she felt better about what was going on in the office. She also felt like she had regained control of her life. Now she could deal with nonessential tasks.

She shut the laptop down and went looking for Mia.

The house was empty. "Where the hell is she now?" Teri pulled on one of the slickers hanging in the mud room and went out to the garage. The cars were still there. She pulled out her cell but realized she didn't know Mia's number. "Damn it. She's intentionally doing this. What a waste of time! She should have left a message telling me if she was going somewhere." Teri's patience was being tested.

When she got back to the house, she searched one more time. Still no Mia. Finally, she realized Bren would have her number. Teri had no other recourse but to call and ask for it.

"Why do you want Mia's number?"

"Why does it matter? I just want it."

"Then I can't give it. Ask Mia."

"I would if I knew where the hell she was."

"What do you mean? Has something happened to her?"

"How the hell do I know? I had some work to do, and when I came out, she was gone."

"Are her clothes still there?"

"Yes." Clothes reminded her to give the blue dress to Mia.

"Then don't worry. She'll eventually turn up."

"She should have told me where she was going."

"Teri, she doesn't need to tell you anything. She especially doesn't need to if you're working. She doesn't work for you."

"I am perfectly capable of multitasking." Teri's voice was louder.

"Everyone is well aware of your multitasking abilities, but that is not what you agreed to do."

"Don't lecture me about what I agreed to do. Trust me, I've been entertaining your little friend." In spite of Mia currently being missing, Teri had enjoyed some of the time with her. When she first couldn't find Mia, she feared Mia had left. She would've missed her. "Now, what is her phone number?"

"Then you need to ask my little friend." The connection was immediately lost.

Teri stared at the phone. "What the hell is wrong with the world?" She put her head in her hands. She was getting a headache.

CHAPTER TWENTY

Mia's shoes were soaked when she finally got back. The walk in the rain had helped her release the anger and anxiety. It was as if her soul had been washed clean. She looked at her sodden feet and smiled. Her clothes would also have been soaked if she hadn't grabbed a slicker before she left. As it was, her sweatpants were damp and needed to be changed. Her top was drier but not much.

The walk into town and then back along the river had restored some calm. She had time to sort through some of her feelings and anger. It was time to let go. There was no way forward without letting go. She pulled off her sneakers and the slicker in the mudroom, intent on getting a hot shower.

"Where the hell have you been?"

Mia was startled by Teri's greeting. "Excuse me?"

"Where have you been? It's nearly four thirty."

"I've been walking." She was not going to elevate her own responses to Teri's. "Is there a problem?"

"I've been looking for you for the last thirty minutes."

"Is there something in particular you needed?"

Teri struggled for words. "Needed? I didn't know where you were and I didn't know how to get in touch with you. I was afraid something may have happened to you."

"As you can see, nothing happened."

"I don't believe this." Teri threw up her hands and paced back and forth. Mia stood in one place, waiting for the ranting to end. "I thought we had agreed that we would do something when I was finished with my work."

"Are you finished with your work?" Mia kept her voice neutral. It took every ounce of control. She was determined to maintain her newly restored peace.

"Of course I am! That's why I've been looking for you!"

"In that case, I'll get ready. Let me get a shower and change and I'll be right down." Mia offered a half-hearted smile. *I can be nice.*

Before Teri could respond, Mia was gone. She stood watching Mia climb the stairs and wondered how she had lost control of the conversation. That seemed to be becoming the standard around Mia.

Any further thoughts were choked off by the visceral reaction Teri was having to Mia's damp clothes clinging to her body. High, taut breasts were easily visible under the white polo shirt. Her wet sweats outlined well-shaped hips and ass. Her hips swayed slightly as she quickly ascended the stairs. The image of Mia climbing the stairs seared into her brain. A current crept through her body. Mia was definitely an interesting woman. *An interesting, impossible woman! An interesting, impossible, desirable woman.*

She sat on the couch and watched local news, unaware of anything being said. Her mind was whirling with thoughts of Mia. Mia was attractive, and Teri had no doubt that the reaction she just had was sexual. She wanted Mia. She also had no doubts about the complications involvement with Mia would cause. Then there was the merger. She had to be focused on business. It had been so long since she had wanted a woman, much less had sex with one.

Teri forced herself to think about the merger. It was safer.

"I'm ready."

Teri turned and found Mia dressed in jeans, her new hiking boots, and a bright, peach-colored, button-down shirt. No matter how she was dressed, Mia was attractive.

"That color looks nice on you." Teri shoved her hands into her pants pockets. The need to touch Mia was not well controlled.

"Thank you." Mia said. "Anything in particular you want to do? I hope I didn't take too long."

Teri looked at her watch. It was after five. Too early to eat. Unless they drove to Orono. "I was wondering if you wanted to drive up to Orono. We could do some shopping and then have dinner. I would like to make up for my earlier behavior."

"I know how much you love shopping." The sarcasm was intentional; Teri was sure of that. "Thank you for the offer. If you're sure, then let's go."

Teri hesitated, but she was the one who offered. "Of course I want to shop."

Mia barely stifled a grin. She turned and walked toward the door. Teri wondered what was amusing.

"Just as long as we're back early enough for me to get some sleep. It looks like the rain has finally stopped."

Teri looked out the window. Indeed there was a hint of sun. "Shall we go then?" She grabbed her wallet and keys and then held the door open for Mia.

"Thank you. I've never been to Orono. What's it like?"

Teri was glad she had recently been to the university. "It's larger than Bar Harbor. The University of Maine in Orono is there. Many restaurants." She looked briefly at Mia. "And lots of different stores for shopping."

"What kind of shopping do you like to do?"

"None!" Teri mentally backed up. She had just committed to taking Mia shopping. "Sorry, I'm not much of a shopper."

"I can't imagine you grocery shopping, but surely you buy your own clothes."

"I do, but I generally have my tailor come to the house and make my suits. She is familiar with the colors and materials I like, and the style doesn't change that much. I just need to decide whether it's a pant suit or skirt suit."

"Color choice must be difficult. Black, black and white, or white."

Teri glared. She headed north on I-95. "You forgot gray and my white blouse with the blue pinstripes."

"And the solid blue shirt you haven't worn yet."

"I'm saving it for our great adventure tomorrow."

"I noticed you didn't complain about the time. Guess it's because you're already up that early."

"When I get up early, I can get a lot done before I go to the office. Generally, I don't have many calls that time in the morning. How do you know I get up that early?"

"I heard you come upstairs the last two nights and then heard you go downstairs yesterday and today. Since I didn't smell coffee or food, I figured you were working."

"I've been doing it for so long. I'm not sure I could stop. What about you?"

"I'm an early morning person but not because I'm hurrying off to work."

"What do you do then?"

"Drink coffee. Enjoy the morning."

"Doesn't that get boring?"

Mia laughed. "Never!" she said with great dramatic emphasis.

Teri turned off the interstate. She couldn't imagine wasting time like that, but here she was driving from one town to another to go shopping and have dinner. "Where to first? There's a mall not far."

"Fine. Let's find a place to park. We can just browse."

"Browse? You don't have anything you're looking for?"

"No. That's why it's called browsing. You just look."

As soon as they parked, Mia was out of the car and walking into the mall. Teri found herself running to catch up. She wished she had worn her new hiking boots. Fortunately, Mia stopped at a nearby shop. It was some kind of toy store.

"Isn't that a beautiful doll? I wonder how much it is." She turned to Teri. "Want to go inside with me?"

Mia was transformed. The look of childlike wonder in her expression, the sheer happiness stirred something in Teri. Mia carefully examined the doll.

"Isn't it magnificent? It's an old-fashioned one. My friend's daughter prefers these. Look at the eyes that blink and the well-made clothes."

Teri had no idea what the differences were between old-fashioned and new dolls. Mia, however, was so enthusiastic that it was contagious. "It's lovely." She looked at it again and realized that the doll had the same bright blue eyes Mia did. "Look, it's your eyes. Beautiful blue."

Mia nearly dropped the doll. Teri grabbed it. She handed the doll back to the clerk and asked to have it wrapped.

"Let me buy it for you," Teri said.

"That's a generous offer, but no. I'll pay for it."

Teri had already pulled out her American Express card. "I know, but I can see how happy it makes you. Please."

CHAPTER TWENTY-ONE

O kay, Teri has complimented me and said please. So, is the world coming to an end? Shit, I need to check my life insurance policies.

Something was going on. Whatever it was, Mia would just enjoy it while it lasted. Which probably wouldn't be that long. "You're much too generous. Please let me pay for it."

"I've already done it." Teri smiled.

It was such a wondrous smile that Mia was both surprised and enchanted. "Thank you." She then made sure the doll was carefully wrapped. It allowed her time to try to understand Teri's uncharacteristic behavior. And her own aberrant reaction.

"Where to next?" Teri asked, picking up her credit card receipt.

"On to the next shop." Mia led Teri in and out of several more shops before her growling stomach caused her to check her watch. "I guess it's time to eat."

"That was loud enough to shake the floor. Come on and let me feed you." Teri briefly took Mia's hand and moved her to the mall exit.

They found a small, highly recommended Italian restaurant. Mia questioned the sommelier on their selection of wines. She selected an expensive Barolo that Teri was unfamiliar with. "You speak fluent French and German and are well-versed in Italian wines. What other surprises do you have?"

"I really don't have any surprises. Trust me; my life's very ordinary."

"Mia, you are anything but ordinary. Where did you learn French? Pamela Milton swears you speak it like a native."

"I think she overstates my skills." *What else did Pam Milton say?*

"So, are you going to tell me how you learned?"

An answer was delayed by their wine arriving. Teri took a sip. "Good choice. I'll have to remember the vineyard and make sure to get a case. Or maybe you'll help me pick out a selection of wines. On that I will trust your judgment."

"Thank you." Mia was really having trouble looking at Teri. The compliments were frequent and unexpected. She wasn't sure how to respond.

"Now, tell me about learning French." Teri leaned forward, looking as if anything Mia had to say was important.

"I had two years of French while finishing my high school equivalent in UK, so I was able to pass the French proficiency. It took an extra year because I transferred from the U.S."

"Mia, I didn't realize."

Realize? Realize that you were uprooting a family and drastically changing their lives. Teri, however, seemed sincere, and she remembered her earlier decision to be agreeable. "I wouldn't have even thought about the Paris Sorbonne if we hadn't moved to Europe. Turned out to work for me."

"You were an amazing kid." Teri paused. "You've become an even more amazing woman."

Mia was speechless. Was Teri flirting? Was this a compliment? "Thank you."

"What did you study?"

Their wine glasses were refilled and dinner served. Before Mia could answer, Teri pulled out her cell phone and responded to a text. *Ah, work. So much for the likeable Teri.* Mia started eating and tried to focus on her food.

"Sorry," Teri said. "I've been waiting for some information. My assistant just sent it by e-mail."

"It's well after five. Does your staff always work late?"

"When there is a lot of work, yes. I pay them well and they are able to flex schedules when necessary."

Mia just nodded and kept eating.

"You were going to tell me what you studied?" Teri said.

"I pursued a liberal arts education."

"A very practical degree." Teri sounded patronizing.

"One of the reasons I went to Paris and chose my major is that I wanted an education that would prepare me for the world around me. A liberal arts education teaches you to think, to explore ideas, to be a citizen of the world. My area of interest was the fine arts, but I learned so much more. Paris is one of the greatest places to study. Voltaire, Proust, Zola, and all the great American ex-pats: Gertrude Stein, Hemingway, Fitzgerald. The architecture, painting and sculpture, the city is full of beauty. The Louvre—I could spend a week there and not see everything. And at night, it is a city of magic."

"You love the city." Her voice was barely a whisper. "I've never felt that way about any place."

Mia leaned forward, her elbows on the table and her chin resting in one hand. "I do. I grew up and found myself there. I accepted who and what I wanted to be and said it was okay." Mia smiled at the memories.

"Wow. What must it be like to be that passionate?" Teri suddenly looked nervous. She avoided looking directly at Mia.

Was she embarrassed to admit something so personal?

"I've never spent much time in Paris. Mostly going from the airport or Gare du Nord to a hotel, but I would agree with you." Teri was back to her unengaged voice.

"I would have thought you would have flown. I can't imagine you wasting time on a train."

"Actually, I like trains. Much more comfortable and I still can get a lot of work done."

"Ah, work." Mia sipped her wine. It gave her time to shape a response. "So, what do you do for fun?"

"Work."

❖

Teri couldn't remember when an evening had been so enjoyable. She was almost sad when they arrived back at the house and Mia said good night.

She went to her desk and turned on her laptop. The room was filled with pictures of her grandparents, her parents, and Teri and her siblings. Memories floated around the room, begging for some life. They finally forced Teri to look at her personal life. For over an hour, she just sat and stared at the screen. Once in a while, she would answer an e-mail. Her concentration was gone. Instead, images from the evening kept popping up. Mia laughing. Mia with sauce on her chin and Teri wiping it off. Mia with her head tilted to one side, the expression on her face one of attentiveness. Mia discussing French history. A subject that had never interested Teri, but Mia made it compelling.

Teri stood and grabbed her glass of Scotch. The room was closing in on her. She didn't have time to waste. But it wasn't wasted. She had a great time. She climbed up to the sleeping porch and sat in the recliner.

No matter how much she tried, Teri was having trouble ignoring the attractive, smart Mia. *Damn, she's a hell of a woman.*

She finished her Scotch and headed for bed. She knew she wouldn't get much sleep but at least she could try. *Oh, shit, we're going to some damn mountain. No, not much sleep.*

CHAPTER TWENTY-TWO

Mia poured coffee into the thermos on the counter. The staff had prepared some cold food and fresh fruit for them. She grabbed her jacket, gloves, and cap. She packed a couple of blankets, the food, and coffee in the Jeep, and pulled it around next to the house. Mia fully expected to see Teri coming out the door. She looked at her watch. It was almost four thirty. She went back in the house.

Teri wasn't in the study, or anyplace else downstairs. Mia finally knocked on Teri's bedroom. "Teri, are you ready to go?" Not hearing a response, she slipped the door open.

Teri sat up abruptly. "Shit." She looked at the clock.

"Teri?"

"I'm awake." Teri pulled the sheet up to cover her naked body. "I'm awake. Give me ten minutes and I'll be downstairs."

Mia knew her grin could have put the sun to shame. And she didn't care. Teri had been asleep. Another indication that something was awry in the Teri the Terror world. *And she sleeps naked. Might be another interesting day.*

Ten minutes later, Teri was rushing down the stairs, her hair still wet.

"Let me get you a towel. It's chilly out there." Mia grabbed a couple of towels from the downstairs bathroom and threw them to Teri as they hurried out the door. Teri was attractive in the blue shirt. *She should wear more color.*

"Why aren't we taking my car?" Teri asked.

"One, this has a tighter turning radius. Two, I checked the map out, and I think it will be better if I drive."

"What's wrong with my driving?" Teri towel dried her hair as she climbed into the car.

"Well, I'm more awake. I've already had one cup of coffee. And I think I have a little more experience driving mountain roads."

"What time did you get up?"

"About an hour ago. Took a shower, got dressed, and had my first cup of coffee."

"Right. Down time when you get up."

"You got it. Hot coffee in the thermos and cream and sugar in the cooler." Mia pulled out and followed the instructions on the printout.

"I've got Mapquest on my iPhone."

"If you want to bring it up on your phone, it would be easier than my trying to drive and read this."

Mia gave her the destination. This quiet, but mindless task didn't require conversation.

Teri put her head against the back of the seat and closed her eyes. When she opened them, they were on a winding mountain road.

"Holy shit! Where the hell are we?"

"Acadian National Park. We're starting to climb Cadillac Mountain. This is why I wanted to drive. Not quite like driving across the Alps, but it can be challenging in the dark if you haven't done it before."

"Can you slow down?" Teri braced her hands on the dashboard.

"Trust me. I'm not driving that fast." Mia was glad it was too dark for Teri to see her grinning. The higher they climbed, the lighter it got. She followed the signs until they reached the top. "Come on. We have a short hike and it's beginning to get light." She shoved the blankets in her backpack and reached for the cooler.

"Can I do anything?"

Mia handed her the cooler and a walking stick.

"Where did you find this?"

"In the garage. Jeremy has several he uses when he comes up here."

Teri grabbed the dark, hand-carved stick. "You know a lot about my brother."

Mia continued to walk ahead. "He's my oldest and closest friend."

"I didn't even know the two of you were still in contact."

Mia nearly tripped over a root. "With e-mail, texting, and Facebook, it's easy to stay in touch." She picked up her pace, determined to watch the sunrise. And avoid any confrontations.

"Can you slow down?" Teri was panting by the time they finally stopped. "I didn't know we were going to jog all the way."

As soon as Mia spread a blanket on the ground, Teri plopped herself down. Mia wasn't even breathing heavily, but Teri was definitely struggling. Mia decided that Teri's exercise was opening and closing her laptop.

Mia pulled out her camera.

"You a photographer?"

"I enjoy it." Mia moved away and took several shots. She walked over to a woman with a camera and compared notes on settings and shots. This woman was obviously familiar with the area and pointed out some other locations for prime shots. Mia kept clicking.

❖

Teri watched as Mia chatted with the stranger. It was not the first time Mia had started up conversations with an unknown person. It seemed so easy for her. Mia moved over to another spot and took more photos. Teri wondered what kind of picture Mia was looking for. She walked over.

"How do you decide what to take a picture of?"

Mia continued to look at the screen on her digital camera, moving it around, snapping, and then moving it again. "I look for the right combination of light, color, and composition."

"How do you know when you have it?"

Mia finally looked at Teri and laughed. "I review all the photos on my computer. Keep a few and delete most of the rest."

"That seems like a lot of wasted effort," Teri said. "Why do you take so many pictures then?"

"How will I know I have the perfect picture if I don't have a lot of imperfect ones to compare it to? Here! You take the camera and move it around slowly until you see a picture you want."

It had been years since she had handled a camera. Teri recognized it as an expensive digital SLR. She moved the camera around, adjusting the focus until she found a shot.

"Go ahead and take two or three more, but move the focus or camera so that you have a slightly different view."

Teri sat on the ground so that she would focus from the bottom up. The object of her interest was a gnarled maple that appeared to have been hit by lightning on one side. She was fascinated by the dichotomy. Green and healthy on one side and darkened and dead on the other. She moved around and took another shot and another.

Realizing she was snapping away with Mia's camera, Teri took one last photo and handed it back.

"Come on, let's go sit down and finish watching the sunrise."

The sun was finally breaking through the mist. Mia poured coffee for them both while Teri unpacked the cold sandwiches and fruit. They ate silently for several minutes. In between bites, Mia snapped pictures. She turned to say something to Teri and was mesmerized by what she saw. Teri's face was bathed in gold. Her knees were bent and both arms were extended across the top of her knees. She appeared lost in the sunrise. The sun made Teri's royal blue shirt warm and brighter.

Mia slowly picked up her camera, aimed it, and took several quick photos, including the one of Teri looking directly at the camera and saying no.

"I'm not very photogenic."

"You're an attractive woman, Teri."

"Every picture I've ever taken I look like I'm in pain."

"Well, maybe you should smile and you would appear less grim."

"I'm not grim."

"You rarely smile." Mia put her hand up. "I know. You have serious work to do." Mia shook her head. "Serious work can still be enjoyable." She noticed Teri shivering. She pulled the other blanket out of the backpack and offered it to her.

"Aren't you a little chilly?"

"Some, but it'll get warmer soon."

Teri moved over next to Mia and wrapped the blanket around the both of them.

The unexpected gesture was disconcerting. Mia felt herself tighten up. There was no way she could avoid their bodies touching. She sat that way for another few minutes before Teri broke the silence.

"It's amazing how different the sunrise looks with every passing second."

"Did you know this is the first place the sun rises in the U.S.? Well, at least part of the year. I'm glad the mist cleared enough to see it."

"Thank you for suggesting this." Teri turned and Mia's face was inches away. Teri's eyes moved down to Mia's lips. She leaned forward and gently, but briefly kissed Mia. "Thank you." She quickly stood.

Mia was bewildered. Teri kissed her and then became impersonal. She arose and began to pack up. The ride back to Bar Harbor was silent. Her thoughts were frozen on a split second of time. *Why had Teri kissed her? Did she regret it as soon as it happened? What happens now?*

"Can I buy you breakfast?" They were approaching the edge of Bar Harbor, and Teri had finally broken the silence.

"Why did you kiss me?" Mia asked.

"Do you regret it?"

"I'll answer your question *after* you answer mine."

"The sun was glowing on your face and I couldn't help myself. Do you regret it?"

"I have no regrets since I'm sure it won't happen again."

"What makes you think it won't happen again?"

"I doubt either one of us wants to make that same mistake."

"How do you know that?"

"You prefer really well-planned. That wasn't. Work is your only passion. Anything personal would be a distant second. I don't take backseats. You won't give up the front seat—work." Mia's barbed comments were designed to sting. Teri never did anything without some plan, some intention. Teri's response made her feel cheap. Again.

The surprise on Teri's face was priceless. Theresa Stanton, heir to the Stanton fortune and business, was being turned down.

"You didn't answer my first question. Can I buy you breakfast? Must be some good places around here."

"Mrs. Davis said she'd have breakfast ready for us when we got back."

"Oh. I'll let her know that we'll be there soon." Teri pulled out her phone. "I don't know the number."

Mia handed her phone over. "Check redial. It's the second or third number. Jeremy had it."

"Of course, Jeremy had it." Teri sounded frustrated. *Jeremy!* Her conversation on the phone was terse. She handed the phone back and stared out the window the remainder of the drive.

CHAPTER TWENTY-THREE

Mia stopped near the front of the house. "I'll let you out here and then park the car."

"Fine!" Teri immediately regretted her tone of voice. "Sorry. I was lost in thought. Can I help with anything?"

"If you can grab the blankets and the cooler, I can handle the rest."

Teri pulled as much as she could out of the backseat and then watched Mia drive around the house. *I should have stayed in the car and helped her. Too late now.*

Before she reached the top step, the door opened. "Good morning, Ms. Stanton. Did you enjoy the sunrise?"

Mrs. Davis was a pleasant, smiling woman who had been hired years ago by her grandmother. Teri couldn't remember the time before Mrs. Davis. She must be close to retirement by now. "It was beautiful. Chilly until the sun came out, but I enjoyed it. Thank you."

She handed over the cooler and started to walk toward the back of the house. She was stopped by a hand on her arm.

"If you give me those blankets, I'll get them cleaned." Mrs. Davis quickly took Teri's bundle. "I hope I'm not out of line, but it's good to see you up here and to see you smiling again."

"Thank you." Teri didn't know what else to say. She was sure she smiled. Often. She went into the dining room and found the pot of coffee. She poured a cup and added some half-and-half. The heat of the cup warmed her hands and helped her to relax. "I do smile."

"Excuse me, Ms. Stanton?" Mrs. Davis had entered with a hot breakfast that she placed on the dining table.

"Just talking to myself. How soon will Ms. Daniels be joining me?"

"She said to tell you to go ahead. She wanted to take a shower first."

Teri nodded and ate in silence. She thought about the phone calls she needed to make. It was almost nine. She could start calling the West Coast soon. She remembered that their office in London would be well into their workday. The number was programmed into her phone. She quickly connected to the director of their European operations, an individual she had personally hired.

"Teri! Good to hear from you."

"I need a favor, Clark. Quite a few years ago, one of our U.S. executives transferred to our London office and he eventually left. I never did find out where he went. We may not even have the information, but if you could check on Thomas Daniels." She gave him the necessary dates and employment history. "If you can't get the information, it's not a problem."

"Has he done something? Do I need to check with the authorities?"

"No!" Teri checked her tone. After all, this was a personal matter and she didn't need to raise anyone else's attention. "No. He was an excellent executive, and I was just wondering what he's doing now. Call me if you find out anything." She chatted with Clark for a few more minutes, discussed their European operations, and then hung up.

"Might as well get some work done." She booted up her laptop, checked her e-mails, and mentally made a list of calls. First was to her sister. Bren was laughing when she answered the phone. "I assume you're not talking about work."

"Actually, Teri, I am. I found the picture of you when you first joined the company after graduation. You really need to get another picture taken. We're working on the Milton presentation and wanted to put the photos of the executives from each company in and only had that one of you. You looked grim."

There was that damn word again. "Thanks. What have you found out about the Miltons?"

Bren filled her in on the latest problems with the solar rechargeable batteries Milton Corporation was putting into mobile communication devices. "The reason why the Miltons were in New York was they were on their way to Washington to see if they could get more development money."

"That could be a game changer. Take Pamela out for lunch. Play golf or tennis with the son. Get as much information as you can. Call me later tonight. I'll be up late."

"Teri, what about Mia? You're supposed to be relaxing."

"I am. We watched the sun come up on some cold, damp mountain."

"Does that mean you had a good time?"

She could hear the mocking tone. "Actually, yes. This is business, however. Mia is fine. Now get busy." She quickly hung up and called her chief financial officer. She wanted him to rerun the numbers. If her gut instincts were correct, she could save several hundred million on their bid for Milton.

CHAPTER TWENTY-FOUR

Mia really liked her shorter hair. It was the first time since she had graduated from college that she wasn't wearing it long. It barely touched her collar in back. She fluffed it with her hands.

Her thoughts wandered to Jeremy and Bren. When the phone rang, she wasn't surprised it was one of them on the other end.

"Should I be on the next flight to Maine?"

Mia laughed. "No. We haven't tried to kill each other yet. Have Jeremy and Elaine gotten to spend much time together?"

"Every spare moment. I've never seen him so happy. He proposed to Elaine and she accepted. He's smiling all the time. Makes me happy just being around them. I admit I'm a little envious."

"I hope it happens to you one day. Maybe Alan will be the one."

"Maybe. I don't think my sister feels that way. Teri called the first day I was here and was furious I wasn't at work at dawn. She needs to get a life. Mia, be honest. Is Teri working or is she keeping her promises?"

"Yes and yes. In her defense, it rained most of yesterday so we couldn't do much. The day before I did take her clothes shopping and actually got her something that was not black, white, or gray. And this morning we watched the sun come up on Cadillac Mountain." Mia waited for several seconds and heard no response. "Are you still there?"

"I'm just picking myself off the floor. You took Teri shopping and she bought clothes? And she went hiking with you?" There was a pause. "Mia, what's going on?"

How did she answer? There was no one word or even two or twenty. "You know your sister. There are times when she's actually enjoyable and then other times there's this three-foot-thick wall between us."

"I'm sorry. I should've never agreed to come out here. I'll be done with what I need to do tomorrow and will be leaving by noon. I can be there in two days."

"Don't worry. I'm leaving here a day early. We can catch up in New York. I'm ready to start the next phase of my life."

"How is Michel?"

"Missing me but enjoying being spoiled by my parents. Can't wait to see him. When I talked to my folks, my dad seemed tired. Hope Michel isn't wearing him down."

"I'll be there soon and we'll have time together. And no interruptions this time."

Mia doubted that, but she also didn't know when she would see Bren again. "I'll look forward to it."

"I gotta go play nice with the Milton siblings. Don't let Teri spend all her time working. Take care."

"You, too." She had just closed her phone when she realized she was not alone.

"I just wanted to see if there was something you wanted to do. Was that Jeremy on the phone?" Teri stood at the door.

Mia wondered if Teri took stealth Ninja lessons. She kept popping up unexpectedly and without sound. "It was your sister. What would you like to do?"

"I Googled the attractions in Bar Harbor. We could go see a lighthouse or the museum."

"Tough choices." Mia didn't even try to hide the smirk. "I bet you had the same difficulty with the decision." She had no doubt Teri secretly hoped she would refuse. "When do you want to go?"

Teri seemed to be making some decision. Mia waited.

"Give me a few minutes to change." She pointed to her linen pants and heels.

Mia sat on the front porch to wait for Teri. She seemed to be waiting a lot. "Like your boots and jeans." Teri was wearing the same outfit she had worn earlier.

"I'm growing accustomed to them. Who knows? I might wear them to work one day."

"Let me know." Mia grabbed her camera and backpack. "I want to take a picture of that."

"Well, my family was telling me I need a new work photo. I'll definitely have you do it."

Teri almost smiled. There was no way Mia could figure her out. She was still confused about the kiss.

"In that case, I know what we'll do," Mia said. "You've had those jeans on for at least two days, and I bet they'll soon stand by themselves." The bewilderment on Teri's face was worth it. Mia snapped a picture before the expression changed.

"What was that about?" Teri asked. "I wasn't ready."

"The look on your face. You couldn't have posed for that. Come on. Let's get you a few more clothes designed for relaxing."

"I have relaxing clothes." Teri was adamant even as she was opening the car door for Mia.

"Taking off your heels and jacket do not count," Mia shot back as she closed the door. She could see Teri mumbling something as she walked around the car but only heard the words "smart ass" as Teri climbed into the car.

"I can't believe we're going shopping again. Thought we were going to look at the lighthouse."

"We are. We have lots of time." Mia bit her lip to keep from laughing. Teri's expression revealed so many emotions, especially the frustration with not being in control of the situation.

"I can't believe I'm going shopping again."

This time Mia could hear the mumbling.

"I haven't been inside a fucking clothing store in five years, now twice in three days. Can't believe it."

Much to her surprise, Teri ended up buying a pair of jeans and two pairs of corduroys, a blue pair and a green pair. She also ended up buying a green fleece jacket and a blue, green, and white plaid cotton shirt.

"Excellent choices, madam," Mia teased her. "And they're all interchangeable."

"Oh, yes. The plaid shirt will go well with my gray pinstriped bespoke suit."

"We could have green pinstriped bespoke suit made with a lovely royal blue scarf."

Teri's eyes were wide. "Never! I have my standards."

Mia laughed out loud. "You must have been an actor in another life."

"I'm an actor in this life." This time her words were somber. "I'm just following the script." As soon as the words were out of her mouth, Teri's expression changed. The brief light in her eyes disappeared. "I'll leave theatrics to others, my brother included."

Mia was surprised. There may be more to Teri than the image she presents. "Why do you think Jeremy is dramatic? I think he's a grounded person."

"If by grounded you mean emotional, I agree with you." Teri seemed to be squirming. "I looked at the lighthouse tours. That could take two to four hours. Why don't we just go to the museum?"

Teri shut down the conversation as quickly as she shut her door. She also seemed to turn down an activity she suggested that might take a block of time. *Was she a total workaholic?* Mia was intrigued. The more she learned about Teri, the more she wanted to know. Yet she knew that was a double-edged sword. The brief kiss on Cadillac Mountain hinted at emotion underneath her well-honed veneer of indifference, yet the conversation following it reinforced the sharpness of wit and tongue. And the emotionally empty persona. Her comments about being an actor in her own life were spoken with irritation. *Interesting? Confusing!*

"On to the museum, then?" Teri offered. "I can't wait to see the Conestoga wagons and pogo sticks."

"I'll be surprised to see either of those. Is that how you got around when you were a kid?" Mia wanted the teasing Teri back.

"Ha, ha. I want you to know that I had my own personal pony to take me to school."

"And people think you don't have a sense of humor."

"People don't think I have a sense of humor? What people?"

Mia saw the muscles in Teri's jaw tighten. She regretted her comments. Obviously, there were some things that got through her reserve. "Teri, this is not worth worrying about."

"Are you trying to handle me?" There was an edge to Teri's voice.

"No. It's just...I'm sorry. I shouldn't have said what I did. I didn't mean anything."

"Did you make it up or did someone say that?"

"I didn't make it up!"

"If you didn't make it up, then tell me what was said."

"It's not that important."

"I'm the one to judge whether or not it's important. Were you one of those people?"

"No!" Mia felt anger and embarrassment simmering underneath. "I know all too well how mean some people can be."

Teri pulled the car up near the museum and turned off the engine. She turned in her seat and glared at Mia.

Teri looked down at her hands and rubbed at an imagined spot. Was Mia hiding information? "I need to know who they were." Disloyalty was anathema to Teri, and she would deal quickly with those who were. She would not have anyone working that close to her who was not completely loyal.

Mia squirmed in her seat. "Teri, that was a long time ago. I bet most of those people aren't with the company now. Besides, I feel uncomfortable with this conversation."

"Then why bring it up?"

"If I had known how you would react, I wouldn't have said anything."

"But you did and now I want to know."

"What difference does it make now?"

"It does and I want to know. Now, are you going to tell me or not?"

"No."

Teri pulled the keys out of the ignition and got out of the car. She had no power to force Mia to give her the information. She walked quickly into the museum, uncaring whether she was being followed. *Why the fuck should I give a damn? It was years ago.*

The answer was simple. Teri's need for complete control. How the hell did she not know? She walked around the museum, oblivious to anything she was looking at until she realized she had walked around the same area several times.

Teri looked around and didn't see Mia. *Where the hell is she? Why the hell did I let those comments bother me?*

Chapter Twenty-five

Mia leaned against a tree and stared at the sky. White cotton clouds floated by, and she tried to imagine faces with constantly changing expressions. She kept seeing, instead, Teri's angry countenance. *Well, I now know she has a limited sense of humor, demands you answer a question she asks but doesn't have to answer yours, and her moods are all over the place. She needs some drugs.*

She watched Teri walk out of the building.

"You keep disappearing." It was an accusation.

"No, Teri, you sped out of the car and were in the museum before I was even out of the car. I walked around and you certainly didn't give any indication you wanted to be interrupted. When I was done I came out here to wait."

"Are you always determined to prove me wrong?"

"No, you can do that quite well yourself." *How the hell does this keep falling apart? Play nice. Remember? Just a little while longer and you will never see her again.*

Teri opened the car door for her and then drove silently back to the house.

Dinner was quiet. Mia filled her plate and ate on the front porch. She didn't care what Teri thought. How many years had she driven herself crazy with unhealthy relationships? How many times had she mourned the destruction of her first love and blamed her life's problems on that event and those feelings? How much longer was she going to continue down that path? She was done. She deserved better. Natalie deserved better. Mia put her plate down next to her, her appetite gone. She put her feet up on the seat of her chair and hid her face. Tears poured out until Mia finally felt empty.

❖

Teri sat alone at the table, calmly eating. She was damned if she was going to let Mia's temper tantrum affect her. She had too much work to do, and Mia was just a temporary distraction. When she finished eating, she went into her office. By two in the morning, she gave up. She had dealt with a number of issues, answered e-mails and voice mail messages, and reviewed several reports. Normally, she could give details of everything she had done. Tonight, however, she had read two reports twice.

Damn that woman. She didn't understand Mia, but she missed talking to her. *Perhaps I overreacted. Mia shouldn't have to report on anyone who works for me.* She would get a couple of hours sleep and then get up and make phone calls. Later, when Mia was up, she would make it up and make sure they had a good day.

❖

At nine, Teri went into the breakfast room. The table was set for one. She looked for the housekeeper.

"Has Ms. Daniels had breakfast?"

"Yes, ma'am. She was grabbing something to eat when I arrived. Then she left for the airport around seven."

"The airport? Did she say where she was going?"

"No, ma'am, just that it was time to be going. I thought you knew. I'm sorry. I should have asked."

"No, that's fine. Don't worry."

Teri went upstairs and Mia's room was empty. Except for the blue dress she left hanging in the closet. Teri had put it there the day after she had arrived. Next to it was the blue shirt. Once again, Mia had turned down her gifts. And now she was gone. "Damn that woman!"

CHAPTER TWENTY-SIX

Mia sat in the Jeep staring out at the surface of the water. The wind had picked up and the waves were bouncing up and down, much the way she had been the last few days. She had intentionally missed the first flight and now saw the next one approaching. She stared out at one of the boats. In spite of the churning, it moved through the water smoothly.

She had learned how to navigate the emotional storms her life, and her work, sometimes put her in. Now she was running away from the one personal tempest that had dogged her.

"Isn't this what you always wanted? Isn't it time to move forward?"

If Mia were honest, she had hoped she would run into Teri during this visit so that she could let go of that frightened, shamed teenaged past. True, that teen was fading, but it was still a specter that hung by a thread and insinuated itself into her dreams, memories and activities at unexpected times.

"Well, are you going to let Teri Stanton chase you away or are you going to leave on your own terms?" Mia turned the Jeep around. She would face, and erase, her ghosts.

The trip back didn't seem to take as long as the trip to the airport. It didn't matter. She had been gone for nearly three hours.

Mia parked the Jeep in the garage and left the keys hanging from the visor. She grabbed her bags and walked toward the back door. What was it she had said to Jeremy? *I'll gird my loins and grit my teeth.*

The housekeeper was preparing lunch when Mia walked in. "I thought you would already be on a plane somewhere. You didn't have car trouble, did you?"

"No. I came back to face my trouble."

Mrs. Davis gave Mia a look of confusion and then shrugged. "Young people today," she muttered. "You staying for a while?"

"Yes, ma'am. I'll be here for another two or three days. I'm just going to put my stuff back in my room, if that's okay?"

"Go right ahead. Lunch is not for an hour."

Mia dragged her two suitcases and shoulder bag to the bottom of the stairs and took a deep breath.

"I'll take those." Teri walked up from behind and picked up the two suitcases.

Mia stiffened. *Take a deep breath and relax.* "Thank you." She marched up the stairs, head held high.

"I heard the Jeep coming up the driveway."

Mia reached the top of the stairs and turned toward her room.

"Mrs. Davis said you left."

Once again, Teri was talking around the subject but not asking any questions. Mia stopped and threw her shoulder bag on the bed. The blue dress and blue shirt were still hanging in the closet. When she turned around, Teri was less than a foot away.

"What do you want to know, Teri?" She grabbed one and then the other suitcase and placed them on the floor.

"Lot of clothes for a few days."

Mia had already decided she would be pleasant, but she was not volunteering any information. "What do you want to know?" The rules were changing.

Teri was transfixed. Her breathing was shallow. She put her hands in her jeans pockets. "I want…."

"What?" Mia asked. "What do you want?"

"I would like to ask you what your plans are. Are you planning on staying or going?" Mia doubted that was what Teri wanted to say.

Now it was Mia's turn to carefully scrutinize Teri. *She looks nervous. What the hell is going on?*

"My plans were to visit until Friday. I have a reservation to fly out Friday morning. Until then, I plan on staying here until Thursday at the latest. Then I'll be in New York until some documents I need are ready. Anything else you want to know?"

"You forgot the dress and shirt." Teri pointed at the closet.

"You bought those, so I left them."

"But I really wanted you to have them. I can't wear them. They're yours." Teri's voice was soft, tentative. Very un-Teri-like.

"Thank you, Teri. That's very nice of you, but I can afford my own clothes." Mia needed to put physical space between them. She turned and moved around to the side of the luggage chair.

Before Mia could grab the handle, Teri had lifted the bag onto the chair. Their hands briefly touched. "I don't doubt that, but they were made for you. That's why I bought them. Where do you want the other one?" Teri picked up the second bag.

Teri was too close. Mia could smell her musk perfume. She could feel the heat of Teri's body radiating against her back. She felt her own heartbeat speed up, and her throat was dry. "In the closet." She could barely speak. "I won't need it this week."

Teri put the case in the closet. "And what's inside that you don't need now?"

Mia finally sat on the bed. "Teri, I have some questions for you and I don't want more questions. I want answers." She waited for Teri to sit in one of the chairs in the room. "First, and this is a yes or no, do you want me here?"

"Yes," Teri answered without hesitation.

The answer was a surprise, but Mia continued. "Would you rather be at work than be here?"

Teri hesitated, but she didn't look away. "I've enjoyed most of this week, but I'm involved in a major merger. I need to make sure nothing goes wrong."

"What does that mean? Do you need to go back to New York?"

"It means I'm trying to balance my work with my commitment to you."

"I'm perfectly content to spend the rest of my visit alone. I again release you from any commitment or obligation you may feel. Please go do you work. It's obvious how important it is. I have no expectations of you."

❖

No matter how much she tried, Teri couldn't detect anything but sincerity in Mia's words. The temptation was strong to accept Mia's offer to go back to the city, but there was also an underlying battle for her to stay. No one had ever made such an effort to get away from her. It was almost a challenge. Even more, she was disappointed that Mia didn't want her to stay.

"My work is important, but I also want to be here."

"Why?" There was no way for Mia to hide her surprise or question. Teri grinned. For once, Mia was on unsteady ground.

"Is it that hard to imagine that I want to be here with you?"

"Yes!" Mia looked surprised at her own answer. "Sorry."

"Am I that impossible to be around?"

"You are formidable."

"Any other questions?" Teri shook her head, wondering what was coming next.

"Why are you wearing jeans today?"

"Don't I look good in them?" Teri stood and turned around.

"That was a question."

Teri moved over to the bed and sat beside Mia. "I was hoping we had something planned for today and I wanted to be ready." Her voice was soft, almost intimate. She brushed Mia's hair back. "I thought we might walk along the river and take a picnic basket. I wanted to make up for my previous behavior." *And convince you that I am worth the effort.*

Mia finally looked at Teri. "You've been waiting for me since whatever god-awful hour you got up?"

"Yes."

Teri watched Mia walk away from her. It was both a physical and emotional separation. Recognition of that was novel to her. Her whole adult life was spent gathering what she wanted, at least on the business level. Her personal life had become nonexistent, but even there she was able to get whatever and whomever she wanted. As long as nothing interfered with work. In that moment, she realized she had forgotten how to want a personal life, much less have one.

Mia seemed undecided. Teri needed to make sure any decision was the one she wanted.

"If you'll change, I'll ask Mrs. Davis to make a picnic lunch for us. We'll be ready in about thirty minutes."

Mia shook her head and grinned. "Give me forty-five."

"Done." Teri nodded and got up to leave.

"What am I getting myself into?" Mia wondered out loud.

Teri grinned. "A great picnic."

CHAPTER TWENTY-SEVEN

Teri stared at her cell phone. She had missed three calls while waiting for Mia to come downstairs. Instead, she had planned the rest of the day for the two of them. *What the hell is wrong with me?*

"Sorry I took so long," Mia said. "I needed to unpack and find some clean clothes."

"Not a problem." Teri nodded, picked up their packs, and followed Mia out the door. "Mrs. Davis would be happy to clean your clothes."

"Thanks. Maybe I will wash a few things later."

"It's not a crime to allow someone else to do things for you."

"I know. I just prefer doing things myself. Besides, there isn't that much to clean right now. Thank you, though, for the offer."

"You're welcome." Teri chuckled. This was one hardheaded woman. Teri welcomed the challenge. "I'd forgotten we had a small boat here. It's full of gas and ready to go. We can actually take a ride up the river if you'd like."

"How about if we just walk for right now? I need the exercise. I've been sitting too long this morning."

"Your job, then, must not be a desk job. You've not really told me exactly what you do."

"You've never exactly asked."

"Touché. What exactly do you do?" Teri smiled. Mia is a worthy opponent. *No, she's not an opponent, but I'm not sure what she is.*

"I work for the Department of State as part of their Education and Cultural Affairs office."

"Does that require you to have cultural affairs, or will any kind of affair do?"

"Ah, the sense of humor is still there. It's just the name of the office."

"Okay, then, what exactly do you do?"

Mia explained about the artist exchange programs and the variety of scholarship programs her agency managed. "It's hard to describe the many functions of our agency in twenty-five words or less. I really do a lot of paper pushing and call answering."

"But you love what you do?"

"I do. It provides me the opportunity to meet lots of interesting people and spend time with artists. I'm amazed at the talent, not only in the bigger cities but the outlying villages and small towns. And the college students coming to study are incredible. I feel optimistic about our future." Mia stopped. "I'm sorry. I'm monopolizing the conversation. How about you? You've had quite a meteoric rise in Stanton Industries. You must be one of the youngest chief operating officers."

"Sometimes I don't feel that young. I think it was always expected that I would succeed my father and that Jeremy would become C.O.O when I moved up after my father retired."

"You don't sound like you're that happy."

"Happiness has nothing to do with the job. It's doing what's expected. I'm the third generation to lead this company. I've tripled its value in the last ten years. We are now on four continents and have developed a vertical integration for many of our products. We are currently negotiating to merge with a company that will greatly expand our base."

"The Miltons?"

"Yes, how did you know?"

"It's an easy guess. The last-minute dinner and party could only be for someone or something really important. Interesting family." Mia barely suppressed a grin.

Teri briefly wondered if Pamela Milton was the cause of that last remark. "That's part of the reason I've been so preoccupied. It's the first time in years that I've been away from the office with these big negotiations going on."

"Do you miss being in the middle of the fight?"

Teri stopped walking. Two days ago, she wouldn't have hesitated. Now she was parsing her answer.

"I enjoy the negotiations, especially with a company like Milton's. Great company; not well run but with strong family control." Teri resumed walking.

"Like yours?"

"Not quite. We're both privately held companies, but I have several top executives I can rely on. My grandfather set the business up that way so that we always have some outside input."

"What if someone recognizes there is a problem but isn't sure how to resolve the problem or not sure how you'll react to the problem?" Teri's pace sped up. "Can you slow down just a little?"

Teri abruptly stopped. "If an executive at that level doesn't have the balls to tell me there's a problem or discuss possible solutions, then he or she should be fired."

"That's a little drastic."

Teri glared at Mia. "No, it's business." Teri started walking rapidly away. She didn't know how far she had walked, but Teri realized that once again she had been unfair to Mia. She turned to apologize and realized Mia was not anyplace near.

"That woman is exasperating." She marched back up the riverbank until she found Mia lying on the ground.

"Are you okay?"

"Clouds are fascinating. When we see images in the clouds, most of the time, it's our imagination at play. If you watch them long enough, they change shapes and then different images appear and disappear."

"Now, you're a meteorologist?"

Mia sat up. "Actually, the study of clouds is called nephology. It's a branch of meteorology."

Teri stared. "Where the hell do you get all this information?"

"I'm interested in many things. A product of my liberal arts education."

A snort was Teri's only response.

"Shall we have lunch? I'm getting hungry." Mia bit her lip. She grabbed the basket and opened it.

"Now you sound like my brother."

"He does have a great appetite."

Teri briefly regretted mentioning Jeremy. Mia's enthusiasm for eating, however, quickly buried that thought. "You must be hungry. You're gulping down the sandwiches."

"Sorry. I am hungry. It's been so long since breakfast." Mia put her sandwich down. "Teri, I apologize for leaving this morning without saying good-bye."

The apology startled Teri. She was not accustomed to having anyone apologize—a person was fired as soon as the indiscretion was uncovered, and no time was given for an apology. Teri never apologized. She was a Stanton.

"Okay."

"Okay? Does that mean apology accepted?"

"Just okay. I assume you'll let me know in the future." Teri didn't want to admit she was briefly frightened when she found Mia missing. She lightly touched the side of Mia's cheek. "Please don't disappear again." It was a plea.

Her cell phone ringing prompted Teri to jump up and pull the phone out of her pocket. She looked at the number. "I need to get this." She walked a few feet away and answered. She listened for a few seconds. "I don't want to hear that. I need the data analysis today." She paused. "What? Shit! When are they arriving? No, send the jet. I'll let you know when we arrive." She hung the phone up and sat back down. She had an inspiration.

"Mia, something has come up, and I need to get back.'

"I'll clean up here and you go on." Mia started putting food and containers back into the cooler backpacks.

Teri stopped Mia's hand. "I want you to come back with me." Mia's eyes were wide with surprise. "I've got a French government official requesting a meeting, and I need an interpreter. That's not the main reason, though."

Mia continued packing. Her shaking hands betrayed her inner turmoil. Teri hoped it was a good sign.

"You must have other people you can use as an interpreter. Surely, someone in your office will do." She quickly had everything packed up.

Teri grabbed Mia's hands. "First, we don't have interpreters on call. We have some people we occasionally use, but they need at least forty-eight hours' notice. I need someone on call for the next one to three days. Second, and most important, this visitor is coming to talk about some work we're doing for the government, and this requires delicate and accurate interpretation and it's very confidential. I need someone I can trust. I trust you." As she spoke the words, Teri knew it was true. "Third, your French comes highly recommended, and I'm sure you will keep everything confidential."

Mia tried to pull her hands away. They were beginning to tremble. Teri held tightly, however.

"Teri, I'm honored, but there must be someone you can depend on. You hardly know me. And I think I would be one of the last people you would ask."

"I don't know why you say that. I do know you, Mia, and I trust you. You're willing to tell me the truth, whether or not I want to hear it, and you're not afraid of the consequences." Teri stood and put out her hand to help Mia up. "Please." *Damn it. Just agree.* Teri was becoming as obsessed with acquiring Mia as she was with Milton Enterprises.

Mia took Teri's hand and stood. She brushed off her pants. "What exactly do you want me to do?"

"First, I'd like you to help me host this official and his wife. Second, serve as their interpreter while they are my guests. Most of all, I want you to be my friend and confidante. I'd like to have you by my side and then I know things will work out."

"Do you always have lists of things?"

Teri laughed. "Not usually. I feel like I have to in order to make sure I'm understood."

"You should laugh more often. You're very attractive when you do."

Teri didn't know what to say. She carried the backpacks up to the house while they talked. The housekeeper had also commented on her smiling more often. "If you agree, I'll fly you anywhere you want to go."

"No need. I have a ticket."

"It's the least I can do especially since I don't know how long they'll be here."

"I may regret this, but I agree. After all, what else do I have to do?" Mia put out her hand to shake Teri's. Instead, Teri began caressing the back of her hand.

"Thank you. Now, let's hurry. The jet will be at the Bangor airport at five." Teri took their picnic packs into the kitchen to talk with the housekeeper. *Step one done. A few more days, and evenings, with Mia.*

Mia was looking too perplexed to speak. Teri made a mental note to smile more often.

Chapter Twenty-eight

Once aboard the jet, Teri offered Mia some wine and something to eat. "It's a short flight to New York, but I thought you might want something light."

"Are you cooking?" Mia asked. She couldn't believe she was flirting.

Teri's eyebrows shot upward. "Are you kidding? I'm lucky to make a peanut butter sandwich. Some food was brought aboard when the plane was fueled. I generally have staff aboard to fix things, but I can probably figure this out."

"Let me see what they have and I'll do it." She smiled and pushed Teri back down in her seat.

Teri grabbed her hand. "Self-preservation or questioning my culinary skills?"

"Both." Mia smiled and stepped into the galley. A few minutes later, she brought out some cold vegetables, fruit, and cheeses, as well as two glasses of wine.

"How about telling me a little more about these visitors."

"I can give you something to read." Teri pulled out a document. "This is the short version of our Executive Summary. I expected this visit but not until next month. It just comes at a bad time because we have more meetings with the Miltons coming up."

There were some technical terms Mia didn't understand but nothing that she couldn't translate. She leaned her head back and watched Teri reading through notes. When they boarded the plane,

Teri was handed several faxes. Whatever she was reading was producing worry lines on her forehead. Her eyes seemed even darker.

"Is everything okay?"

"What?" Teri looked up. "Sorry, I'm just reviewing a new analysis of the merger. Something doesn't feel right."

"Do you usually judge your business deals by feel? I thought you said you are always prepared."

"Being prepared gives me the ability to make informed choices. There are times when my decisions are tempered with my instincts. I've learned to trust those instincts. Like knowing I can trust you." Teri paraded her business smile only briefly and then went back to reading, a more somber look occupying her face. Mia wanted the real smile back. By the end of the flight, Teri was laughing and teasing Mia.

Mia was confused. Teri Stanton was a complex person, she decided. And she was beginning to enjoy her company.

It was a little after eight when Mia was again unpacking. This time she had been moved to a room in the main house. The guesthouses would be occupied with visitors by noon the next day.

"Are you comfortable?" Teri stuck her head in the door. "I realize you won't have as much privacy and there isn't a kitchen."

"I'm fine. I would love a coffee pot if there is one to scrounge up."

"How about one of those individual cup makers?" Teri was gone as silently as she had arrived.

"I've got to ask her how she does that." Mia unpacked and then showered. All the traveling and tension were taking their toll. She needed to get a good night's sleep. She had just gotten in bed when there was a knock on the door. Before she could get to the door, Teri came in with a coffee pot, cups, coffee pods, and everything else she needed to make coffee.

"Sorry, I didn't know you were going to bed so early. I'll just set this up and leave. Do you want anything to eat?"

Mia shook her head and crawled back in bed. "Thank you for getting the coffee maker."

"I know how important your morning coffee is." Teri smiled and quickly set up the coffee. She walked over to the bed and sat down. "You're hair is still wet." She pushed some of the strands away.

Mia felt the touch as a caress. She turned her face into Teri's hand. Her eyes closed as Teri's hand slid slowly down the side of her face. She felt Teri cup her chin. When she opened her eyes, Teri's face was inches away. Mia closed her eyes and felt Teri's lips press gently against hers. Teri's mouth was soft and the kiss tender. Mia pushed away the screaming warnings. This moment was too precious to not enjoy. The kiss became more demanding. Teri's tongue slid in and began to explore Mia's mouth. Suddenly, Teri pulled away.

"I'm sorry. You just…you were so irresistible. I know we agreed this wouldn't happen again. I'm sorry." Teri jumped up. "Good night," she whispered and then left.

Mia was numb. Her body was aroused and her brain was whirling. Teri had initiated the kiss and then abruptly ended it. *What the hell is going on? She seemed so unsure, and yet I know she wanted me. Could I be wrong about that?*

Mia thought about their recent interactions. *No, I'm not wrong. What do I do about it? Do I even want to do anything?*

CHAPTER TWENTY-NINE

P hillipe, I don't give a damn where you were. Why didn't I know that Garson was coming?" Teri drummed her fingers on the top of her desk. She was getting tired of his excuses. As soon as the merger was over, she was flying to France and firing him. "You knew this review was coming up and you chose to take a two-week vacation. That is not acceptable. I'll handle this myself from now on." She slammed down the receiver. She called her brother. "Jeremy, I need you back here right away."

"Don't tell me you're missing me already?"

She could hear the amusement in his voice. "Always. Now when can you be here?"

"How about an hour? We just left JFK airport."

"We?"

"We. Bren, Elaine, and I."

"You're in New York?" She looked at her watch. "That's perfect. Can you wait there? Auguste Garson and his wife are arriving on the ten thirty Air France flight. There's a limo at the airport to pick them up. Can you meet him and his wife and entertain them until they arrive at the hotel? I'll have the helicopter waiting at the usual place to fly you out here."

"I don't mind doing this one task, but I promised Mia I would spend some time with her."

"Not a problem. She's here at the house. I'll talk to you when you get here. Who's Elaine?"

"I'll introduce you when we get there."

"Fine. Just take care of Auguste." She hung up and called her office. She made plans for the rest of the day. It was the only way to not think about Mia. Mia made her forget work. Mia made her forget everything except how much she wanted her. She picked up the phone and called her P.A. "Cancel coming out to the house. Meet at the office at two." She hung up without waiting for an answer. "Now to find Mia."

❖

Mia looked at the clock and wondered who was pounding at her door. It was only eight thirty. She had slept nearly twelve hours. "Hold on!" she shouted back at the impatient knocking. She grabbed her bathrobe. Sometime during the night, she had shed her sleepwear.

"I didn't realize you were still asleep," Teri said.

"Obviously, I'm not. I'm standing here holding the door open. What's so urgent?"

"I thought you were an early riser."

"I am." She moved aside and let Teri in. "My body clock, however, is demanding a reset."

Teri's eyes burned with desire. How many times had Mia dreamed about this moment? Teri's hands were tight balls. Mia looked in the mirror near the door. Her hair was a mess and her robe was barely held closed. Her breasts were begging to be free. "Come on in." Mia pulled the robe closed, but not before Teri took a beeline to the coffee maker.

"What kind of coffee do you want?" Teri asked. She never glanced at Mia as she rushed by.

After the kiss last night, Mia expected a warmer welcome. *Did I misinterpret? No. She has the same look in her eyes now.* She stood behind Teri and waited for her to turn around. Maybe Teri was waiting for her to make a move.

"What kind of—"

"What kind of kiss do I want? How about a long one?" Mia pulled Teri into a tight embrace. She claimed Teri's lips before any other words could be spoken. She was surprised when Teri's lips opened and a moan rolled through. The kiss deepened. Teri pulled her closer. Her hands started exploring Mia's back.

"No, I can't do this." Teri pulled away and straightened her clothes.

"Can't do what? Is this some kind of game?" Mia pulled the robe tightly around her. She couldn't believe this was happening again. Was Teri going to accuse her of leading her on?

"No! This is not a game." Teri walked across the room and leaned both hands on the desk. "You have no idea how much I want you, but I can't do this. Not this way."

Mia was numb. "What do you mean 'not this way'? After you kissed me last night, I thought…Maybe that's the problem. I thought the kiss was special."

Teri remained with her back to Mia. "It was. It is. It's just that—"

"Just what?" Mia stood next to Teri. She desperately wanted to touch her.

"Just that I can't."

"Sorry." Mia was angry with herself. "This time I promise it won't happen again. Now, if you'll excuse me, I need to take a shower and get dressed. I know you have work to be done. That's it, isn't it? I'm just here for the business."

"No, that's not it, but, yes, I do have business." Teri's voice had softened. She sounded upset. Well, good. Mia wasn't happy, either.

"Please leave."

"Mia?"

"Leave." As soon as the door closed, Mia climbed into the shower. She let the water wash away her tears. As soon as this business arrangement was over, Mia was leaving. If she never saw Teri again, it was too soon. She was ready to let go. Completely.

PART TWO
LOSING TIME

CHAPTER THIRTY

A cold shower and a change of clothes and Teri was clearheaded. She put on her gray pinstriped suit with a white silk blouse. She chose her matching gray heels. Putting on her work clothes was akin to putting on her armor. She was invincible. And protected.

She had wanted Mia. Then when Mia offered herself, Teri couldn't follow through. This had never happened before. In those few moments she realized she didn't want Mia for a few moments or even a night. She wanted Mia forever. That thought scared her. It didn't fit in with her current life.

She continued to work in her office until right before lunch. It was what she needed to refocus. Finally, a little after twelve, she went downstairs. Laughter was coming from the formal dining room. She recognized the voices right away. Bren and Mia. She pushed the door open and found them just finishing lunch. Bren was dressed in a tan, silk pantsuit. Mia was wearing a royal blue suit with a pale yellow blouse. She was beautiful.

"I see you're both ready to go. Where is Jeremy?"

"He'll be joining us this evening," Bren said.

"The car is outside." She barely looked at Mia as she walked through and then out the front door.

"What is that about?" Mia asked.

"That's Teri in her work mode. All the niceties of social convention are put on the altar of making money." Bren looked at her. "I'm sorry she dragged you into this."

"Don't apologize. I agreed to this insane partnership." Teri was standing by the open door waiting. "Come on. She may just decide to make us walk or sit in the trunk."

❖

Teri was on the cell phone during the drive to the helicopter. The flight into the city was too noisy for much conversation. The drive to the office involved Teri telling someone what she wanted to happen during this visit. Mia just nodded. Her job was easy. Translate.

While Bren and Teri were involved in a staff meeting, Mia lounged in the break room, drinking coffee and reading American magazines.

"Ms. Daniels, can I get you something else to read or something cold to drink?"

"I'm fine." Mia stopped. She recognized the older woman who had come in. "You worked with my father, didn't you?"

"Yes, I did. I remember you and your father. Your father was one of the best bosses and mentors I've ever had. We were surprised when your father requested the transfer to London. I'm retiring later this year, and hope I can visit your parents when I do. Please give them my regards."

"I have no doubt my parents would be pleased to see you." After the woman left, Mia sat fuming. *Dad requested the transfer? Who spread that lie?* Mia shook her head. Silently, she hoped it wasn't Teri, but she couldn't rule that out. She needed to take a walk.

"Would you tell Ms. Stanton that I'll be back in an hour?"

Mia was longing for a small café to sit, sip wine, and think. The last several days had not allowed her much time to reflect on the various events nor the panoply of emotions she had experienced. She walked slowly, staring into windows but not really seeing. *I don't understand her. One moment she's demanding, cold, and distant. The next she's taking me on a picnic, kissing me. Maybe she's bipolar. No, Teri doesn't have the time. She just takes people for granted. When things are going well or going her way, she behaves like a queen tossing a few favors to the masses. When things are not going well, she's a bitch.*

That's not fair. You don't know what's going on inside her head. And she certainly hasn't made any effort to talk about what's going on. I'm so damn mad right now, I'm not sure I care.

She stopped in the middle of the sidewalk while crowds surged around her. "This is getting me nowhere." Instead, Mia focused on finding something appropriate for a Stanton dinner party that she could also wear for work events. It didn't take long for her to find the right dress. She only needed shoes. She only needed to survive a few more hours.

CHAPTER THIRTY-ONE

Does your family have the entire top floor?" Mia asked as they rode up in the elevator.

"The top floor is two penthouse apartments. One belongs to my parents and the other is my sister's."

"Why don't you have one, Jeremy?"

"I don't spend as much time in the city. Besides, I'm not a city person. That's another thing I love about Elaine." He grabbed his fiancé's hand.

"It's one of many things I love about Jeremy." Elaine's love was written so plainly across her face. Mia was happy for Jeremy.

The elevator stopped. Mia reluctantly admitted she was nervous. She was confident of her translation skills. Her ability to get along with Teri was not as reassuring. Her feelings for and about Teri were everywhere. "Well, here goes."

"You aren't worried about doing this? If this makes you uncomfortable, just say so. She can figure some way to get a translator."

"I'm fine." The double doors to the parents' penthouse suite were open, and already Mia could hear the sound of voices. This is just a work cocktail party, she reminded herself. She had attended many of those. She took Jeremy's proffered arm. "Shall we put on our work faces and pretend we're having fun?"

❖

Teri looked at the open doorway again. For the last thirty minutes, she had expected to see Mia and Jeremy come walking in. She turned to talk to one of her guests when she heard Madam Garson gasp.

"Mia!" She moved quickly across the room and embraced Mia.

It was Teri's turn to be surprised and aroused. She was surprised to see the easy familiarity between Madeleine Garson and Mia Daniels. They were chatting animatedly and, obviously, knew each other quite well. It was Mia's knee-length, black cocktail dress, however, that was bringing heat to her body. The sleeveless dress had a V neckline that offered a hint of cleavage and a flowing skirt that moved easily as she walked. It wasn't until she realized that Auguste was also greeting Mia as an old friend that Teri shook off the fog of desire. *This is about business.*

Teri walked over to the group. "Mia, I see you've met our guests."

"How do you know this charming lady?" Auguste Garson asked.

"We've known Mia since she was a youngster."

"Enough! Next you'll be telling embarrassing stories." Mia turned and spoke in French to the Garsons. They laughed and responded back.

"Somehow, I think you're the one telling stories, Mia," Teri said.

"Sorry, I was telling them that Jeremy and I have been friends for a long time and that we grew up trembling in fear of the older sister."

Teri grinned, but it didn't reach her eyes. "Most teens have difficulty with any authority. Jeremy, please introduce your lovely guest."

"Elaine, this is my older sister, Teri. Teri, this is my fiancé, Elaine Johnson."

"Fiancé? Welcome, Elaine." Teri stared briefly at Jeremy. "We'll chat later. Please come in and let me get you a drink." She was cordial, but the greeting wasn't warm. Teri escorted Mia and the two couples to the bar. Her world was tilting again, just as she thought she had it balanced.

Teri handed out champagne. *When did he have time to get engaged? Why didn't I know he was even seeing someone?* She plastered her business smile on, then turned and spoke softly to Mia. "Walk around with me while I introduce the Garsons. I'll make the introductions in English and you can translate."

Mia leaned close to Teri's ear. "They speak English quite well."

"Are you going to do this?" It was more a command than a request. Mia's soft breath whispering in her ear had ratcheted up Teri's desire to a combustible level. It was taking every ounce of self-control to even speak.

"Of course." Mia walked around the room with Teri and the Garsons. Her assistance was rarely needed, but it did allow for Mia to catch up with the Garsons and mutual friends whenever there was a break in introductions. When the introductions were done, Madeleine Garson grabbed her arm and walked with Mia to the balcony.

"Mia seems to be very familiar with our guests," Teri's father said. "She may be very useful." He patted Teri on the back. "Good decision to bring her here. You can keep an eye on her and she can leave when they do." He raised a glass in toast. "Who's that with Jeremy?"

"That's Elaine, his fiancé."

"His what? Why didn't we know about her? Find out what you can. We need to concentrate on this merger. Theresa, I want that girl out of here as soon as possible."

"Father, what is your objection to Elaine? We don't know anything about her."

"Exactly. Jeremy needs to show more responsibility toward the family and our business. I want Jeremy to make a desirable match. I need one of you to marry, and it doesn't seem that you are so inclined. I want acceptable heirs to continue to run this family." He walked away and began talking to a New York congressman. He didn't expect an answer.

Teri wanted to go in search of a Scotch. *Am I that cold and calculating? One day, Mia is an unwanted guest, and the next she's an asset. Just as quickly, she is again persona non grata. Even worse,*

Father is only interested in whether or not we produce heirs. She saw Mia out on the balcony laughing at something humorous that Madeleine Garson had said. In the summer twilight, she appeared as a chimera with her face, neck, and bare arms clear in the moonlight. There was a definite strength to Mia, but there was also an inner peace that Teri didn't understand or possess. *She's beautiful, inside and out. What the hell am I doing with her? Am I just using her?* For the first time in her adult life, Teri wanted something, or someone, more than she wanted work.

Once dinner was over, a small orchestra set up to play music. Auguste asked Mia to dance and led her out to a small dance floor. Mia was an excellent dancer. When the next song began, Jeremy led Mia back to the floor. For the next twenty minutes, Mia danced with different partners. Whether fast or slow, Mia had no trouble following. Teri was envious of every partner and aware that Mia was beginning to occupy a piece of her heart.

By midnight, the crowd had thinned to the Stantons, Mia, and the Garsons. Teri's parents excused themselves. Teri moved the small group across the hall to her suite. Coffee was served and conversation was pleasant. Finally, she brought up the purpose of the visit. "I'm looking forward to our meeting tomorrow. If it's okay with you, Auguste, I've invited Ms. Daniels to join us so that we won't have any translation difficulties."

"Non, although I think my wife was looking forward to the two of them shopping."

"In that case," Teri said, "I'll try to conclude our business as quickly as possible." She looked at Mia. "I know Ms. Daniels enjoys shopping."

When everyone stood to leave, Teri asked Mia to stay for a few minutes. "I just wanted to talk about a couple of things."

Mia was tired but acquiesced. "Only for a little while. I promised to catch up with Jeremy and Elaine."

"Are you staying with Jeremy tonight?" Teri asked once they were alone.

"Yes. What do you want to talk about?"

Teri began to pace. Too many thoughts were running rampant. "Did you know about Jeremy's engagement?"

"Yes."

"What do you know about her? What does she do? How long have they known each other?"

Mia walked toward the door. "I know they love each other. Anything else you want to know, ask you brother."

"Wait!"

Mia hesitated. "Why?"

Teri had no ready answer. "You're a lovely dancer."

Confused was the only descriptor for the expression on Mia's face.

"Dance with me?" Teri held out her hand.

"No." Mia put her hand on the doorknob. "It's time for Cinderella to go home."

"Stay here tonight," Teri said.

"No!"

"Why not?"

"Why?"

"That's not an answer."

"I gave you an answer. No."

"Doesn't it matter that I want you to stay?"

"Teri, I don't know what you want from me. Worse, I don't think you do either. There was a time when that, or any, invitation would have been so quickly accepted. The last few days have been a roller coaster. It just reminds me of my promise to myself. Let go."

Mia opened the door and left.

The door closing sounded like something in her heart shattering. Teri stared at the closed door. *What did she mean "let go"? That can't be about me.*

Teri couldn't remember the last time she was forced to face a problem she didn't know how to solve.

CHAPTER THIRTY-TWO

Mia walked quickly out the door and then leaned against it. "What the hell am I doing?" She walked to the elevator and pushed the down button.

Mia found Jeremy and Elaine waiting for her. She went to the mini bar and found the cabernet. She poured the wine and watched it swirl, like her inner turmoil. Too many disparate images of Teri Stanton floated around in an undefined collage. There was no way to put together a coherent image. Sanity demanded that she get out of town as quickly as possible.

"Sorry, I'm so late." Mia sat next to them. "I saw you arguing with your father. Is everything okay?" From the grim expression on Jeremy's face, things were not okay. "What happened?"

"It's okay," Elaine whispered. She grasped Jeremy's hand.

Jeremy took a deep breath. "My father made it clear he wants to know the pedigree of any future mother to a Stanton. I'm expected to produce the future prince of the kingdom." Elaine caressed his cheek. "I'm sorry, El." He turned to Mia. "This is one of the reasons I never said anything. He knows Bren and Teri don't want kids or to get married."

Elaine and Jeremy continued talking, but Mia was no longer paying attention. Why was she surprised? Did she really think Teri would change for her? Did she really believe those kisses meant something to Teri?

"What do you think?" Elaine asked.

"About?" Mia was back down to earth.

"Jer wants to find a job near me and never come back here. I don't want him to lose his family."

"Elaine is right. Your sisters love you. Don't sell them short. Even Teri."

"The only person Teri cares about is Teri. The only thing Teri cares about is work. She hasn't done anything with Bren or me in years unless it was related to work."

"Jer, in spite of that, Teri does care about both of you. I don't know how I would have survived the last eighteen months without my family and my friends. I'd hate for you to completely cut yourself off from your family. Whatever you do, love one another. I'll let you two talk." She hugged them both.

Alone in her room, she allowed the barely contained tears to escape. She cried for all her losses. At the beginning and end was Teri Stanton. She was letting go in pieces. Fortunately, not many were left.

❖

The meeting with Auguste Garson went so smoothly that Mia and the Garsons were being entertained at a late lunch by Teri while Teri's assistant completed the final versions of the new contract.

Once coffee and dessert were served, Mia asked to be excused and she and the wife of the French official headed off for an afternoon of shopping. She was determined to end her visit to New York on a happy note. She couldn't wait to go home. Hopefully, Michel's passport would arrive soon. *One more party tonight and I can leave Teri and this madness behind.*

Mia packed her clothes and waited for Bren. Teri had offered to fly Mia out in the helicopter, but Mia politely declined. She needed less of Teri. The drive out to the North Shore allowed her to relax. By the time she arrived at the Stanton estate, she and Bren were laughing hysterically.

"Unfortunately, he rushed into the courtroom without his usual suspenders. I stood up to ask for a continuance. He stood up and shouted 'I object,' and his trousers fell down. I promptly objected, and the judge granted the continuance. Her comment was that the plaintiff's attorney obviously needed more time to address the court."

"Bren, that is a YouTube moment."

"Well, we're here. Why don't you come back to the city with me tomorrow and stay at my place? Jeremy and Elaine will join us for lunch. We're plotting a coup."

Mia laughed. "I'll gladly ride back with you. I'll leave plotting to the Stantons, though." No matter what happened this evening, Mia would enjoy herself. Letting go had been freeing. Michel was a big part of that. If she found love, that would be great. If not, life would go forward.

"Come on, let's change clothes and swim before the hordes start arriving."

❖

"Oh, no. I didn't know she would be here."

Bren looked around and saw Pamela Milton walking toward them. "You know her?" Bren whispered.

"Unfortunately."

"Bonjour." Pamela Milton sat in a chair next to Mia. "So good to see you. I was afraid the evening would be boring." She tried to move her chair closer. She lowered her voice and switched to French. "I hope we can have a little private time. I'm in one of the guest cottages."

"Hello, Pamela. I see you've met my guest."

Mia looked at Bren and winked. She'd forgotten Bren spoke French fluently.

"Have you seen my sister recently? I know she wanted to talk to you as soon as you got here."

"I'm sure she will find me."

Bren stood and grabbed Mia's hand. "Come on, honey. We have an hour to rest before we need to dress." She quickly led Mia away. "What a barracuda! She was openly making a pass at you."

"Well, you gave her something to think about. She already thinks I'm sleeping with Jeremy and Teri." Mia told her the story of her encounters with Pamela Milton.

"I'm going to have a chat with Teri tomorrow. Pamela Milton is a barracuda. I have zero tolerance for that, and right in front of her new business partners."

"Please don't say anything. I don't want to cause problems."

"Trust me; you aren't the one with problems."

"Bren, please. If anything goes wrong with the merger, Teri will blame me. I just want Michel's passport and to get out of here."

CHAPTER THIRTY-THREE

Teri watched Mia and Bren come into the house. She couldn't believe Pamela Milton went to get a drink and then headed out to the pool. She would talk to Bren sometime this evening and find out what was going on. Meanwhile, she needed to make sure all their overnight guests were cared for. It was the only way to push back the image of Mia. Mia in sweats. Mia in a cocktail dress. Mia with warm sleep surrounding her. Mia in a bathing suit.

By five, Teri was finally alone. She had only said "hi" to Mia all day. She was definitely missing her. *Maybe when this merger is done....No, I need to concentrate on the merger.* She made phone calls, answered e-mails, and finally dressed for the evening. She chose a black, Donna Karan outfit. The pants were soft and hung well on her tall frame while the shell top emphasized her broad shoulders. The V neckline gave enough hint at the firm breasts beneath. She applied her makeup with care.

She looked at herself in the mirror and liked what she saw. She never had time for exercise, but her body was still in great shape. She wondered what Mia thought of her. That led to wondering what Mia would be wearing. Staring in her mirror, she realized she had chosen this outfit because of Mia. It was the kind of outfit she often wore when she was younger and into a seduction.

"Maybe I need to change." She picked up her Cartier Rose Gold watch. It was almost seven. She strapped the watch on. "Too late now."

People were running around everywhere. Large tents had been set up for food and bar at both ends of their large garden. Teri knew more than two hundred people had been invited, including the French ambassador and the French consul general in New York. Protocol dictated their presence when a high-ranking emissary such as Auguste Garson arrived to conduct business on behalf of his country. That also meant the U.S ambassador to France would be present, several dignitaries from the State Department, the mayor of New York, plus numerous other New York and Washington guests. Teri was also aware of the large number of residents from this end of Long Island as well as the financial and corporate leaders. Normally, this was the kind of evening she relished. Tonight, something was different.

Teri did a walk around. She only needed to greet her guests. Why, then, was she looking for one particular guest? By eight, the Miltons and about a hundred guests were wandering around. A large group of French officials, including the Garsons, were just exiting the main house. In the center of the group was Mia, laughing and talking, as if she were with old friends. She was stunning in an off-white, strapless evening dress. One side of the dress appeared to be lace, and Mia's leg was definitely visible under the see-through lace skirt. The low cut neckline provided enough glimpse of breasts that Teri forced herself to look up at Mia's face. Teri couldn't help smiling. She walked toward the group. Her shortness of breath was not from the walk.

Mia made rapid introductions. "Sorry if you already know everyone."

"You continue to amaze me," Teri said. "Is there anyone in France you don't know?"

"Absolument." Mia's eyes roamed Teri's body, only increasing Teri's excitement. "You look…gorgeous."

"You…you are stunning."

"Thank you." She linked her arm in Teri's as they walked toward one of the bars. Mia lowered her voice. "Reminds me of the many times your brother and I hid up there." She pointed to the upstairs terrace. "I remember how beautiful you looked and your equally beautiful dates."

"Ooops. Didn't know anyone was paying attention. I promise my behavior will be much better tonight." Teri began handing flutes of champagne to the group.

"Too bad." Mia laughed. This definitely was unexpected.

Teri handed Mia some champagne.

"Thanks, but I'll pass until I get something to eat."

Teri excused herself and walked with Mia over to the food. She handed Mia a plate. "Thank you for being here."

"Teri, all these people speak English fluently."

"I know. I just felt more secure knowing you're here." Teri briefly touched Mia's arm. "Thank you."

Mia was close. Her head was slightly tilted, her expression one of intense interest. Teri wanted to kiss her. Capture those full lips and hang on for dear life. She took a step back. "Get lots to eat. We always have too much left over. I'll catch up with you later. I see my sister has just arrived with her handsome date in tow."

Teri walked away as quickly as she could. Her body was pleading with her to turn around, grab a bottle of champagne, take Mia by the hand, and pray no one noticed them climbing aboard the boat tied up on the dock. Her nipples ached. Her center was throbbing. It had been so long since she had wanted someone this much. Her body craved to be touched. Her heart pleaded for more. She walked faster trying to will the desire away. Tonight had to be about business.

She greeted Bren. "Where's Jeremy?"

"Right behind me. Teri, this is Dr. Alan Crain, the new trauma head at the hospital. Alan, my sister."

Teri chatted briefly and then joined Jeremy and Elaine. She only had a few moments to spend with them, but she didn't need long to realize that they loved each other. She couldn't remember ever seeing Jeremy this happy. And she was sure Elaine wouldn't meet her parents' muster. One more thing to deal with later.

Her emotions were back under control.

CHAPTER THIRTY-FOUR

This party couldn't end soon enough. Mia was emotionally and physically exhausted. The time with Jer and Bren was definitely supposed to be relaxing. Then everything fell apart. She knew Michel's passport was due any day. Maybe she could have Bren send it to her. *No, I can't take the chance of it being lost or delayed. Just a few more days and I'll be gone. I'll stay with Bren in the city until then.*

She said good night to the last of the French guests and looked for a place to hide and rest for a few minutes.

"Ms. Daniels." Teri's father. Mia recognized the old discomfort overtaking her. It had been her frequent companion when she lived around here when she was younger.

"Mr. Stanton. How are you?"

"Thank you for assisting us tonight. Whatever amount you and my daughter agreed to for your help the last couple of days, I'll make sure our office makes out a check to you tomorrow. If you'll leave your address with one of the staff here, I'll have it delivered tomorrow. I'm sure you're anxious to get back to whatever you were doing before we interrupted. Good night."

He was gone as quickly as he arrived. Mia felt cheap. She was just hired help and she had been royally dismissed. She was tired, angry, and close to tears. She found a bottle of cold water and climbed to the upstairs terrace. She looked at her watch and realized it was still too early to call her family. She missed them and her much more stable life. As soon as she got Michel's passport, she was going home and never coming back to this area.

She sat and waited for Bren or Jeremy to come get her. Mia laughed. All those nights she hid up here with Jeremy and dreamed of being all dressed up and being one of the guests. Well, here she was all dressed up and sitting on the upstairs terrace. Alone. Initially, this evening, Teri had reacted to her arrival. The rest of the evening, Teri mostly ignored her. Dealing with Teri was like trying to walk along the beach. Waves in and waves out. In either direction, it could knock you down. *Her father just knocked you down.*

Heels clicking on the stairs alerted her that someone was approaching, but it sounded more like one set of footsteps. *Maybe it's Bren.* The head quickly appearing, however, was Pamela Milton's. *Shit.* There was no way she was going to be alone with Pam or give Teri ammunition for wild accusations. She stood and greeted Pam.

Pam offered her a glass of champagne. "No." She held up the bottle of water.

"I saw you come up here and thought this would be a great place for us to meet."

Mia needed every ounce of will power to not groan and dump the rest of her water on the intruder. "Pam, I'm not interested. I think I've made that clear. If you'll excuse me."

Pam grabbed Mia's wrist as she walked by. "I know you want me."

"Actually, I was just getting ready to leave. Let go." Mia's politeness would only extend so far.

"Or what? Come on. I know when a woman's interested."

Mia quickly rotated her wrist toward Pam's thumb, causing the grip to be broken. "And when a woman says no, what do you do? I'm saying 'no' and I have no interest in knowing you at all."

Pamela Milton moved closer. Her eyes were dark pinpoints. "I've never had anyone say no, so this is a challenge. What is it? What do the Stantons have to offer I don't?"

Mia tried to step away, but Pam pulled her close and tried to kiss her. Mia's instinct was to turn quickly and put Pam into a chokehold until the bitch was flat on the ground. This was not the time or place.

She was determined to get away safely and not have Teri Stanton have one more thing to complain about. She grabbed Pam's thumb and bent it back, forcing her to back up. "I'm leaving. Good night."

"Who the hell do you think you are? Do you have any idea who I am or what influence I have? The Stantons want my family's business. I don't think they would appreciate your behavior." Pamela Milton was now the predator, and Mia's patience was gone.

"I don't care about what the Stantons want, and I care even less about you."

Mia pushed Pam away. She had taken three steps when she felt a hand on her upper arm. This time the grasp was tight. "Let me go!"

Pam tried to pull Mia hard against her. "You want me and I want you. So stop pretending."

She relaxed enough that Pam Milton loosened her grip and, with a sharp jerk, Mia was able to pull free. The effort resulted in her stumbling and losing her balance. She leaned forward, panic setting in. Her foot slipped and she began falling forward toward the steps. She had only seconds. She put her right hand out to break the fall and tried to lean away from the stairs at the same time. The stairs were cold and hard. A sharp pain shot through her right arm as she slipped down another step. That was followed quickly by her head slamming against the step. She had no way to stop herself from going down the stairs. Somehow, a hand caught her, stopping her tumble.

"I've got my medical bag downstairs with my clothes." It was Alan Crain. Mia closed her eyes. She was in pain, but she would be okay.

Chapter Thirty-five

Have you seen Pamela Milton? Her father's looking for her."
Bren and her date interrupted Teri's conversation. Teri
was saying good night to one of their guests. It was after midnight.

"I just saw her heading upstairs to the terrace." Before she
could finish, Bren grabbed her date's hand and walked quickly
away. Teri wondered what was so damn urgent. She wasn't happy
about Pamela's actions but decided to wait until her guests were
gone before finding out what was going on. There was no reason for
Pamela Milton to be on the upper terrace.

She turned back to a local banker and his wife. She still had
business responsibilities. "Thank you for coming. We'll talk next
week." Several others wished her well and departed. The next ten
minutes were spent with her parents thanking their guests. She had
just said good-bye to another couple when her cell phone went off.
It was her sister. She ignored it. That was followed by a notice of
text message.

On the way to hospital ER with Mia.

*What the hell? Mia, emergency room? Who was hurt? What
happened?* Too many questions were swirling, and they had nothing
to do with work. Teri was torn between concern for Mia and her all too
familiar responsibilities. Once again, she chose her responsibilities.
It was the easiest path. She kept looking over at the steps but forced
herself to concentrate. Her vice president of operations and his wife
stopped to chat. He was flying to visit several of the Milton facilities.

"Make sure you take the brief I prepared." She continued to talk to various guests. Finally, she saw Alan and Bren running down the steps. Her guest was saying something, but Teri was having trouble concentrating. "Sorry, what's that?" She half-listened, but she was looking for Mia. She wanted to run to Mia, yet every fiber of who she was required she finish this job first.

A group of executives approached and chatted about work. She half-listened and thanked them for coming. "See you on Monday." Her phone vibrated. She ignored it. The Miltons were nearby. Teri glared at Pamela. She could read nothing in her facial expression. "I understand you'll be spending a few days upstate."

The senior Milton nodded. "We're leaving early. Have a ten o'clock flight."

Pamela smiled, and Teri wanted to strangle her. She didn't know why. Her phone went off again. "I'll let you know if there are any unresolved issues. We'll have the limo take you to the airport in the morning." Pamela walked to the cottage, laughing and talking to her parents.

"Theresa, nice work tonight." Her father patted her on the back. "What happened to Jeremy and Brenna? I expected them to at least be here until after all our guests were gone. You need to make sure those two, especially Jeremy, understand their roles in this family."

Teri looked at her father and wondered when she became her siblings' parent. "I'm sure they are taking care of our guests." Her phone vibrated. She couldn't decide whether to throw it away or answer. She was so damn frustrated.

"Your mother and I want Jeremy to take more of an interest in the business. We also need to introduce him to some of the eligible daughters of our friends out here."

"He's engaged, Father."

"Not as far as I'm concerned. He needs to make a suitable match, and this gold digger is not suitable. Make sure she leaves when your little friend leaves. Let's meet in the morning after the Miltons leave. I want to close this deal before the end of the third quarter."

"Father, that's impossible." Teri glared at him. Could he really be that cold and calculating? He knew nothing about Elaine or Mia. Teri stopped. What was it she had felt when she first saw Mia and Elaine? She'd even referred to Mia as her sister's little friend. For the first time in years, she felt a niggling regret for her own behavior. The image of a very different Theresa Stanton was congealing in her brain, and it made her uncomfortable. She pushed it away. She had work to do. "The merger's scheduled for completion by the end of the fiscal year."

"Get it done. I know you can." She was left standing alone, wondering why she was talking about the impossible. As soon as her parents were gone, Teri was ashamed of her own spinelessness. *Why didn't I stand up to them? When did I become such a coward?* It was a word she had never associated with herself or her life, yet it seemed to fit snugly, like a well-broken in shoe.

Distraction and action were her salvation. She called Bren. No answer. She tried Jeremy. No answer. *What the hell is going on with them?*

She checked her phone and listened to the voice messages. There had been an accident. She needed to change quickly. She ran up the stairs. It was the quickest route to her part of the house. At the top of the steps was the type of detritus that she expected from a medical emergency: bloodied bandages, an empty glass vial, discarded containers from various wraps and bandages.

Teri panicked. Mia was hurt. She pushed the debris aside and ran into her room. It took less than five minutes to change before she was running out the door with car keys in hand. She started the engine remotely, jumped into the car, and raced out the gate. *Why was no one answering the phone?* She again tried voice dialing on her car's Bluetooth. Still no answer. "Damn it. Someone answer."

She was well above the speed limit, but didn't care. She was on autopilot, well aware that her behavior was irrational. All she could think about was Mia and the need to make sure she was okay. "This doesn't make any sense." She wasn't even sure that anything was wrong with Mia.

Her voice was the only thing keeping panic at bay. "Probably just a minor cut. Otherwise they would have called for the ambulance."

No matter how much she tried, logic did not ease her fears. She had barely spoken to Mia all evening. Suppose something serious had happened. She had put feelings for Mia on a back shelf. Work was logical. Emotions weren't. She didn't doubt that, buried under her Stanton persona, were deep-seated feelings for Mia. She just didn't know what to do about it. Or if Mia felt the same way.

Her throat tightened and she couldn't swallow. Panic was setting in. Teri hadn't felt this type of emotional pull in so long she wasn't sure she could name it. Suddenly, an old children's game came into mind. Name it and claim it. Teri didn't know how.

Seconds stretched into minutes. Teri wondered if she had missed a turn. The *hospital's much closer*. Finally, she saw the lights up ahead. Jeremy's car was in the parking lot. "No wonder I couldn't reach him."

Bren, Jeremy, and Elaine were sitting in a corner of the waiting room. "Where's Mia?"

Bren crossed her arms across her chest. "Where the hell have you been?" Her voice was cold and accusatory.

"Taking care of business, as if you or Jeremy cared." Teri was angry. How dare Bren challenge her? "Tell me what happened and where she is."

"Why? What difference does it make to you? Mia doesn't have anything to do with Stanton Enterprises. Since when did you care about anyone?"

Her jaw was hurting from clenching her teeth. She couldn't believe anyone would dare talk to her this way, much less her sister. "Of course I care about her. She's a friend."

Jeremy laughed and stood inches from Teri's face. "You don't have any friends. If it's not related to work, it's not important. The only time you have any interest in my life or Brenna's is when you want to talk about business."

"That's bullshit." Teri leaned closer. She didn't have to put up with this. "Just tell me where Mia is and what's going on."

"She's in radiology," Elaine said.

"I tried to get you, but you didn't answer." Bren's voice was becoming strident.

"You know as well as I do that we had guests. Someone had to be responsible." Teri was pissed. *How dare they question me like this? I didn't see them taking care of business.* As soon as that thought flew through her brain cells, Teri knew she was wrong. Bren and Jeremy had spent much of the evening talking to people. "I got here as quickly as I could."

"Nearly an hour after we tried to contact you." Jeremy sounded disbelieving.

"Please lower your voices. This is a hospital," Elaine said. She put her arm through Jeremy's. "Can we just deal with Mia right now?"

"Thank you, Elaine, but this is between me and my family." Teri liked Elaine but resented her interfering. Jeremy stood in front of her. He was angrier than Teri had ever seen him. His fists were tight balls and, for the first time ever, his behavior frightened her.

"Elaine is family, or soon will be. Don't ever, and I mean ever, talk to her like that."

Teri stepped back. *What the hell is going on?* "I apologize, Elaine. I didn't intend to upset you. I just wanted to find out what was bothering my sister and brother." She looked at Bren and Jeremy, took a deep breath, and spoke. "I saw Pamela Milton coming down the stairs with all of you. What does Mia have to do with Pamela Milton?"

Silence. She looked from one to another. "Will someone please tell what's going on?" Her own voice had become louder than she intended. She took a deep breath and lowered her volume. "Can someone tell me what happened tonight?" Elaine whispered something to Jeremy. He shook his head and whispered something back. "Jeremy?"

"I'll tell you." Bren was now inches from her face. It was only then Teri noticed the bloodstains on her dress. "Let me put it in legal terms you'll understand. Pamela Milton, a prospective business partner, has been sexually harassing Mia Daniels, our guest and friend. She has approached Mia on more than one occasion, including at public functions. Tonight, Pamela refused to take a polite 'no' and, as a result, her behavior resulted in injury to Ms. Daniels. Extent of injuries unknown. Is that clear enough for you?"

Teri was stunned. "What do you mean sexually harassing?" Her fists tightened.

"Come on. You know what that means. Mia has had to put up with unwanted comments and inappropriate touching. Touching that escalated tonight into injuries. And I can tell you that Mia was polite, but consistent in her refusals.

"Are you telling me tonight was not the first time?"

"No, Teri, it wasn't." Jeremy's emotions were barely controlled. "From the first time she met Pamela Milton, Mia has had to put up with the unwanted attention. The only thing we could do was run interference because Mia knew how important this damn merger is to you and she didn't want us to tell you."

"Why?" Teri was struggling to keep her own emotions under control. She didn't know what made her angrier: not knowing what had been going on or knowing that Mia was injured. "Is Mia going to sue us? Is she going to be all right? Has anyone talked to Pamela Milton?"

Bren ran a hand over her forehead and paced across the room and back. "You're my sister and I can't believe you sometimes. What happened to your heart?"

Teri slapped her hand on her chest. "It's still beating. It's the same heart that has beat for the last thirty-seven years. It's the same heart that went to work each day while you two were finding yourselves. So just answer my damn questions."

Bren and Jeremy looked at each other and then turned away. Elaine shook her head and began to speak. "Mia is not going to sue you. You're the reason she asked that you not be told. Apparently, you accused her of doing something when she was a teenager that was not true, and she was afraid you would blame her for Ms. Milton's behavior."

"You don't know what you're talking about." Teri couldn't believe this stranger was pretending to know more about her life than she did.

Elaine's voice remained calm. "I know she has remained close friends with your brother and sister and always been your champion when they have been angry with you. I know she's a very special friend. So if you want to know why Mia didn't want you to know, then you need to ask her. She asked Jeremy and your sister not to tell, and I'll respect that. Now, I'd suggest you all lower your voices and talk to each other like brother and sisters."

"You sound like a teacher."

Elaine smiled. "I am. Kindergarten."

"Ouch." Teri relaxed. She saw her brother and sister, both with arms folded, glaring at her. "Is Elaine right?" Both nodded. "Everything?" Again, they nodded. Teri thought back to that night all those years ago. Could she have been wrong about Mia then? Could Mia have been a victim then as she was now? Too many long-held beliefs were being challenged, and she wasn't able to sort through them.

"You know I won't tolerate this kind of behavior in our company. Someone should have told me." Teri knew she was just trying to justify her own ignorance. And behavior. Then a thought came gushing out. *Could Mia think I've been harassing her, too?*

"And if you had been the kind of person that Mia, or for that matter, anyone in the company felt they could trust, you would have been more aware and more approachable." Bren glared at her as she continued speaking. "Teri, I used to look up to you, but you've changed. You've put blinders on, and the only truth is what you declare to be true. I can't remember the last time you gave an inch on anything. Do you have any idea how many top managers you've fired because they didn't do what you wanted when you wanted and the way you wanted it? You've turned into a carbon copy of our father." Bren stopped. For a moment, Teri thought she saw a tear in her eye. Instead, Bren looked away and pointed to Jeremy and then herself. "Neither one of us feels comfortable talking to you about anything that's not directly related to work, and then only about what you want to hear."

Bren's words stunned her. Yet, it was the same thing that Mia had said to her in Maine. And she had gotten angry at Mia. Teri's view of herself had always been one of a fair but tough manager. It was beginning to sound like fairness got dropped off somewhere. "Jer, Bren, I'm sorry. I don't know what's happened to us, but I don't want any more secrets."

"Then you've got a hell of a lot of work to do because I'm done trying," Jeremy said. Bren shrugged. Any changes from this point on would have to come from her.

She turned to Elaine. "I apologize if I've said or done anything to upset you. Thank you for telling me the truth." Teri's view of the world had been shifting. Tonight it was in crumbles.

"Mia Daniels' family?" A woman in scrubs had just walked into the waiting area. Teri walked up to her. "Dr. Crain should be right out. I'm Dr. Barrett, the orthopedic surgeon. Ms. Daniels will be here at least overnight. The MRI showed some tearing in her right wrist, and there's also a broken bone. She's probably going to need surgery. Her other injuries will heal with time. We're moving her to a room on the ortho-neuro floor. You can visit her in a few minutes. We'll try to get her in for surgery as quickly as possible."

Teri was on overload. Pamela Milton's behavior was unacceptable. Hers had not been that much more honorable. If she were totally honest, Mia had done nothing to warrant the rudeness or denigrating behavior Teri had exhibited. When she wasn't mistreating her, Teri wanted to seduce her. Somewhere along the way, Teri had traded pieces of herself for her parents' approval and sold her soul for the rewards of financial success and power. She not only had to decide what to do about Pamela Milton, but she also needed to examine her own life and choices.

Once upon a time, she had felt closer to her siblings. Now she felt a great chasm separating them. Pamela Milton could be handled later. More immediate was how she was going to win her sister and brother back and apologize to Mia. Like the children's nursery rhyme, Humpty Dumpty had a great fall. She wondered how she could put herself back together again.

"Bren, are there any witnesses to Pamela Milton's behavior?"

"Are you questioning Mia?"

"No! When I confront the Miltons, I want to avoid them questioning Mia."

"Alan and I both saw part of what happened tonight. Plus, I also overheard Pamela Milton proposition Mia in front of me. She was speaking in French and didn't know that I understood every word. There were well-marked bruises on her arms that could only have been made with someone's hand. Alan insisted that the emergency department take pictures. Tonight, Pamela tried to use her standing with the company as leverage for her behavior. We were just coming to the top of the stairs. I confronted her and she tried to blame Mia, saying Mia was trying to disrupt the merger."

Teri's fists were clinched. Every muscle in her body was taut. She felt a slow burn in the pit of her stomach. She couldn't remember ever being this angry. Most of that was aimed at Pamela, but Teri also deserved some measure of blame. "Can you get a written statement from Alan and the E.R. staff and copies of those pictures?"

Bren nodded. "Pamela Milton will not be allowed to get away with this. I'll make sure of that." Teri paced. Bren stared at her. "Is there something else?"

"Why is Mia afraid I would blame her again? For what?" Teri listened as Brenna explained that August night fifteen years ago. All those years ago, Mia was being bullied, and Teri just heaped further insult by being cruel and calling her an uncaring liar.

"I never knew." Teri felt something inside snapping, like a twig bent too far. She wasn't sure she wanted to look too closely at her past.

"She never wanted you to know. She thought you moved heaven and earth. And you were so wrapped up in yourself and your frequent affairs. She knew you would just laugh at her."

Teri sighed. *Mia was right. I probably would have laughed. When did I become such a shit?* She knew the answer. *Fifteen years ago when I started doing my family's dirty work.* She shook her head. *I can't think about that now.* "Bren, what do we need to do now?" Putting on her work persona was as easy, and as automatic as getting dressed each morning.

"We can talk to Pamela Milton and let her know this behavior will not be tolerated, or we can walk away from the merger." Bren hesitated.

"Bren, I want your opinion and help."

"Legally, we can't afford to have anything to do with Pamela Milton. I can't imagine any deal with the Miltons without the daughter wanting an executive position. I would toss the merger. The decision is up to you and Father, however."

Teri took a deep breath and absorbed Bren's suggestion. Her father fully expected the deal to go through and wouldn't give a damn about Mia. "Let me work on this. I don't want Pamela either, but I've got to figure out how."

Bren nodded. Neither Jeremy nor Bren seemed convinced.

She chatted briefly with Bren as they rode up on the elevator. If she resorted to logical analysis of the events, it was easier. Get the data. Make sure Pamela Milton never held any position in the merger. But how?

As soon as she walked into the hospital room, Teri was speechless. She backed up and stood just outside the door. Her physical reaction to seeing Mia was a like a lightning bolt searing through her body. Mia was sitting up in the bed with a bandage covering most of her right arm. Skin over and around one eye was swelling, and her upper arms were turning purple and yellow. Mia looked bruised and in pain, both on the outside and inside.

Teri remembered Bren's words. "Mia has had a rough time. Don't make life difficult for her. The only way I'll go to California is if you reassure me you won't give her a hard time."

What had Teri said? "Mia can take care of herself."

Teri felt a deep, soul-searing rage growing. She wanted to be angry with Pamela Milton, with her father, with anyone but the person she needed to be angry with: Teri Stanton. She forgot what it was like to care about someone other than herself.

Mia was vulnerable. It wasn't just the injuries. Mia's masks were down. She was talking to people who cared about her. She felt safe. Safe enough to be vulnerable.

Why hadn't she noticed? She knew the answer. She was so intent on her own agenda. She had this preconceived image of Mia and refused to be dissuaded. Until she ran into the brick wall of contradictions. Beautiful Mia. Smart Mia. Gracious and graceful Mia. Sensual Mia. Desirable Mia. Harassed Mia. *Obviously, Mia doesn't feel safe with me.*

Mia finally looked at her. "Nat?" Her voice was hopeful.

"It's Teri," Bren said.

"Teri? What's she doing here?"

It was more a question than an accusation. Teri wondered the same thing. What was it about Mia Daniels that got under her skin? What could Mia possibly see in her? What could she give her?

"She's worried about you. Just the like the rest of us. How are you doing?"

"I'm tired." Mia wiped a tear, and Teri felt a rip in her heart. She remained glued to the door, unable to move forward and unwilling to go back. She listened to Mia's every word, wanting desperately to know more about this woman who was stealing her heart. This woman that she had treated so unfairly.

"Go home. All of you. It's late and I'm okay." Jeremy and Bren protested, but Mia was adamant. "I'm fine. Thank you for rescuing me tonight."

"We'll let you sleep. Call if you need anything. I'll be back tomorrow." Bren hugged her, then Elaine, and finally Jeremy. They were lined up in a protective phalanx around Mia. "Teri, are you coming with us?"

"Go on. I just want a few minutes with Mia." Teri ignored the glares from her siblings.

"May I speak to you?" Elaine's voice was lowered, but it was obvious she expected Teri to follow. Teri did.

"I know you told me your family is none of my business."

Teri put up her hand. "Elaine, I'm sorry. I can see how much you love my brother, and I was way out of line."

"Let's just move forward, then. Mia won't admit it, but she really hates hospitals. She may be sending us home, but she doesn't want to be alone. She's also having a rough time. She needs support right now. Please be gentle with her."

Teri nodded.

"By the way, I do love your brother." Elaine walked out of the room followed by Jeremy and Bren. Teri was surprised that even Elaine knew so much about Mia.

As soon as they were alone, Teri sat on the edge of the bed and held Mia's uninjured hand. "I'm so sorry."

CHAPTER THIRTY-SIX

F or what?" Mia didn't understand.

"For so many things." Teri stroked Mia's cheek. "Why didn't you tell me?"

"Tell you what?"

"That Pamela Milton was harassing you."

"Pam made some comments and I was able to avoid her. Until tonight." Teri's touch was unexpected. There was tenderness in the stroking that soothed her and helped Mia to relax even more. She groaned. "Besides, it had nothing to do with you."

"I disagree. Can I help with something?"

"Will you see if there's another pillow in the room?" Mia was fidgeting and couldn't get comfortable. "My arm is throbbing and the pillow behind my head is slipping."

Teri found a pillow and then placed it under Mia's right arm. She sat on the bed and reached across Mia to adjust the pillow. Her face was inches away from Mia.

"Thank you," Mia whispered. She was feeling groggy.

"You can stay here as long as you want or need."

Mia was having increasing trouble focusing. "Thanks, but I don't like hospitals."

Teri smiled. "I'm not referring to this place. I mean you can stay at my place in the city or any other place. Just tell me and I'll take care of it. "

"I just want to go home. I'm missing my parents and Michel."

"Michelle? I didn't…I mean…is she a girlfriend?"

A halfhearted laugh was the best she could do. Teri seemed definitely taken aback. So different from her usual somber, unyielding self. "Michel is the French equivalent of Michael. Michel is my son."

"Your son?" Teri's eyebrows flew up. Mia was sure they would have flown off her face if they weren't attached. "You have a son?" Teri perched on the edge of the bed, speechless. Mia would have been more amused if her brain weren't so foggy.

"Yes. No. Actually, he's Nat's son, but I've legally adopted him." Her brain was mush. She was revealing personal information, and she didn't seem to have much control over it. "Nat was an amazing woman. I didn't deserve her, but she loved me. In spite of me."

"Nat is an unusual name. Is she your girlfriend?" There was something almost desperate in Teri's question.

"Her name's Natalie. Was Natalie. She was my partner."

"Did you two break up?"

"No. She promised to never leave me."

Tears escaped. Mia didn't know if it was the pain of the injured arm or the pain of the lost love. "Will you stay until I fall asleep? I've changed my mind. I don't want to be alone right now. Even if it is you."

"Of course." Teri's voice was gentle. "What happened to Natalie? Where is she? How did you meet?"

"Natalie was a nurse. She worked for a French phys…phys… doctor. Sorry, I'm having trouble with my words."

Teri stroked Mia's hand. "You're fine. Natalie was a nurse."

Mia could almost hear Nat's laughter, see her teasing brown eyes, hear her lilting, melodious voice. *"I love you, and I know you haven't forgotten Teri. Ten years from now, you'll still be with me and we'll both be saying 'Teri who?' I'll be teasing you about your three gray hairs. And you will be as madly, deeply, hopelessly in love with me as I am with you right now."* She fought back the tears.

"She was the most giving, loving person I've ever known." Mia began to cry. Teri moved closer on the bed.

"What happened?"

Mia shook her head. "She died." Mia sniffed and tried to wipe her eyes. Her right hand was too heavy to lift more than three to four inches off the bed.

Teri brushed the tears away. "Can I hold you?"

What a strange request. Mia just nodded. Teri and Natalie were merging. She was having trouble separating them.

"When did she die?"

Teri's body felt good next to her. "Eighteen months ago." Mia sighed and closed her eyes. "I'm so lost without her." Mia felt empty. She was afraid she was forgetting what Nat looked and felt like. She wasn't the only one. "Michel cried every night. I would put him in my bed and rock him to sleep. It was three months before he could sleep in his own bed through the night." Her voice betrayed her. She was back in Paris with Michel. "Now, sometimes, he asks me to tell him about his mother. He can't remember what she looked like. So I show him the picture of the three of us."

Mia turned her head and looked into Teri's eyes. "She knew about my crush on you, but she loved me in spite of you. Unconditionally."

"I don't understand."

Mia giggled. Was Teri really that dense? The pain medications were really kicking in. She was talking too much. "You were the first girl I had a crush on. From the first time Jeremy and I hid on the terrace, I thought you were the most beautiful, magical being in the whole world. I wanted to grow up and be beautiful and funny and sophisticated so that you would notice me. And one day, you would ask me to dance and kiss me under the stars."

Mia's speech was slurring. She was getting sleepy. "But you broke my heart and called me a liar." Mia tried to raise her right hand. She wanted to touch Teri's face. The hand wouldn't move. "I don't want to hurt anymore."

CHAPTER THIRTY-SEVEN

Pieces of her past came flying back. Teri had gotten so many things wrong. "I don't want you to hurt anymore." She gave Mia a gentle, lingering kiss, enjoying the softness and the connection. "I never knew. Mia, what do you need now?"

"Hold me." The words were barely above a whisper. Mia was falling asleep. "I do love you, Nat."

She thinks I'm Natalie. Her heart was in shreds.

Teri lay there for some time, holding Mia and replaying scenes in her head. She now understood Mia's protests and Jeremy's accusations when Mia's family was sent to London. Mia was a teenager with a crush, but not on her brother. *And I'm the one who shot her down. No wonder she didn't want me to know about Pamela Milton. I wouldn't have trusted me, either.*

What surprised Teri the most was the recognition of the growing feelings she had for Mia and the nascent hope that it was mutual. *After all these years. Yet, this Natalie had loved her in a way I don't understand. Or could. And she still loves her.*

A light came on, and Teri buried her thoughts and feelings. She wiped away a solitary tear.

"Sorry, I didn't realize anyone was in here." One of the nurses walked up to the bed. "I just need to take vitals. Are you her partner?"

Am I anything to Mia after the way I've treated her? "Yes." *Why did I say that?* "Didn't know if there are visiting hours?"

"Immediate family members can stay overnight if you want us to make arrangements. We do need to get some paperwork taken care of. She didn't have any insurance information when she came in, but Dr. Crain said someone would be by to take care of that. I guess that's you."

Insurance, of course. Teri put her business face on. "Where do I need to go?" She stood and straightened out her clothes.

The nurse gave directions and Teri was gone. Thirty minutes later, she had a cup of coffee in hand and walked back into Mia's room. The couch had been made into a bed and Teri sat down. She watched Mia sleep and wondered what life would have been like if she had taken a different road.

Doesn't matter. I made my choices. Mia was a kid and the family deemed her unacceptable. I dealt with it. It's obvious she's still not acceptable even though she has the education and social skills to excel in so many different worlds. Then there's Elaine. Father has hinted that relationship must be discouraged. I can see how happy Jeremy is. Would I give up so much to be with someone? Would I give this up for Mia?

Teri didn't have an answer. For her brother, she would do whatever was necessary to support him and Elaine.

❖

At six, the orthopedic surgeon came in and talked with Mia. Mia was more alert and was asking questions. Teri was grateful. It was obvious she was anxious to be back in France. The surgical procedure was explained, and she was reassured she would be able to resume her life soon and have all her follow-up at home. Mia signed the surgical consent forms. Teri's head acknowledged the need for Mia to leave. Teri's heart wanted her to stay.

After the surgeon left, Mia noticed her. "I didn't know you were here. Have you been here all night or did you just get here?" She was friendly, but none of the intimacy of the previous evening was even hinted at.

"I came in last night and then came back." *Why am I lying? Why not talk about last night? Mia is the stronger person. You, Teri, are a coward.* "How are you feeling?" Teri stood by the bed. She felt as if Mia was a stranger that she was meeting for the first time. A stranger she wanted to be close to. One she just lied to. *Can I change?*

"I think my toes and nose are the only parts of my body that don't hurt." Mia's efforts to smile ended in a groan. "I don't remember exactly what happened. I remember being at your party and being tired. After that, just brief images. I know I'm in a hospital, but how did I get here? I remember all of you being here for a while."

Teri outlined the briefest details of her fall and being brought to the hospital. She didn't mention Pamela. That would be saved for another day when they could have a longer talk.

"Is there anything I can do?"

Mia's face scrunched up. "Did you ask me that last night? I get bits and pieces, but nothing makes sense."

Teri brushed hair away from Mia's face. "You'll remember in time."

Two people in scrubs wheeling a gurney came in. "We need to get you down to surgery." The person speaking turned toward Teri. "You can follow us down to the surgical waiting area and we can let you know how she's doing."

Teri nodded and followed. As soon as Mia was wheeled away, she got out her phone and started making calls. She still had a business to run, and she wouldn't rest until something was done about Pamela Milton.

CHAPTER THIRTY-EIGHT

Teri was almost manic in gathering every ounce of information she could on Pamela Milton, the Milton family, and their businesses. Integration of the Miltons' company into her business could increase profitability. It could be worth billions. Stanton Enterprises could expand into Asia. They might even have taken the company public. Pamela Milton's behavior had cast a pall on everything. She needed to be meticulous in handling this transaction.

She looked at her watch. She had time to run home, shower, change clothes, and still be at the office before eight. She wasted no time getting to her car. She left her morose thoughts about her relationship with Mia where they belonged—behind her. She surgically removed them and left them on the hospital floor.

❖

Her senior staff were busily making notes. "We've been working on this acquisition for over a year, and we find out today they have some major legal problems. Anyone want to explain?"

No one even made eye contact. Teri was furious. She wanted to rant and yell. She took a deep breath. "Pretend like we're just starting out. I want every fact, every dollar, every product, and product recall rechecked. It's three o'clock. I want an update by six. No one goes home until then."

The room was vacated so fast Teri didn't even have time to stand up before she was alone. "Fuck!" Teri slammed her hand on the table. No one had uncovered a small factory in India owned by the Miltons that burned down killing three hundred employees.

"Theresa!" Her father looked very unhappy. "Why are we stalling this takeover? This damn factory has nothing to do with us. We're not purchasing that part of the business."

How could she explain? Was she just looking for any excuse to break the deal, or was she frustrated because she hadn't come up with a way to keep Pamela Milton out of the picture?

"Fix this." It was an order. "And I want this Elaine person gone. Why isn't Jeremy here today?" Her father walked out. He didn't want an answer. He wanted action.

Teri realized how much she *was* becoming her father. Was this the road she wanted to continue on? She turned her computer on and checked her e-mail. Nothing yet on Pamela Milton.

She turned the computer off. She wanted to run to the hospital and be with Mia. She needed to run the company. Of the two, running the business was the one she was more comfortable with, and more familiar. *This is how I got where I am. Making the sacrifices. Including your soul? Come on, Teri. Aren't you being a little dramatic?*

It was almost six. Her staff floated back in. She shut down mentally—everything except what she needed to run the meeting. She could deal with the abstract later.

"All right. Who wants to start?" She listened to each person's report. "I want all this in writing by nine tomorrow." Not much new. She sent her staff home. "Maybe I should check on Mia."

Teri drove to the hospital, her mind going around in circles. Mia. Work. Mia. Work. Then, for some diversion, she threw in some guilt. It was getting her nowhere. Being around Mia was making her crazy. She stopped the car and briefly thought about turning around and driving back to the house. She could work at home just as easily. But she wouldn't see Mia.

It was getting late. Maybe she could see her tomorrow. *No, I need to see her now.* Teri kept driving.

❖

Mia was laughing. She looked much better. She was easily entertained by Bren, Jeremy, and Elaine. "How are you feeling?"

"Teri! I'm fine." Mia was obviously surprised. There was something else. She looked puzzled. Maybe it was that the room had become quiet.

"You left the office early," Bren reminded her. "Does this mean you came here since I didn't come to the office?"

"Actually, I came to see Mia." She joined the conversation around the bed. Even banged up, Mia was still beautiful.

Bren and Mia began telling stories about Jeremy growing up, much to his chagrin. "Okay, enough. Elaine thinks I'm a great person, and now you're telling her all my secrets." Jeremy put his arm around Elaine. "I assure you they're exaggerating. I've always been an angel."

Teri humphed. "What my little brother means is that he pretended to be an angel and hoped he didn't get caught. The only reason he had such good grades was because Mia was so studious and she made him study with her."

"How did you know?" Mia and Jeremy asked in unison.

"The oldest knows." Teri didn't try to hide a smug smile. "You'd be surprised at the things I knew you three were into." She looked at Bren. "I even followed Bren and Mia when you two decided to run away from home."

"Oops," Mia said. "Guess we weren't as sneaky as we thought." Her smile was amazing and welcoming. Teri hoped it was meant for her. No wonder she was having so much trouble focusing on work. Again, she stayed after the others left.

"How did your surgery go?"

"It's over. I couldn't move my hand much before. Now I can't move it at all. Swollen. Everything's fixed. Whatever that means. How's work? Real work, that is."

"Nothing seems to be going right, but I don't think you really want to talk about that." She talked about anything but work. Anything to get Mia to smile. Finally, she became more somber. "Mia, I want to make up for so much."

"I'm sorry if I...when Bren was talking about last night, I started remembering pieces of what happened. As soon as I get some paperwork I'm waiting for, I'll be going back to Paris. I won't cause any problems."

"Mia, stop. You haven't done anything wrong. I know you're waiting for Michel's passport. You're welcome to stay at my place, if you choose, for as long as you need or want."

"I told you about Michel, didn't I?" Teri nodded. "Ugh, I thought I had dreamt that conversation." Mia picked at her blanket. "I'm embarrassed. I don't usually dump my personal life on someone." She turned away and stared out the window.

Teri sat on the edge of the bed and turned Mia's face back toward her. "Please don't. I'm glad you had someone who loved you that much. I'm the one who needs to apologize, but we can talk about it some other time."

CHAPTER THIRTY-NINE

Mia had no doubt that Teri was sincere in apologizing, but she was puzzled by her unwillingness to talk about what happened. She had remembered telling Teri about Natalie, Michel, and, worst of all, her crush on Teri. Was this making Teri uncomfortable? The kiss seemed very natural and comfortable. Was she again regretting kissing?

This visit had not been what she planned, but she was glad it happened the way it had. The next page of her life was calling.

"Bren has already offered her place. It probably would be easier if I didn't run into your parents or the Miltons."

"Are you determined to turn down all my offers?" Her face was serious, but there was teasing in her voice. "That's fine. If you'll feel more comfortable. The Miltons left today, and we don't expect them to be back any time soon."

"Jeremy didn't expect you to be home the day I arrived."

"Again, you're right." Teri smiled, and this time it reached her eyes.

"You're attractive when you smile. You really should do it more often."

Teri reached for her good hand. "Maybe I don't often have a reason to smile. I should let you get some sleep." She kissed Mia on the cheek and quickly left.

"Why is it you change the subject or run away any time we start personal conversation? Is that why you disappeared this morning?"

Maybe someday she might be able to actually ask Teri, but she doubted it.

❖

At six in the morning, Teri was back. Mia was determined to keep the conversation on friendly, but neutral terms. "Good news today. I can leave tomorrow. The surgeon wants to see me in seven to ten days, check on the swelling, and then put a hard cast on. Hopefully, I'll be gone by then."

"Are you that anxious to leave?"

"I didn't plan on being in this area this long. I came to see Jeremy and Bren. Then I wanted to go look at places to live."

"Are you moving back to the States?"

"I'd like to move back with my parents and Michel. Just haven't quite figured out how yet. How's work? You seemed distracted earlier."

"Work is good. Well, mostly. A part of my life that is definitely controllable." Teri sat on the bed. "I feel like I have a half dozen fires that I'm trying to deal with at the same time."

"Am I one of the fires? Bren reminded me of my encounter with Pamela Milton."

Teri's fists tightened. "She shouldn't have."

Mia grabbed one of Teri's fists, rubbing it until her hand relaxed. "Teri, why not? I had bits and pieces of the evening, and she filled in the blanks. I couldn't remember what happened right before my fall. I know now it was an accident."

"It was not an accident. She should never have touched you, especially when you told her to leave you alone." Teri's voice was strained. She was obviously struggling for control. Control must be Teri's mantra, Mia decided.

"It was an accident." Teri just glared at her. There was no way Mia was going to convince her otherwise. *No need trying.* "Anyway, I'm getting out of here sometime tomorrow." Mia smoothed out her blanket. "Teri, what's going on between us?"

"What do you mean?" A brief look of fear passed across her face before Teri put on her unreadable expression.

"You've kissed me. More than once. You bought a very expensive, and lovely, dress for me."

"One you haven't worn."

"One I haven't worn. You spent the night in the hospital with me. You actually were lying in bed next to me but lied to me about it." Teri stared down at their hands and pulled hers away.

"Mia, there's nothing going on. I've just been concerned about you."

"Are you afraid I'm going to sue you?" Mia wasn't sure she wanted an answer. She prayed the answer was no, but she needed to know.

"No. What makes you think I even believe that?"

"Bren said that was the first question you asked her when she told you what happened."

Teri began to pace. "My sister can have a perverse sense of humor. I practically had to beg to find out what happened. Brenna, in her most regal and legal voice, informed me what had happened. I briefly wondered if she was trying to tell me that you planned on suing. I didn't believe it, but I had to ask." She returned to sit beside Mia. "I don't believe you're that kind of person."

"What kind of person am I?"

"Do you need me to tell you?"

Mia's gaze was steady. "Yes."

"You're an amazing, talented, beautiful woman. Whether it's a result of your liberal arts education"—here, Teri smiled—"or just who you are, I've never met anyone quite like you."

"Then I ask you again. What's going on between us?"

"God, Mia, I wish I knew. I've never known anyone quite like you. I hope we can be friends, Mia. Good friends."

It wasn't what Mia wanted to hear, but at least it helped her to take another step to a healthier life. Teri obviously was married to her work. Mia would be out of the hospital soon and probably wouldn't see Teri again.

CHAPTER FORTY

Teri knocked on Bren's door and was surprised when she opened it. "I didn't think you'd be home this early."

"Are you here to talk business or see Mia? If you're here to see Mia, she left earlier today."

"Is she okay?" Mia hadn't said anything about leaving when they talked last night. Had Michel's passport arrived?

"What's going on with you and Mia?"

It was the same question Mia asked several days ago. "What makes you think something's going on? Can't I just visit?"

"Teri, I've lived in this place nearly six years. In that time, you've been here less times than I can count on one hand. Since Mia got out of the hospital five days ago, you've stopped by at least once every day. You've ordered food delivered here. You've brought Mia's clothes here."

"She's a friend."

"A friend you're falling in love with?"

"No!" Teri paused. "Yes. Maybe."

"What are you going to do about it?"

Teri now stared at her. "Nothing. I've got a company to run." She walked out as quickly as she could.

❖

No matter how much she tried, Teri couldn't put Mia into a mental box and lock her away. Mia was residing in her heart. She stared at her phone and wanted to call but again realized she didn't know where she was or how to call her. A week had passed and she knew nothing about Mia's sudden departure.

Teri remembered the call she had made to the private investigator. Why hadn't she heard back? He usually had information of some sort within two to three days. It had been over two weeks. She dialed his number.

"I gave it to your sister. You weren't in the office and you usually have me provide her a copy."

Teri was stunned. "When did you give it to her?"

She hung up as soon as she got the answer. Was there some kind of plot? How dare Bren keep the information? She marched into Bren's office and slammed the door shut. "Where's the damn report?"

Bren put a large brown envelope and a smaller white one on the desk. "Which one do you want?"

She stared at the two envelopes, wondering what the hell was going on. "Why didn't you give me the report when it came in?"

"You weren't here. Someone had to sign for it and I did. I thought it was about a business matter. Imagine my surprise when I find it's more personal." Bren stood in front of her. She held the white envelope up. "What right do you have to look into Mia's family? Her father is no longer a part of our company. Mia, obviously, is not that important, so I don't think you should read this."

Teri was vacillating between curiosity and frustration.

"If you really want to know why Mia left, then open the envelope. But then I want to know what you're going to do. Then maybe I'll give you this other envelope."

She didn't hesitate. She grabbed the envelope and read the report inside. She sat quickly in a nearby chair. "How long?"

"I don't know. Her father was just diagnosed. That's why Mia flew back quickly. She's trying to move her parents back to the States and she can't leave until she has Michel's passport." Bren held up the other envelope. "It arrived today. I've got the jet waiting for me at the airport. It's fueled and the pilot is on standby. I planned on flying the passport to her and bringing them to my apartment until they can find a place to live. Then I'm flying her brother and his wife to New York." Bren tapped the small envelope against her other hand. "Well? Do you love her?"

"I've got the merger to deal with."

"Do you love her? Don't go unless you do because I won't allow you to hurt her again. Not after what she's been through."

"How does she do it? How does she keep living each day and yet seem to be so positive?"

Bren took her by the arm. "She puts one foot in front of the other and hopes the next step will be better. She also surrounds herself with people who love her. You should try it." They had reached the door. "The jet is ready. I've got my clothes packed. What do you want to do?"

"What makes you think she'd even want to see me?"

"She may not, but I think she still loves you. Only you can convince her that you love her."

"I don't know how." Teri hated to admit it. "I know how to negotiate and to play hardball. I don't know if I know how to be a friend, much less how to win her."

Bren put both envelopes in her hand. "Maybe it's time for you to find out."

PART THREE

MAKING TIME

CHAPTER FORTY-ONE

Teri was glad she always kept some clothes in the office. It was the only thing she was grateful for. Mia's father had pancreatic cancer. Mia's mother was recovering from a heart attack with some mild heart damage. Dealing with sick people made Teri uncomfortable. Visiting Mia in the hospital had been an effort.

Mia had a five-year-old boy, and Teri knew nothing about children. She never wanted to know anything about children. They were best kept at a distance—a long distance.

Teri was getting closer to forty and still had never had the kind of relationship Mia had with Natalie. From what Teri had learned, Natalie was a saint. A dead saint. There was no way to compete with dead saints. She didn't understand why, but she wanted to try.

There were some things she could do. She could make sure Mia had Michel's passport. She could fly the entire family back to the States. She could arrange a place for them to live. These were black or white activities. They either happened or didn't. No need for lots of conversation or discussion of feelings.

The five-hour flight to London gave her time to make some phone calls. She made several to Jeremy and Brenna. Brenna knew Mia was looking for a transfer to the States. Teri knew a few people and actually found a State Department job for her in New York. It paid well and she could work there until she found something that might be more interesting. Teri secretly hoped Mia would stay in New York. She even got a realtor looking for housing.

"Ranch style," Jeremy said.

"Why?"

"So no one has to climb up and down stairs."

It made sense, but Teri hadn't thought about it. There was so much Teri had taken for granted in her life. "Thanks, Jer." She hesitated, gathering courage. "I love you. And I want to get to know Elaine. Talk to you soon." She hung up the phone. *When was the last time I told my sister or brother that I loved them?*

She called the realtor and insisted that she wanted a house to move into before the end of the week. Money was no object.

Teri leaned back in her seat, pleased with her actions. Except now she needed to deal with Mia's parents and their health problems. How was she going to find a specialist? Alan Crain. Brenna provided the number. He gave her the names of three oncologists and two cardiologists. He also offered to call and open doors. Teri was surprised at his willingness to help. "Thank you, Dr. Crain."

"Alan. After all, Brenna and I have been dating two years. Call me when you get back to the U.S."

Two years? Bren has been dating Alan for two years. My brother is engaged to someone we just met. Mia has a five-year-old child.

Teri felt very alone. She assumed that, since they hadn't shared any information, that Jeremy's and Bren's lives were uneventful and they had no personal lives. How wrong she had been. Not only had she missed out on sharing important parts of their lives, she had given up on one of her own.

She rested her head on the back of the seat. What was she to do when she arrived in London?

❖

Teri knocked on the door of the two-story English country house. She had stood outside for almost ten minutes trying to decide what to say.

"Teri! What're you doing here?"

Mia looked like she had been crying. Her hair was barely an inch long and obviously not combed. Her clothes were in disarray and flour, or some white substance, covered the front of her clothes. Teri's brain had stopped functioning. Emotions were creeping in. "You got your hair cut. It's short."

"Yes, Teri. I'm glad you came this far to talk about my hair." Mia looked away. "I'm sorry. It's been a rough morning. Want to come in?"

"I just happened to be in the neighborhood and thought you might need this." She couldn't tell Mia that she had been in London for three hours. "Michel's passport."

Hints of a smile appeared at the corner of Mia's mouth. "I'm sorry, but I don't believe you just happened to be in the neighborhood." Mia opened the door wider. "Thank you for bringing this." Mia wiped her eyes. "It's six in the morning, Teri. Come on in. Everyone else is still asleep. I'll be fixing breakfast soon."

Teri looked around and admired the warm feel of the place. It was small and cluttered compared to the places she called home. The living room could barely hold the residents, much less a larger crowd. The furniture was not new, but it looked comfortable. The rugs were faded. Still, it felt welcoming. "I thought you lived in Paris."

"I do. This has been my parents' house for the last two years. Before that they lived in a three-story flat." Mia seemed to be nervous. "It got to be too much for them so they moved here. There are two bedrooms on this floor and two upstairs and bathrooms on both floors. Want some coffee?"

"Ah, yes. The early morning quiet and coffee. You've cut your hair really short."

Mia pointed to her right arm and sling. "It's much easier to care for. Sorry, I haven't had a chance to get properly attired yet."

Mia led her into a small kitchen. Pots and pans hung on one wall. The counters had a variety of boxes and containers of food. The refrigerator was half the size of the one in her penthouse. On one counter were the obvious ingredients for breakfast, including a bag of flour.

"You look great." Actually, Mia looked like a charming pixie, and Teri was enchanted. Something, however, was bothering Mia.

Teri hoped it wasn't her presence. "I'd love a cup, and I promise to sit quietly."

Mia finally smiled. "No need. Have a seat. I'll turn the BBC news on in fifteen minutes." She poured coffee for them both then sat at the table. She held up the passport envelope. "Thank you for this. You could have overnighted it and it would have been cheaper."

Teri shrugged. "I overnighted it and I also get to see you." *That was lame.* If she didn't make the effort, she could lose the chance. "I've missed you."

"Thank you." Mia waved the envelope. "I don't know want to say." She played with the envelope and looked anywhere but at Teri. Teri wanted to still those nervous hands. Finally, as if there were nowhere else to look, Mia made eye contact. "I don't understand why you're here. I find it hard to believe you've missed my arguing, but I'm willing to take your words at face value."

It was not the response Teri expected. Nor the one she wanted. Her initial reaction was to ask what the hell that meant and wonder why Mia wasn't more grateful for all she had done and was doing. Then she remembered that was the old Teri. That wasn't the Teri she wanted to be. Nor would it be the person to win Mia's heart.

She took a deep breath. *How do I carry on a conversation, then?*

"Believe it or not, I've missed you. Not long ago, you asked me what was going on between us. At that time, I didn't know how to answer the question. Or I was so obtuse with an answer that even I didn't know what I was saying. My whole world was being turned upside down." This was harder than Teri thought it could be. She had learned how to get what she wanted at work, but forgotten how to ask for what she wanted personally. "I don't know what's going on between us. Whatever it is, I want to find out. I've missed you, more than you can possibly imagine. The thought of not seeing you again—" Teri stopped. She couldn't finish the thought. "I'd rather be here arguing with you than anyplace else."

Mia was carefully scrutinizing her. Teri had to work hard to maintain eye contact. "I don't know what to say." The way Mia was biting her bottom lip worried Teri. Was she about to be turned down?

"Isn't it ironic that I've been working so hard to forget you? Just when I think I'm at that point, you show up."

"If you want me to go away, I'll leave right now. I just want you to know that you've changed me. You are amazing, and I want to be better because of you. Even if you send me away, I'm a different person."

"I'm not sure what you want and, right now, I'm not sure what I'm capable of giving. This is so unexpected. Teri, I…."

Teri nodded. Time to learn about love. The unconditional kind of love Natalie had. "That's okay. I'm willing to wait and willing to accept what you can give."

"Who are you?" Mia laughed. "Never mind. I don't think I want to know right now. I'm fixing pancakes and sausages. Want some?"

"Yes. Can I help?"

"Please. I've been trying to get this stuff together and I'm hopeless." She pointed to her shirt. "I'm wasting more than I'm mixing. This was Michel's request." A sniffle gave away Mia's frustration.

"Look, two hands." She wanted to put her arms around Mia and promise to fix whatever was wrong. Instead, she let Mia put her to work mixing the pancakes. She sat and watched as Mia cooked the sausages.

"It took us a while to get used to English sausage, but now we enjoy it. Pancakes are my father's and Michel's favorites. You arrived just in time. I'm not sure why you're here at this particular time, but today you're a lifesaver." She held up her right arm and the cast that now covered it past her elbow. "Thank you, Teri." Mia briefly hugged her. "Time to get everyone up. Are you leaving right away or can you stay for a few days?"

"I'd like to stay if you don't mind my being under foot. My luggage is outside the door. Just one bag. Can I bring it in?" Mia nodded and Teri felt relief. She had a reprieve, for at least a few more days.

Teri brought in her one bag and was shown to a guest room. Mia gave her some towels and showed her where the upstairs shower was. When she returned to the kitchen, Mia's parents, Thomas and Lisa Daniels, were sitting at the table with Michel in between. Teri was surprised at how thin both were and how tired Thomas Daniels seemed. Smiles, however, filled their faces as they played with Michel.

"Good morning, sir, ma'am. Hope I'm not interrupting." Teri was again the young, impetuous college student, too cocky and self-assured. Thomas Daniels, however, was her kind, patient, and generous mentor. She learned more during the time they worked together than four years of college. She had forgotten the people lessons all too quickly while the financial ones became ingrained.

"Teri, good to see you." Mia's father hugged her and led her to the table. Mia's mother was more reserved in her greeting.

"This young man is Michel, my son." Mia stood behind the dark-haired boy. Teri was surprised that he didn't look more like the fair-headed Daniels' clan. "Michel, this is my friend, Teri Stanton."

"Bon jour, mademoiselle." He moved to stand behind Mia.

"Good morning, sir." Teri was completely at a loss at what to say next.

"Michel is shy when he first meets new people." Mia hugged the boy and gestured toward the table.

Breakfast was enjoyable with conversation centering around Michel, the weather, and plans for the day. When breakfast was done, Mia's mother left to help Michel dress for school.

"Teri, I hear you've done great things with the company. Congratulations. I've followed your career. Big merger in the works. What tears you away to visit our humble abode?"

She had always liked Thomas Daniels's directness. She now understood where Mia had inherited that trait. "I understand you folks are looking to move back stateside and I wondered if you needed a ride."

"That's nice, Teri," Mia said, "but we don't have a place to live. I have a job and responsibilities here. I'd love to take a rain check when we're ready. If the offer would still be available."

"Of course." Teri had never been turned down as many times by one person. She was undaunted. On to Plan B. "I'm also here to ask you, Tom, if you would serve as a personal consultant to Stanton

Enterprises, to me, while we go through this merger. There have been some complications, and there were some lessons you taught that I seem to have forgotten."

Mia's father looked first at Mia and then his wife. He appeared deep in thought.

"Dad, whatever you decide will be fine with us." Mia's mother nodded agreement.

"Theresa, I'm honored. I need to tell you that I was recently diagnosed with advanced stage pancreatic cancer. I've been told my life expectancy is relatively short. I've started treatment and it's not fun. I'm not sure how much I can help." He looked at Mia. "And I plan on spending as much time as I can with my first grandchild and my two children."

The finality of the statement hit Teri harder than she thought it would. She knew the disease was often aggressive and life expectancy was short. Hearing the words spoken drove a stake into her heart. She had forgotten how much this man had meant to her when she was just beginning at Stanton Enterprises. He had been patient and forgiving. She had been obnoxious and impatient. How easily she had discarded those memories!

She swallowed hard. "Sir, I'm so sorry. I still would appreciate any help or advice you would feel comfortable and well enough to provide. I can even put you on our insurance plan and make sure that isn't a worry."

"Theresa, that's very generous of you, but unnecessary. I have great coverage. From what I've been reading about the merger and your career, you seem to have things well under control. What's the real reason you're here?"

He stared at Teri and then at Mia. Teri noticed Mia's face begin to turn red. "Mr. Daniels, Mia is certainly your daughter. That's the same question she asked me earlier. And please, call me Teri. That's what you used to call me."

Thomas Daniels took Mia's hand. "Honey, how would you feel about us moving sooner than later? I think I'd like to work with this youngster one more time. See if there is anything I can still teach her."

Teri held her breath. Her future was tied to the answer.

"Dad, if that's what you want?" He nodded. "I need to contact my boss and I need to get my stuff from Paris."

"I've got the Gulfstream. I can fly you there or we can take the train."

"I think the plane would be better. More room for my luggage." Mia's smile was warm. "Thank you. How soon do we need to do this?"

"Do what?" Mia's mother asked. "Let me get Michel to school and I'll be right back. Don't decide anything until I get back."

"Now you know who the real boss is." Mia grinned at her mother.

By noon, Mia was cleaning out her apartment in Paris. Teri had her white shirt sleeves rolled up and was packing boxes. "What about the food?"

"I'll leave it for my friend next door. She doesn't get out much." Mia packed the food and took it downstairs. When she returned, Teri was holding a photograph.

"Is this Natalie?"

"Yes. That was taken not long after Michel was born." Mia took the photo and wiped dust off. "It was our first Christmas with him."

Teri just stared at Mia. No other questions were asked. Natalie looked enough like her that she easily could have passed for Teri's sister.

"You've lived here quite some time. Will you miss Paris?"

Mia stared down at the picture. "There will always be a part of Paris in my heart." Mia wrapped the photo and carefully packed it. "I know my parents need me now." She resumed packing, but Teri had no doubt that Mia was leaving more than a physical place. She saw the tear that Mia quickly wiped away. Teri turned away and allowed her a moment of privacy.

"Why don't we take a break and get some lunch? I'm looking forward to sitting someplace and enjoying your recommendations." A hint of a smile crossed Mia's lips. Teri wanted to see more. "Take me to your favorite place. Wherever it is. I'm looking forward to exploring good food. And a leisurely lunch."

A broad smile now decorated Mia's face. "Then let's clean up and go."

Teri allowed Mia to order. True to her word, she ate slowly, enjoyed the wine, and found herself laughing at Mia's stories. The warm September sun added to her feeling of well-being. She held Mia's hand as they walked back. "I don't know when I've had a more wonderful lunch. Great food, great company. Thank you." She kissed the back of Mia's hand and then reluctantly let go. "I can't believe how quickly time passed. I feel like I could take a nap, and I never nap."

"We'll quit early tonight." Mia unlocked the door. "I'd like to get as much packed tonight as possible, though."

All Teri wanted was to sit and hold Mia. Every moment spent with Mia increased the infatuation. And the confusion. Mia had admitted to a crush, but what did she feel now? "Where do you want me to start? I've got a couple of more hours in me."

Mia laughed and started opening closets. "Well, let's get packing."

"What about your car? Do you want it sent ahead?"

"Car? You're kidding. I don't own a car."

One more thing she learned about Mia. How did anyone survive without a car?

❖

By seven the next evening, they were landing back in London. Teri made sure the luggage and boxes were carefully stowed on the plane and the plane locked. "Now, let's pack up your parents. Ship what we can and then pack what's needed."

"You're formidable when you undertake a task. Why are you here?"

"Is it so hard to believe that I want to spend more time with you?"

"Yes, Teri. Maine wasn't that long ago. You spent every free moment working."

"I'm trying to change."

"I hear your words, but I'll judge your actions."

"Fair enough."

When they got back, Teri convinced the family to allow her to arrange for packing and transportation of personal property to New York.

"That's expensive," Mia said.

"It's what we do for top staff. Let me do it. Besides, professional movers are much more efficient and you'll have less to repack of anything I pack."

"Packing is not your forte."

"What is? My charm?"

Mia laughed, a deep soul-cleansing laugh. "Giving orders." She leaned against Teri. "You've got that mastered. Speaking of which. I just got a call from my boss telling me that there's a job, with a higher pay rating, in New York City, if I want it. You didn't have anything to do with that did you?"

"Must be destiny. You're meant to move." Teri grinned. Mia had been in a teasing mood all afternoon and Teri was enjoying it. Mia rolled her eyes and resumed sorting Michel's clothes.

"My dear, surely you know Teri. Once she sets her mind on doing something, nothing stands in her way." Her father laughed. "She was that way as a youngster."

"I'm learning." Mia backhanded Teri's stomach. "Okay, what else have you done? Do we have a huge house with forty servants and boats aligned on the dock?"

"No, that's my house. Yours is the little shack at the dead end." Teri winked and continued packing.

Mia collapsed on the couch. "I need to rest. My arm's beginning to hurt."

Teri was immediately by her side. "What can I do?" She sat next to Mia. "I shouldn't have had you doing so much work. Let me get you something to drink." Teri brought her a bottle of cold water and her medications.

"No, that will put me to sleep and I need to fix dinner."

"There must be someplace we can order from." How had she not noticed how tired Mia was? Teri berated herself.

"Teri, come with me." Lisa Daniels was walking toward the door. "There's a great Indian restaurant around the corner."

Teri put her wallet in her pants pocket and followed Mia's mother. She was sure food was not Lisa Daniels's primary concern. It didn't take long to find out.

"You care about my daughter."

In face of such a definitive statement, Teri had only one answer. "Yes, ma'am."

"You've caused her a lot of pain. She was at an impressionable age when you broke her heart. I realize it was just a crush and she was only fifteen. You, however, were twenty-two and knew better. Or should have. I suspect you, or your father, were responsible for the transfer to Europe."

Teri would regret that day, probably for the rest of her life. She was equally determined to make up for it. Even if it was for the rest of her life. "I can't tell you how much I regret that and how selfish I was acting when that happened. I'm trying to do things differently now."

"Do you love my daughter?"

Why did that question keep coming up? "Mrs. Daniels, I care for your daughter. I'm hoping she can teach me about love."

CHAPTER FORTY-TWO

Mia was amazed at Teri's determination. She spoke to her office once a day. The rest of the time was spent with Mia's family. It was obvious Teri wasn't sure how to deal with a child. She often seemed awkward and unsure of what to say or do. Mia found her antics amusing. She was grateful, however, for Teri's take-charge behavior. In ten days, Teri had arranged for all the furniture and household goods to be shipped to New York, found a house for Mia and her family, and even provided medical referrals for her parents and a school for Michel. The last two nights were spent in a suite in an expensive hotel. Teri refused to let Mia or her family pay for anything. All the physical labor had its toll on Teri, but still she stayed up, frequently asking what she could do to help.

They were finally boarding the flight to New York. Teri chatted with the pilots and the cabin crew. She sat next to Mia and took her hand. "I would love to come back someday with you."

Obviously, Teri planned to stay around. Mia would wait and see. She would miss her life in Europe. Whatever the future would bring, it would be an adventure. And she was determined to bring Michel back to Paris as often as she could. They both needed that connection. If Teri was a part of her future, then Teri would be part of the journey.

Once everyone was aboard the plane, she saw how tired her parents were. When the plane was safely airborne, she asked them if they wanted anything to eat or drink.

"Mia, sit down. I'll get it."

"You're still giving orders."

Teri laughed. A real laugh. "Yes, I am. I arranged for easy to prepare foods. Our staff can take care of this. Rest."

Mia shook her head and watched as Teri arranged for food and beverages.

"Teri, thank you for making all this possible." Thomas Daniels wiped at his eyes. "Lisa and I wanted to get back and spend time with both our kids." He looked at Mia. "My only regret, honey, is that I won't get a chance to walk you down the aisle. If only Nat had lived."

Mia knew how excited her parents were when she told them Natalie had proposed. "I know. You have a grandchild. That was one of the things on your bucket list—spoil a grandchild. You just didn't think it would be mine."

Mia's parents began to tell stories about Mia learning to change diapers. "Please," Mia said. "There must be some things that are sacred and private."

Laughter filled the plane. Mia forgot everything except the happiness she was experiencing at the moment.

The limo was waiting for them at the airport along with the customs people. Teri had arranged for the entire process to proceed smoothly. Again, Mia was amazed at how thoughtful Teri was being in caring for her entire family. Teri even carried a sleeping Michel. Something was going on. Mia wasn't ready to completely trust, but she was willing to be open. Besides, right now Teri was making her life so much easier.

"The house is wonderful." Mia stepped out of the limo and admired their new home. The ranch style house was recently completed and had five bedrooms and six bathrooms. The floors were a light oak, except in the bathroom and kitchens where decorative tiles added color. All the kitchen appliances were black and stainless steel in color. And easy to clean. Especially with an active little boy. All their personal belongings had already been delivered from the airport and placed in their respective bedrooms. It was more house than she had ever lived in and certainly couldn't afford. That she would work out with Teri. Right now, it was going to provide her family with room and comfort. It was also close to schools and medical centers.

The best surprise, however, was seeing Jeremy and Bren sitting in the kitchen with a table full of food.

"Teri called us when the plane landed." Jeremy hugged Mia tightly. "I can't tell you how happy I am that you're back in the U.S."

❖

A crew of people helped them unpack and settle in, including a wide variety of groceries. The rest of their belongings had arrived the previous day. Mia doubted she could have accomplished as much by herself in a month, much less in one day. There were still things to unpack and put away, but she felt they could survive and survive well. By seven, her parents and Michel had readily headed for bed, exhausted from the hectic week and the long day. Now she was sitting in the kitchen with friends. Teri was included. Mia still wondered when the terror would return, but for now, she was willing to suspend disbelief one more time.

"How much stuff can a kid have?" Teri asked. "I've run out of room for those little blocks."

"They're Legos." Jeremy laughed. "You didn't particularly care for mine either."

"They were always everywhere but put up. More than once I slipped on one of your contraptions." Teri feigned disdain but ending up laughing when her brother made a face. "Careful your face doesn't get stuck."

"Nana used to say that," Bren said. "You almost sounded like her."

Teri grimaced. Mia wondered what prompted that reaction.

"Well, I certainly can't cook like her." Teri walked over to the refrigerator. "Anyone else want something to drink?"

"I'm fading." Mia stood and stretched. "You're all welcome to stay here tonight. I think we have plenty of room. You'll just have to help me find sheets, towels, and the places to sleep."

Jeremy and Bren quickly rose, declaring early morning meetings requiring their presence in the city. "I probably should go, too." Teri seemed to be vacillating. "I can stay a little longer if there is something you need help with."

Mia hugged Jeremy and Bren and walked with them to the door. Teri was still standing in the same place in the kitchen. *This is awkward. She's been running around commanding for the last ten days, and now there's nothing left to command. Do I ask her for help or try to figure this out myself?* Mia really had little choice.

"I wouldn't ask except my mom's asleep." Mia hesitated. "I need help getting undressed. There are some things that are hard to do one-handed." Teri was not looking at her. "I wouldn't usually ask, but I've been in these clothes for nearly twenty-four hours."

Teri finally made eye contact. "How can I help?" Teri's expression was confusing. Mia couldn't ever remember her being so nervous and unsure. What happened to the self-assured obnoxious terror? She had to admit she preferred the newer version. Still, Teri's current lack of enthusiasm seemed problematic.

"That's okay. I'll manage." Mia turned to walk Teri out. A hand on her shoulder stopped her.

"I said I'd help. Do you need help or not?"

The Boss was back. Teri was in her commanding mode. This person she could deal with. "Yes. You just seemed uncomfortable."

"Tell me what you want me to do. I don't want to be unwelcome, and sometimes I'm not sure what to do."

This woman is definitely bipolar. Command, uncertain. Command, uncertain. Mia smiled. "I need some help."

Mia slipped the sling off her arm. "I need help getting my shirt off and unhooking my bra." She walked to the master suite, not waiting to see if she was being followed.

Chapter Forty-three

Teri's hands were tight fists. That was the least of her problems. She had spent almost every waking moment of the last two weeks with Mia. The more time she spent with her, the more she wanted Mia. The more she wanted Mia, the less she knew how to achieve that goal. Mia was such an enigma. There was a gentleness and humanity about her that Teri was drawn to. Mia brushing hair out of Michel's eyes, rubbing her father's shoulders, or pushing aside her own fatigue and pain to keep everyone laughing and talking. The unguarded moments when Mia looked at her parents or Michel and Teri could read the sadness so clearly written on that precious face. These were the emotions that were tearing her apart, and Teri didn't know what to do to make things better.

She followed Mia into the bedroom. She had no choice. She was beginning to need Mia. She hadn't been aware she needed anyone or anything. Work was much easier. She was in control. With Mia, she was out of control.

Mia threw the sling on the dresser and began tugging the sleeve over her cast. Teri walked up behind her and pulled the top over Mia's head. She leaned into Mia, enjoying the heat radiating off Mia's back.

"I desperately need a shower." Mia's voice was more a moan. "I can't get the cast wet."

Teri found Mia's neck too irresistible. She briefly rubbed Mia's neck. She would have preferred kissing it. "Let me get something to cover your cast." She needed to slow down.

She sat on the toilet while Mia showered. Helping Mia undress had almost been painful. Mia was so damned determined to do as much by herself. All Teri wanted to do was do it for her. And touch her.

As she sat and waited for Mia to finish showering, Teri realized how little time they had spent really talking to each other. They had spent so much time talking about the move Teri still knew little about Natalie or the relationship. Mia was right. She could become so focused on a task that she lost the ability to have a conversation. She was determined to keep her desire in check. She wanted to get to know Mia.

"I'm done." The shower door opened and Mia was smiling. "I can't tell you how good it feels to be clean." She was clutching a towel and trying to dry herself. Teri grabbed another towel and finished the task. She then helped Mia into her bathrobe.

"Do you want your hair dried?"

"Not much to dry. Just want to get some sleep." Mia climbed into bed. "Thank you."

Teri sat on the edge of the bed and played with Mia's wet hair. "It's really short. It's cute. Looks good on you." She put her hand back down. "You never told me how you met Natalie."

Mia started laughing. "She threw up on me. We both had a morning meeting at the same restaurant. She was in line right in front of me. I noticed that she didn't look well, but I was so concerned about the meeting. Suddenly, she says, 'I need to sit down.' I walked her over to where some chairs were and she just threw up. I had a new suit on. Nat was so upset. I walked with her into the restroom and she threw up again. I cleaned myself up the best I could, but I knew there was no way I could go to work. Natalie was so apologetic. She was in the first pangs of morning sickness. I ended up taking her back to her place. She gave me her number and insisted on getting my suit cleaned. We ended up spending most of the day talking, and I didn't make it into work that day."

"Well, that's a new way to get a date. So Natalie was pregnant when you met her?" Mia nodded. "Have you always wanted children?"

"No! I've not been great with relationships, and I couldn't imagine parenting."

"Natalie being pregnant didn't scare you, then?"

"You needed to know Natalie. Anything she did she did with such enthusiasm. She was infectious. It was a part of who she was. If you loved her, you loved the things she did and that included her child. Michel has much of his mother in him. Parenting was never a question. It just was." Mia's smile began to fade. "I still miss her."

Mia reached for Teri's hand. "Stay with me tonight. I'm not on drugs and I will remember I'm asking."

"Are you sure?"

"Just hold me."

Teri pulled off her shoes and nodded. She crept into bed and soon Mia's head was resting on her shoulder. Teri was in heaven. "How did Natalie die?"

"She worked for physicians who were active in Doctors Without Borders. She was injured by a landmine in Afghanistan. When she arrived in Paris, she was almost gone. She hung on for another three weeks. I lived at the hospital." Mia snuggled closer. "I didn't realize how much I loved her until I sat there realizing she was never coming back. Then one day the machines started beeping, and I knew Natalie didn't want to live on a machine. I had to let her ago."

Teri brushed tears away. She couldn't imagine losing someone you loved that much. Teri looked at her own life and realized how easy it had been. Mia had lost her lover and become a single parent. At the same time, she was facing the loss of one parent and nearly lost the other. Teri put both arms around her, as if that single act could push away pain and protect Mia from hurt. Teri then remembered her own behavior. She had been as guilty of causing Mia pain.

"Natalie must have been an incredible person. You must miss her."

Mia closed her eyes. "I do love you, Nat."

Teri's heart could have stopped. It was the second time Mia had said that. Did she miss Natalie so much that no one would ever fill her place? As soon as Mia was asleep, Teri left. She was beginning to hurt. She couldn't stay away and she couldn't stay.

❖

Staying away from Mia for a week did little to resolve her feelings for or about Mia. Teri was short-tempered with staff, had trouble focusing, and had to reread even her e-mails several times.

"Theresa, why aren't we closing this deal?" Teri just stared at her father. "I wanted this done before October first, and it's mid-September. You haven't been focused."

"Father, Pamela Milton is a liability and the company has hidden assets. We cannot proceed until I'm absolutely sure we won't end up acquiring their problems."

"From what you have told me, Pamela Milton hasn't done anything to jeopardize the merger."

"Damn it, her behavior is unacceptable. Harassment is not tolerated in the corporate world."

"She was at a party. We don't know if there hadn't been something going on between Pamela Milton and what's her name?"

Teri slapped her hand on the table. "As long as I run this company, we will have zero tolerance for sexual harassment, in any situation. Mia Daniels did nothing to deserve the behavior, and I have sworn statements that Pamela Milton was the aggressor."

Her father stood in front of her. "I don't care about Mia Daniels or Pamela Milton. Do whatever you need to do to fix this and close on the merger. Do you understand me? I want it done. The board wants it done. And I want Jeremy to break off his engagement. Are you going to take care of this or do I need to?"

"I'll take care of this in my way. Jeremy has already set the date for his wedding. If you choose not to go, then you'll be the only one to blame if Jeremy and Elaine don't come for a visit."

"I'll talk to him then. What's gotten into you lately?"

"I'm going to run this company the way I want until I'm removed from office."

"That may happen." Her father stormed out of her office.

"What's going on?" Bren walked in without waiting to be announced. "Father looked furious."

Teri shook her head and sat down. "He doesn't care about Pamela Milton's behavior. He wants Jeremy to end the engagement. And"—

Teri felt every inch of her body tense—"he wants to blame Mia for the unwanted attention from Pamela." She looked down at her hands. Her knuckles were white. "How dare he try to blame Mia?" She looked at Bren. "He even threatened to remove me as C.O.O."

Bren stood behind her. "The board will never go along with that. I'll start feeling them out. Maybe it's time for Father to retire."

"Maybe it's time for me to step down. I don't want to keep doing things this way. I won't let anyone hurt Mia again."

Bren sat on the edge of Teri's desk. "You're in love with her! I can't believe you're actually considering stepping away from all this. My sister's in love. I don't believe it."

"This isn't about Mia."

"The hell it isn't."

"I don't want to end up like our parents. Such snobs. And I will not tolerate Pamela Milton. I'd rather pass on the merger." Teri got up and looked out at the city. "Milton has quite a reputation, and there's no way we would ever consider having her in any position in our company." She turned and looked at Bren. "I don't know Elaine, but I see how happy Jeremy is. I told Father that it was his choice whether or not to support Jeremy's decision. I want Jer to be happy and Elaine makes him happy. He's so lucky to have Elaine."

"And what about you and Mia?"

"Bren, I don't know what to do. She's still in love with Natalie. I don't know if I can give her that kind of love. I don't know how. Besides, she doesn't readily accept anything I do for her."

"That's not true. She let you bring her family here. Her brother and sister-in-law are arriving tomorrow."

"That's it. All those things are for her family, not her."

Bren stared at her. "You idiot. That's what's important to Mia now. Don't you realize how much that means to her? Why aren't you spending time with her? Why are you sitting here?"

"Because she loves Natalie. I remind her of Natalie."

Bren smacked Teri on the back of the head and walked toward the door. "Come with me. I need to show you something."

Teri followed Bren into her office. Bren pulled out her cell phone and started scrolling. "Here's a picture of Jeremy, Mia, and

Mia's college sweetheart." Teri looked at the picture of three young faces. "Here's another girlfriend. And another. Here's her English girlfriend. Here's Natalie. What do you think they all have in common?"

Teri was numb. Each one looked enough like her that Teri could easily have imagined herself in each photo.

"Mia kept falling in love with you—or someone who looks like you. Natalie called her on it but loved Mia in spite of you. I don't doubt that Mia and Natalie would have made it work if Natalie had lived. Natalie was so in love with Mia, and Mia was finally allowing someone to love her. Teri, Mia needs you. She may not want to admit it, but she does."

"What can I do for her? She sometimes seems like a porcupine."

Bren laughed. "You should talk. She needs to know that you'll be there for her. She needs to trust you."

"And how the hell do I do that?"

"Do something for her family. Show her that you not only care for her but the people she loves."

Teri remembered the conversation on the plane. "Her father wants to walk her down the aisle. They were talking about it when we were coming to New York. Her parents wanted to spoil grandchildren and walk Mia down the aisle."

"Then if you really love Mia, marry her. But only if you really love her and plan on a long-term commitment. And realize Mother and Father may not be happy."

"I don't know if I can love her the way Natalie did, but I'm willing to try. I'm willing to spend the rest of my life trying to make her happy, if that's what it takes." She turned to Bren. "What do we need to do? What about the merger?"

"One step at a time." Bren's smile was reassuring. "Let's get you married. You need to ask Mia first, but you better get a ring."

For the first time in years, both Teri and Bren left the office early. Bren helped Teri pick out a ring, then picked out something for Teri to wear. Teri was nervous, but somehow, she knew Mia would make her happy.

Teri drove to Mia's. She needed to talk with Mia's parents first. Mia's father was old-fashioned enough to expect Teri to speak with him first.

"Teri, come on in." Mia's mother opened the door. "We hadn't seen you since we got settled in. Tom and I want to thank you."

"Is Mr. Daniels available? I'd like to talk to you both."

"Is something wrong?"

Teri couldn't remember the last time she had been this nervous. What if Mia's parents objected? They certainly had reason. "No!" She fidgeted in the doorway. "I just need to ask you something important."

"Mia isn't home yet. Do you need to speak to her?" She led Teri into the home office where Tom Daniels was reviewing merger documents. "Tom, look who's here."

Teri looked at her former mentor and time stood still. Tom Daniels had shown her such kindness and gentleness, even when she knew she was having temper tantrums. She was reminded of her grandmother's unconditional love. He had given her the same love and respect. Tears threatened. She took a deep breath and gathered her courage. She did know about love but had forgotten.

"I know how important Mia's family is to her. So I'm asking your blessing. I want to ask Mia to marry me. I'm well aware of our past history and that Mia would never do anything that her family didn't approve of."

Teri now knew what the defendant in a trial felt like, awaiting the jury's decision. Her life was on hold. She looked from Mia's mother to her father. Time seemed to drag as they looked at each other. Teri couldn't read their expressions. Her happiness was in their hands. This was a rare and uncomfortable position for Teri.

Finally, Tom Daniels spoke. "Teri, you haven't been around much this week."

"No, sir. I could claim that I was busy at the office. Even though that's true, that's not the real reason. I care so much for Mia that most of the time I feel like a bumbling teenager. Worse, I've realized that I behaved selfishly and without cause too many times around Mia. Why she doesn't hate me I don't understand. I also doubted that I would know how to love her the way she needed. That's sounds so lame, but it's true."

"And now?"

"I've been miserable all week. The only time I'm happy is when I'm around her. She makes me laugh. She makes me forget that I'm a Stanton. She makes me want to be the kind of woman she could be proud of." Teri looked down at her trembling hands. "So many years ago, you both made me feel part of your family, welcomed me into your home, and helped me to belong. I almost forgot that. There's a possibility that my father may try to remove me as C.O.O. I want to let you know that financially, I'll still be able to take care of my new family. You and Mia are more important than any job or title."

"I hope that doesn't happen. If it does, it may mean a big change in your life."

"Sir, I know that. I'm not sure how I will deal with it, but I choose Mia over work."

"Jobs will come and go." Lisa Daniels's voice was just as steady as her eye contact. Teri had no doubt she was referring to the abrupt job transfer years ago. Teri didn't look away. "You can get some temporary feeling of joy from them, but the job will not heal a wounded heart. It's not going to give your life the inner strength that love can." She reached for her husband's hand. "We've taught our children to put family and their personal lives first. I have no doubt you care about Mia. I've seen it in the way you look at her, the way you talk to her. I just didn't think you knew it. If you can put her first, you have our blessing. Thank you for asking even though we know Mia's the one who has to say yes."

Teri took a deep breath and relaxed. She welcomed the hugs from both Mia's parents. Mia's father pulled out the Scotch and poured them all a drink. When Michel arrived home from school, she sat on the floor with him and played with his Legos. They had just completed building a large castle when Mia arrived.

"Where's my camera?" Mia said. "Here's Teri Stanton in her very expensive clothes and shoes, sitting on the floor, surrounded by plastic building blocks."

"Mama," Michel jumped up, causing the not too stable castle to cascade down on Teri's lap.

Mia's smile was worth the shoe filled with blocks and the chocolate milk stain on her pants leg. A heat was building inside her chest. She loved Mia. She made a silly face and Mia laughed.

"Now I definitely need my camera. That picture should go on your corporate website." Mia put out her hand to help Teri stand. "That would certainly put a different face on Theresa Stanton's image."

Teri was standing close enough to smell Mia's sweet scent. She closed her eyes briefly and memorized the smell. "I'm not sure Stanton Enterprises is quite ready for that big a change. I'll remember your offer though." She took in all of Mia. "You look wonderful."

Mia's expression became more serious. "You disappeared."

"Yes. I had some things I had to take care of. I won't be disappearing again." Teri knew she had an uphill battle, but she was ready. "How's your arm?"

"I go next week and they'll x-ray it. Hopefully, the cast will be off permanently or at least a shorter one. This long one has more to do with my wrist than the broken bone." Mia's scrutiny made Teri uncomfortable. "You haven't even called. You said you wouldn't disappear. Is this a way to get even?"

"No. Getting even is the last thing on my mind." She stroked Mia's good arm. "I'm sorry. I didn't want to wear out my welcome."

"Have I or my family done something to make you feel that way?"

"No! It was me not you." Teri squeezed Mia's hand. Her hand was a lifeline to a world that Teri no longer was a part of. A world of people, family, friends. This was an awkward moment, and she didn't know what to do. "Do you need to change clothes? Your mom is fixing dinner. I can help you change."

Mia's head tilted as if she wanted to ask a question. She just stared. Finally, Mia nodded.

Chapter Forty-four

Mia had missed Teri. Walking in and finding Teri sitting on the floor had been a pleasant surprise. Once she was over the initial shock of seeing Teri, her reserve kicked in. What did she want from Teri? She no longer knew. She was sure she had put the infatuation away.

"Thank you, Teri. I'll get my mom to help."

"I think she's deep in flour or something. I don't mind."

Something was different. Teri didn't seem as arrogant or assured. "Fine." She brushed Michel's hair. "You wait here and let Mama change. I'll be right back."

Once in her bedroom, she was nervous. She had spent so much time alone with Teri, and still, she was unsure of what was going on between them. She lifted the sling off her neck. Teri gently pulled it off. Teri's every movement screamed tenderness. Mia felt treasured. She was able to undress and get dressed without any feeling of awkwardness. Teri sat on the floor and tied Mia's tennis shoes. The look on Teri's face was priceless. Her tongue was sticking out of the side of her mouth as she tied the laces.

"Thank you." Mia lifted Teri's chin. "For everything." Something was changing. Mia could feel healing beginning. "Let's go see what my mom's cooking."

Teri remained sitting on the floor. "Wait!" Mia stopped at the door. "There's something I need to talk to you about." Teri stood and stuck both hands in her pockets. Teri looked everywhere but at her.

"Can it wait until after dinner?"

"I need to do this now."

"O-kay."

"Mia, you are the most amazing woman I have ever known. This past week I've been miserable missing you. I know there's no excuse for my not being in touch, but I was afraid you might not want to see me. Not much scares me, but I would've been devastated if you told me to go away. Again. Being away was worse. I want to spend every free moment getting to know you. Every song you love to sing. Every wine you like to drink. Your favorite books. If you snore at night."

"I don't snore!" Mia smiled anyway.

"I don't care if you do or not." Teri pulled a small Tiffany box out of her pocket and opened it. "I've fallen in love with you, and I don't want to imagine a life without you. Marry me, Mia Daniels."

"Marry you? Teri, most of the time I wasn't even sure if you liked me."

Teri reached for Mia's good hand. "Why would you think that?"

There were so many things she could point to, but Teri's declaration of love was totally unexpected. "Teri, what happened to my being a manipulative liar? What about my being so difficult?"

"You can't imagine how sorry I am for any and all the things I've said. Even more, I'm sorry I've been such an asshole. To you, to Brenna and Jeremy. To so many people. You've made me realize there is so much I've been missing in life. Knowing you has made me want to be a better person."

"I had no idea you felt this way."

"No one has dared to even suggest taking me shopping, and I've been shopping more times with you than in my whole life. You got me to buy jeans and hiking boots and dragged me up some mountain at zero dark thirty. I know how much you loved Natalie, and I didn't think you could feel that way about anyone else. Especially me. But, Mia, I don't care. I've been miserable this week and made everyone else miserable. I've felt empty without you. You're a breath of fresh air in my black-and-white life. Please tell me I haven't ruined a chance to show you how much I love you." Teri moved the ring closer to Mia. "Put color back in my life."

Mia was speechless. Teri was standing there with an obviously expensive engagement ring in her hand. It was a large, marquise cut solitaire diamond with smaller emeralds on either side. It had to be at least one carat. Mia recognized the look on Teri's face. She expected to be turned down. For the first time ever, Teri looked vulnerable.

"Why now?"

"Because I'm miserable without you. I didn't even know I wasn't happy until you. I've fallen madly in love with you. I can't think. I can't work. No, change that. I don't want to work. I want to be with you."

"You don't want to work? I'm speechless. You've never said anything. I even asked you what was going on between us and you said we were friends."

"I know. I've been so confused. To be honest, I didn't trust what I was feeling. At first, I thought it was just lust, but it's so much more. Marry me?" Mia was hesitating. "Wait! One more thing. I do remember your father saying something about his bucket list. He wanted to walk you down the aisle. And I want him to have that chance."

The fact that Teri remembered her father's wish touched Mia. She felt tears come unbidden. She put her arms around Teri's neck. "You've been so wonderful. Thank you." Teri's embrace was tentative.

"Is that a yes or a no?"

"It's a 'Can I think about it?' answer."

"I'll beg."

Mia kissed Teri on the check. "Please don't beg. I can't give you an answer. I'm still trying to deal with all the changes in my life." Mia's life had been tossed into a tornado and the winds just increased. *Teri wants to marry me?* "This is definitely unexpected."

"So does this mean I have a chance?"

"I've learned no door is ever closed as long as you're alive. Come on. Let's see what's for dinner."

Mia's emotions were roiling. There was no doubt in the sincerity of Teri's offer. It was so sudden. Just as she had finally let go of her infatuation with Teri, Mia found Teri asking for her hand in marriage. Was this some obscene, perverted joke? Mia doubted it.

The remainder of the evening Teri was both attentive and affectionate. She would walk by and touch Mia's arm. When they were sitting next to each other at dinner, she was frequently feeding Mia or teasing her. She helped with the dishes and then sat next to Mia afterward. Mia liked the attention but wondered whether Teri would be there the next day or the day after that. After all, work was always more important.

By nine, Mia was alone with Teri. The rest of her family was sleeping.

"I've always wanted short hair. It looks great on you."

"Teri, I'm confused. You and I haven't been able to spend a day together without arguing. You hardly know me."

"We've spent most of the last month together and only argued three times. I know how wonderful you are. More, I know how bare my life is without you."

"What kind of music do I like? What are my favorite foods? What have your parents said?"

"I plan on telling my parents tomorrow. I don't care what they say."

Mia was stunned. Could Teri really do something without her parents' permission? She leaned her head against the back of the couch. "I'm tired tonight. I have an early day. I'm going to call it a night."

"Do you want me to leave?" Teri was stroking her hair.

"Yes." Teri felt so good. "No." Mia sat up. "I don't know. I don't understand."

"Tell me what you want me to do. I'll stay or leave."

Could Teri change? Was she capable of caring for someone? "If I ask you to stay, can you do that as a friend?"

"If that's what you want."

"Right now, I just want to get some sleep. Stay if you want. I'm not making any promises. We'll just see how things go." Mia sat up. "Come on. Let's make up a bed for you. You may need to get some clothes."

Teri smiled. "I'll be all right for tonight. Thank you." Teri kissed Mia on the cheek.

Mia was determined to not get her hopes up. She would trust what Teri did.

❖

A week had gone by, and every evening Teri was at the house shortly after five. She changed clothes and played with Michel or helped with dinner. After her parents were in bed, they sat up and talked. Mia was enjoying the time with Teri more and more. "Who are you?"

"I'm someone who loves you." Teri put her arm along the back of the couch. "And I'm happy to be sitting right here with you."

"Are you moving in or are you just staying for a while?"

Teri leaned closer and kissed Mia. It was such a gentle kiss that Mia wondered if she imagined it. When she opened her eyes, Teri was inches away. Teri was waiting for her to make the next move.

"I can't do this." The hurt look on Teri's face revealed so much about the intensity of Teri's feelings. Mia rushed to finish her thought. "The last time you kissed me that's what you said. Why did you say that? What's changed?"

Teri looked confused.

"I was staying at your place when the Gastons were visiting."

Teri nodded. "I remember. I woke you up. That was the day I realized how much I wanted you. It wasn't just about sex."

Mia's eyes were wide. "What was it about? I felt you were saying that I was interfering with your work."

"No. I was attracted to you from that first day I saw you. That day, however, I realized I didn't want one night. I wanted lots of nights. I wanted you, and I just didn't know what to do."

"I don't understand. You wanted me?"

"Work has been my life for most of the last fifteen years. Suddenly, I realized I wanted you in my life almost as much as I wanted to go to work. I couldn't just want one night when I wanted much more. For the first time, I was actually wondering what it would be like to be in a relationship. A relationship with you."

Mia was quiet for some time. "Back to my question. Are you moving in or just staying for a while?"

"I'll do whichever you want. I want to stay. I want to see if I can convince you that I love you. I want to find out what all this relationship business is all about. If you ask me to leave, I will." Teri's voice broke. She looked away.

"Teri, look at me." She waited until Teri's gaze was steady. "I need to know what *you* want to do. Are you staying or just visiting? I need you to tell me."

CHAPTER FORTY-FIVE

Every time she brought more clothes over, Teri asked herself the same question. "I'm trying to figure that out. I know that the past week I've been happier than I thought possible. Not only you, but your parents and Michel."

"What about your parents?"

Teri shook her head. "They're not happy, but I don't care. I go to work, but now I can't wait to leave and be back here with you." She looked down at her hands, now restless in her lap. "I don't know how to have a girlfriend, much less a wife. You challenge me. I want to do things differently." She finally looked at Mia. "I even miss finding Lego blocks in my shoes."

Mia laughed. "Your timing couldn't be worse. For half my life I've had a crush on you. When Natalie came into my life, I began to think I could love someone else. And I've been working hard to get over you. It's obvious I haven't succeeded as well as I thought." She became serious. "I need to trust you. I need to know you're going to be there. Natalie taught me how important that is. Especially now. I have a son, a parent with heart disease, and a parent who is dying. I don't want to fight with you. It's taking every ounce of my reserve to get up each day. I lost Natalie. I'm losing my dad. I can't take any more losses. If you can't commit for the long term, then we don't have a chance."

Mia turned away. Teri saw the tears forming before Mia hid her face. Bren and Jeremy were right. She hadn't taken care of anyone except herself. She'd never worried about anyone's feelings.

Relationships, she was discovering, were definitely harder than she ever imagined. She preferred the black-and-white of her work world. It was easier, but it didn't make her happy anymore.

"I don't want to fight either. I can't imagine what you've been going through. In fact, I don't understand how you get through each day. I want…I want to be part of your life. I know this is a hard time, and I'd like to do whatever I can to make it better."

Mia's tears tore at Teri. She didn't know what to do. She tentatively touched Mia's shoulder. Mia turned and leaned against her. Teri held her.

"Sorry. Sometimes I feel so overwhelmed." Mia sat back, pulling herself from Teri's embrace. "I need to get some sleep." She kissed Teri on the cheek and left.

Teri watched Mia walk away. The emptiness in her arms was nothing compared to that in her heart.

Teri was alone. She realized she had been alone for a long time. "Why didn't I care before?"

She went to bed. Alone.

❖

As soon as she arrived at the office, her father met her. "Theresa, we need to talk." Teri nodded and led him into her office.

"You're here rather early."

"I feel this is important, and I want an answer today." He sat on the couch in the office. "Sit here." He pointed to the other end of the couch. "It's almost October and the Milton deal is not anywhere near closed. Your mother and I received a notice about Jeremy's wedding to some girl in California. We don't know her parents or who her family is. I came in yesterday afternoon at four thirty and you'd already left. I've never known you to not carry out my orders. What the hell is going on?"

Teri stood up. Time to decide. That was easy. "Jeremy and Elaine love each other, and I will not interfere in that, regardless of what you or Mother want. The plan all along was to complete the Milton acquisition by the end of the year. At this point, I'm actually looking at other possibilities because having Pamela Milton as an executive in our new company is a deal breaker as far as I'm concerned." Teri took a deep breath and continued before her father had a chance to protest. "And I'm leaving work at the end of the work day. I have asked Mia Daniels to marry me, and I'm spending my non-work time with her and her family."

Her father stood up. "Have you lost your mind? You've really let me down, and I'm beginning to think you no longer have what it takes to be the chief operating officer. I had been thinking of announcing my retirement at the end of the year and promoting you. Now, I may need to find someone else. You have until the end of the day to make up your mind. There are plenty of the right girls for you to marry. Girls who understand how important work is. Obviously, Mia Daniels doesn't. I want an answer by three. Either you want to be C.E.O. or you don't want to work here anymore."

Her father turned to leave. Teri had wanted the C.E.O. title for too many years. Now, she wanted something, or someone, more. "I'll give you my answer now. If taking over your role means giving up Mia and her family, I'm turning the offer down. Jeremy will marry Elaine, and Bren and I will be there. Pamela Milton will not serve as a vice president as long as I am chief operating officer."

He stopped at the door and stared at her. "Then you may not be in the job much longer." The door slammed as he left.

The rest of the morning went much better, but Teri couldn't concentrate. At the afternoon staffing with all the top-level managers, she kept staring at Bren and Jeremy and wondered how she had lost touch with them. She wondered what she would do when she no longer worked for Stanton Enterprises.

"We'll meet again next week. Good meeting." She turned to Bren and Jeremy. "Can you two stay after the meeting?" They nodded.

"Is everything okay?" Jeremy asked.

"Why are you asking?"

"Because you said good meeting."

Teri sighed. "Work is fine. I just wanted to talk to you both. I realized that we haven't spent much time together." Bren started to speak. Teri put up her hand. "I mean outside of work. We were close once, and I don't know what happened."

"I'll tell you what happened." Jeremy's voice was filled with regret. "You chose work over us. You chose to do whatever our parents wanted over us. You chose you over us. I'm damn tired of being a Stanton." He spun around in his seat. Teri wanted to speak but sat quietly and waited. Finally, he looked at her. "I'm done working for Stanton Enterprises." He started for the door.

"Jeremy, wait." Teri met him at the door. "Please. I'm sorry. I'm trying to change. What can I do?"

"You can start by telling our parents that I plan on marrying Elaine, no matter how much they threaten me."

"I understand. Please don't leave." Teri walked with her brother back to the table. "They're giving me the same story."

"What do you mean?" Bren asked.

"I told Father that I was going to your wedding and that I plan to marry Mia."

"You what?" Bren and Jeremy said in unison.

"Since when?" Jeremy asked.

"I asked her last week."

"What did she say?" Bren asked.

"She said she needs to think about it." Teri told them about that evening and her conversations with Mia. "I don't know how to win her, but I'm not giving up."

"What did our parents say?" Bren seemed almost excited. "I can't imagine Father wanting to come back to run the company."

"He's threatened to remove me as C.O.O. and hire someone outside. They've been insisting for over a year that I date the daughter of one of their friends. They're sure I'll come to my senses."

"Great!"

"Great? Do you have any idea what it's like to listen to them every day?"

"I do," Jeremy said.

Bren was smiling. "Between the three of us, we own thirty percent of the company. We only need to talk our uncle and aunt into supporting us and we have majority voting control."

"What're you talking about?" Teri looked at Bren and wondered if she were hallucinating.

"One of the first things I did when I became legal counsel was to divide Dad's share so that we each had ten percent and he had thirty percent. It was part of the agreement for me to come to work here. Father felt that having some ownership was motivation. Aunt Betty and Uncle Joe each have twenty percent since they refused to work for the company. That was Nana's influence."

Jeremy and Teri started laughing. "You mean we can unseat Father?" Jeremy was grinning from ear to ear.

"What makes you think our aunt and uncle will support us over their brother?" Teri asked.

"Well," Bren started, "Aunt Betty has been living in my condo in South Beach with me since her husband left her for a much younger woman and Father refused to help his own sister. Uncle Joe has refused to talk to Father since he refused to help Aunt Betty. He and his wife come down to Miami twice a year to spend a couple of weeks with our aunt."

Teri shook her head. "Why didn't you ever say anything?"

"You were Father's shadow. I didn't trust you."

"I'm sorry. No more secrets?" Jeremy and Bren nodded.

"I'll talk to our aunt and uncle," Bren said. "You two be happy meanwhile."

"I love you. Both of you," Teri said.

"That's the first time you've said that since we were kids." Bren hugged her. "I love you, too."

"Jeremy? If you want to do something else, I'll help you however I can. I'd ask you to reconsider leaving, though. I'm going to need both of you to run this company. I want to spend more time with Mia. Her father isn't doing well. And I just want to be with her."

"Well, let us know if we can help." Jeremy smiled at her.

Teri was grateful for the offer but wondered what it would take to convince Mia.

CHAPTER FORTY-SIX

Teri hadn't been over in two days. She had called and said there was an emergency at work but would be in touch. Mia hadn't heard from her since her call on Thursday. Now it was Sunday and not even a text message. Mia was wondering if Teri could put a relationship before work.

She sat down in her office to pay bills when she realized she hadn't received any information about her payments for the house. Mia was sure she hadn't misplaced any bills. Why hadn't she asked Teri? She knew. The whole process of moving back to the U.S. had occurred so quickly that she hadn't thought about it. "Damn! Now I have to call her." Mia sighed and picked up her cell phone.

Teri answered after several rings. "Sorry, I'm having some trouble with the Bluetooth in my car. I've missed talking to you."

Mia ignored the last comment. "Teri, I haven't received a payment book for the house."

"I'm outside. We'll talk about it when I get in."

Mia heard the key turn in the door. She hoped Teri was in a good mood.

"You look ready for bed." Teri sat at the table. She patted Mia's hand. "Don't worry about the house. I paid cash for it. I didn't want you to worry about payments."

The good feeling from the day was slipping away. "Teri, that's very nice, but I can't accept that. I can't live here and not pay rent or the mortgage."

"Mia, I'm trying to make your life easier. You already have so much to worry about."

"Thank you, but I can take care of myself and my family. We can't live in your house. I thought you had arranged for me to rent or buy the house."

Teri slammed her hand on the table. "What's wrong with me buying the house? What's wrong with me paying for anything? Don't you know how much I love you?"

"There's no need to raise your voice. The family is sleeping."

Teri took a deep breath. "I'm sorry. You're right. I don't doubt your abilities. In fact, you amaze me every single day. I just want to help."

Mia relaxed. She didn't want a fight. "Thank you again. I appreciate that, but I don't want to be obligated or for you to feel obligated."

Teri sat back in her chair. "Obligated? Mia, I asked you to marry me. I'm in love with you. I want us to share a life together." A look of pain crossed Teri's face. "Do you dislike me that much?"

What did she feel for Teri? If she were honest, she was angry because she had begun to depend on Teri and to care about her. She was even imagining a future with her.

"Teri, you've disappeared twice in the six weeks since we've been back in the States. You've told my father you wanted him to help you, but you haven't talked to him in almost a week. Michel asked when you were coming back. I can't allow you to pop in and out of our lives. I've told you I needed stability. I don't need your money. I need you."

Mia picked up her papers on the table and closed her computer. She fought back the tears.

Teri moved closer. "What's wrong with my giving you this house?"

"How do I know you won't disappear again and then I get a notice we need to move because you need to use the house for business or decided to sell it?"

"I wouldn't do that." Teri's voice was strained. "You don't think much of me."

"Just the opposite. I think too much about you. There's no way we could've moved here without you. I don't believe it was chance or fate or whatever that I got the job I did. You've made sure my parents have made all their medical appointments when I couldn't. You've even asked me to marry you. I still don't understand why. Surely, there must be someone you would find more acceptable."

❖

The week had been one of the most emotional ones of Teri's life. It was nothing compared to what she was experiencing now. The only thing that had gone right was reconnecting with her brother and sister. She had to find some way to connect with Mia.

Teri looked at Mia. She was beautiful. No makeup. Her hair a damp mess. Every time she looked at her, she got this tingling feeling in her stomach. When that happened, she didn't care about work, her father, anything, except Mia.

When Mia sat back down, Teri reached for hand. "This past week hasn't been just about work. The reason I haven't said anything to your father is that I wasn't sure I would be working for Stanton."

"What? What happened?"

"Ever since I told my parents I was going to marry you, they've been unrelenting. My mother actually showed up at the office with her family photo album to remind me of our heritage. My father let me know that I was a huge disappointment. Two weeks ago, he told me that I had until the end of this month to finalize the merger and get rid of you and Elaine. I refused. There's no way I'd have Pamela Milton be a part of the merger. And until you tell me otherwise, I'm determined to marry you and be a part of Jeremy's wedding to Elaine. I've not been here the last couple of days because I was trying to figure out who would take over and to make sure the Milton merger didn't go through."

Mia squeezed Teri's hand. "Teri, I'm so sorry. Why didn't you tell me?"

"It was my problem. I needed to fix it."

Mia let go of her hand. "You ask me to marry you, but something this important you don't share. You don't know the first thing about being a friend, much less being a partner. I don't think—"

Teri put up her hand. She was afraid Mia was going to tell her that she didn't think they should marry. She leaned forward and wrapped her hands around Mia's good one. "I've heard the lecture from my sister and brother. I'm sorry I haven't been a better friend, especially after I promised I would. I'm trying. Please give me a chance."

"You are trying and how many chances do you want?" At least Mia was smiling.

"As many as I can get." Teri grinned and pulled Mia close. "As many as I can get. I love you, Mia Daniels. If you still don't want to marry me, I'll go away and drown myself in a bathtub of expensive Scotch." Teri hoped she was hiding her fear behind her humor. "Please?"

"You aren't ordering me?"

"Somewhere along the way, I've forgotten how to ask. You reminded me of that. Please? I'm begging."

"What are the rules?"

"No rules unless you set them. I just want a chance. You're important to me, and I don't want to lose you. In fact, as of tonight, I'm off of work for the next seven to ten days." Teri couldn't remember the last time she had truly taken time away from work. The thought of being gone for a few days was terrifying. Yes, she had spent several days with Mia in Maine, but Mia was right. She was still able to work. The fear of losing Mia was devastating, and she would do anything to prevent it. Mia had found a place in her heart. For the first time in her life, Teri wanted a life outside work. She wanted a life with Mia.

"I don't know how you're managing work, your folks, Michel, and taking care of the house. You won't let me hire a housekeeper. And you're still doing most things one-handed." Teri pointed to the new shorter splint. "Maybe, if I hang around for a while, I'll figure it out."

Mia looked down at her arm. She looked tired. When she looked up, tears glistened in her eyes. Teri wanted to hold her and put a protective wall around her. She knew that wasn't possible, but if there was some way to make life easier, she would do anything to make it happen.

"I don't know what to say." Mia wiped the tears from her eyes. "I don't think I could take anymore disappointments. You promised to spend time with me in August and you spent most of that time working. When you weren't working, we were arguing. I honestly don't think I can handle you disappointing me again. You have no idea how much I missed you this week. I begin to trust you and you disappear."

Mia moved across the room. "I can't do this." Her words were swallowed by sobs.

Every fiber of her being screamed for Teri to walk away. Her heart pulled her forward. She stopped Mia and pulled her into an embrace. The tears flowed until Teri felt a wet place on her chest over her heart. Her body was absorbing some of Mia's pain and she felt the ache. "I'm so sorry. Mia, I never knew. I could make excuses, but that's all it would be. Please, sweetheart, forgive me."

Mia's reddened eyes looked up in surprise. "What did you say?"

"I asked you to forgive me."

"Before that. You called me sweetheart."

Teri couldn't remember what she said. For the first time in a long time, her heart was speaking without her head to filter. "That's the way I think of you. My heart has been empty for a long time. All I've needed to do was make decisions. That doesn't require emotions. Until you and now you're everything I want."

Mia pulled away. "I need to blow my nose." She didn't look at Teri. She walked back into the kitchen and grabbed some tissues. She finally sat at the table. Teri sat next to her. "One more try, Teri." Her sigh was more a sign of resignation.

Teri's heart was breaking. Jeremy and Bren were right. Mia was strong, but she was also vulnerable. Words were sticking in her throat. "Mia, I'm so sorry. You deserve to be special. I'm so sorry. If I could do it over, I would do things very differently." She needed Mia to believe her.

CHAPTER FORTY-SEVEN

Mia was mentally, physically, and emotionally tired. She needed sleep. She was struggling to cope with everything going on in her life. All she wanted right now was to be taken care of, even if for one day.

She also desperately needed to be held. Teri's arms felt so good. There were so many reasons not to trust Teri, but right now, she needed physical comfort more. She needed someone else to be in charge. She needed someone else to say things are going to be all right, even if they weren't.

"Apology accepted." Mia hesitated. Her emotional needs were greater than her clear thinking self. "Would you mind staying here tonight and just hold me?" She put her hand out and prayed Teri would just say yes and not expect more.

"Absolutely." Teri took her hand and led Mia to the bedroom. "Let me go to my room and change and I'll be right back." She started to leave then stopped. "Promise."

Teri's smile lifted some of the load bearing down on Mia. *Maybe this can work.* She put on her blue nightgown and crawled into bed. She would shower in the morning. She had just gotten comfortable when the door opened and Teri came in.

"I guess I took my sleepwear to be cleaned. This is all I could find." Teri was standing in the middle of the room wearing the black-and-white checked shirt they had gotten in Maine.

"Well, you'll be ready for an early morning drive. Or almost ready." Mia finally smiled. Teri's bare legs were in sharp contrast to the checked shirt. They were long and attractive. Mia briefly wondered how Teri had managed to remain single. This line of thought was not productive. She pulled the covers back. "Let's get some sleep."

Teri got into bed and pulled Mia close. Mia closed her eyes and rested her head on Teri's shoulder. Mia felt safe. The heat from Teri's body was both distracting and comforting. Mia's only thoughts were of how good this felt. She relaxed and felt sleep claiming her.

Mia stretched and looked at the clock. It was six thirty. She had slept much later than usual. Sometime during the night, Michel had crawled in bed next to her. Mia was more content than she had been in a long time. She turned and found Teri with her head propped up on one arm. "How long have you been awake?"

"Long enough to appreciate how beautiful you are." Teri's hand stroked the side of Mia's face. Mia leaned into the caress. "I can't believe I slept this long. I woke up once and you were so damned cute and snuggled so close, I didn't want to get up. I fell back to sleep right away."

The look in Teri's face left her feeling warm all over. Mia felt a lightness creeping in and a sense of hope. How long had it been since she had felt this good?

Michel stirred and his eyes slowly opened. "Mama, I had a bad dream." Whenever it was just the two of them talking, he always spoke in French.

Mia hugged him. "You're all right now," she answered back in French. "Were there monsters?" Mia teased him.

His smile lit up her day. "No, Mama. I couldn't find you and I was scared."

Mia pulled him closer. "I'll always find you." She knew it was a promise she would do anything to keep even though she needed someone to find her.

"I'll go get dressed." Teri inched out of bed. "You two stay there. I'll see what I can do for breakfast."

"I think I better get breakfast." Mia laughed at the face Teri made. "Saturday is a day off from work, and I don't want my mom and me spending the day cleaning the kitchen."

"Oh, ye of little faith."

"No! Ye of little cooking talent." Mia rubbed Michel's head. "Go get dressed and we'll have breakfast." As soon as he was gone, Mia got up and grabbed her bathrobe. She reached for Teri's hand. "Thank you for last night. It's been a long week."

"Thank you for letting me make it a little better. Is Michel okay?"

She explained about his dream. "Seems like this has been hard week on all of us."

"I'm so sorry. Let me make it a better week for you. For all of you." Before Mia could reply, Teri darted out of Mia's bedroom. She was left wondering what Teri was up to.

Mia walked into the kitchen and started fixing breakfast. It wasn't long before her mother was helping her pull it all together. Mia began humming.

"Honey, it's been a long time since I've heard you singing. I know you've tried to be strong for all of us. It's good to see you smiling." Her mother gave her a quick hug and started making pancakes.

The atmosphere at breakfast was relaxed. Even her father was laughing. It was the best Saturday morning in at least two years. She looked at Teri. She was laughing and being silly. Mia walked behind Teri and hugged her. "Thank you," she whispered.

"What shall we do today?" Mia asked. Several suggestions were made, but no plan had overwhelming support. Teri offered to fly them anywhere they wanted to go, but Mia's parents didn't want to travel far.

Mia hugged her parents. "Let's see what Michel wants to do."

Michel wanted to go to a movie. It was something that didn't require much effort, and Mia's father wasn't exhausted when they got back to the house. The day had been so perfect, she kept waiting for Teri to answer the phone or for the Terror to return. Instead, Teri paid for the tickets, the drinks and popcorn, and bought dinner. She did everything she could to make sure Mia's dad was comfortable and that Mia didn't have to do anything.

Once her family was in bed, Mia wondered if Teri's behavior would change.

CHAPTER FORTY-EIGHT

Teri sat on the couch opposite from Mia. If she sat closer, she was afraid she would forget her promise to take things slowly. As much as she had enjoyed this day, she was aware of what a commitment it was to be a part of the Daniels family. Tom Daniels had less than a year. Mia's mother would never be able to live alone. Michel was a cute little high-energy boy. Mia would have others to take care of for a long time. Teri wasn't responsible for anyone except herself. And Stanton Enterprises. As much as she wanted Mia, she wondered how she could handle all the responsibility and work. Teri didn't know how Mia did this day after day.

"Thank you for today," Mia said. She picked at the pillow on her lap. "I'm sure there were more important things you could've been doing, but I appreciate you taking the time. My parents appreciate it, too."

Had Mia read her mind? She hoped not. "I had a great time today." The more time she spent with Mia, the more she realized how incredible Mia was. *She spends every day juggling work and her family, and I'm exhausted after one day.* "How do you find the energy each day to do all that you do? I know you're not on drugs."

Mia was smiling when she looked at Teri. "It's no problem. I love my family."

"Tell me about Natalie. You told me how you met but not how you became involved."

The look on Mia's face spoke volumes about how she felt about Natalie. *Will you ever look at me that way?*

"Natalie was high energy. Trust me, I felt like a slug next to her. She had my coat cleaned and brought it back and asked me out for lunch. It was impossible to say no to her." Mia leaned her head back against the couch. She seemed to be lost in her thoughts. Finally, she looked at Teri. "We went from lunch once a week to having dinner on weekends to my being her birthing coach." Mia laughed. "She was the one who kept me calm during the process. I was so nervous. By the time Michel was six months old, we were already living together. I don't know how it happened, but she was a force to be reckoned with."

Mia brushed a tear away, and Teri felt as if she was intruding on a private moment. Seconds later, Mia stood. "I'm tired. Will I see you in the morning?"

Teri nodded. She felt relief and disappointment that Mia hadn't asked her to share a bed. Sleeping with Mia was incredible. Their bodies fit so well together. Teri never thought she would want to share a bed with anyone all night, but Mia was different. She enjoyed Mia's scent, her feel, her warmth. She felt empty when she had gotten up. At the same time, she wanted more than to hold Mia. Mia wasn't ready.

When Mia got to her bedroom door, she turned and waved. "Good night."

Teri waved back. "See you in the morning."

What the hell was she doing here? She looked at her phone. There were five unanswered messages. When she logged on to her office e-mail, there were twenty-two e-mails and seven marked urgent. She had only been away from the office twenty-four hours and already she was feeling as if a part of her life was missing. Yes, she had committed to spending time with Mia and her family, but she hadn't realized how consuming that could be. This was the best time to learn.

Teri looked down the hall to Mia's bedroom. She wanted to devour Mia, body and soul. She also wanted to run out of there as fast as possible.

"You don't run from anything. You fix things." Teri couldn't figure out what she could fix. "What the hell do I do now?"

She looked at her phone. That was something she could take care of. "Besides, everyone else is asleep. It doesn't make any difference if everyone is sleeping."

She walked to her room, plugged her laptop in, and got busy. These were things she could control. These were tasks that she could fix. This is what made her comfortable. Not happy but comfortable.

❖

Teri looked at the clock. She had slept for three hours. She showered, dressed, and was at her computer by five. Her head of marketing for South America had sent his monthly report, and she was not happy. She needed to get down there and see what was going on. She would wait until nine and then have her assistant get her plane and pilots ready.

"Shit!" She slammed her hand on the desk. She couldn't go to South America. She made a promise to Mia. "Why did I do that?"

Teri knew why. She was in love with Mia, and she didn't know what to do about it. Mia came with responsibilities. Mia came with a child. Mia came with parents who depended on her.

A knock on the door disrupted her ruminations. "Come in."

"I saw the light under the door." Mia stood at the door, wrapped in her pale blue, fuzzy robe. Her bed hair stood out like a sexy halo. Teri felt a rush of desire. "You're dressed. And working." There was disappointment clearly etched in her face and in her tone of voice.

"I just thought I would catch up on some e-mails while waiting for everyone to get up." She looked down at the screen and clicked save on an unfinished e-mail. She then turned off the machine. "How about some coffee?"

"It's already made. Help yourself." Mia turned and walked away.

Her first inclination was to let Mia work it off. Mia, however, had shown a resilience and determination that very few ever demonstrated around her. "Hey, wait up."

Mia turned around and hissed. "My parents and Michel are still sleeping. Please lower your voice!" Mia grabbed her coffee cup and sat in the sunroom.

She kicked off her shoes, poured a cup of coffee, and then sat near Mia. "This is a beautiful room. When the realtor sent pictures of this place, I could imagine you sitting here with your coffee watching the sun coming up."

Mia just nodded and sipped her coffee.

"You said you didn't want kids until you got involved with Natalie. What changed your mind?"

"Are you asking for you or are you asking for information?"

Teri turned on the couch and tucked her feet under her. She could stare at Mia without feeling obvious. "I just want to know more about you. You started to tell me about how you got together and that Michel was just a part of Natalie."

Mia leaned her head against the back of the wicker chair. "By the time we moved in together, I knew I wanted a life with Natalie and Michel." A corner of her mouth went up. "It wasn't easy that first year. Michel was one and walking and we rarely had time to make love. She would do things, little things, every day to let me know she loved me. Sometimes it would just be a hug. Maybe it was getting up and fixing coffee for me. She even hid small surprises in my shoes or coat pocket. When she knew she would be gone for a week or two, she would arrange to have something delivered to me, at home or work, every day until she got home." Mia turned away.

Teri could see her wipe a tear away. "I didn't mean to upset you."

When Mia turned back, Teri could see tears glistening in her eyes. "When she was brought back to Paris, she was conscious for only a couple of days. Each day she asked if I had gotten my surprise." Tears were flowing freely now. "She was dying and she was concerned about my gift." Mia wiped the tears and stood up. "I'm sorry, but I need to shower and get dressed."

Before Mia could leave, Teri grabbed her hand. "Mia, please don't go."

"Why? I'm sure you have many more important things to do than listen to me talk about Natalie, Michel, my parents, and me." Mia was angry. "Teri, why don't you just go back to work today? Leave after breakfast and just stay away."

"Because there is nothing I want more than to be with you. I made a promise and I'm trying to keep it."

"The same way you spent time with me in Maine?"

"No, this is different."

Mia put up her hand. "Stop! You have important work to do. I know. Work will always be important to you."

Teri was struggling not to raise her voice. "That was true. Not anymore," she said. "You work."

"You're right, but I've learned to put things in perspective."

"What does that mean?"

"It means I've learned to make time for what is important in my life."

"I'm trying."

Mia walked back into the kitchen and sat down. "I was once like you, so afraid to commit, I kept ruining relationships."

"This has nothing to do with my working."

"It does. You work so you don't have to make an emotional commitment to anyone or anything." Mia finally looked up at Teri. "You wanted to fire an employee just because he or she brought a problem to you without an answer. You don't even stop to consider the person involved. What makes me think you're going to consider my feelings or needs? Any time I've disagreed with you, you've nearly bitten my head off."

"That's not true!" Teri stopped. Her voice was raised. "Sorry. I just proved your point." Teri bent down near Mia. "Mia, I love you. I've never felt this way about anyone. What more do you want?"

"Love, Teri. Unconditional love. I want to be your number one priority. Natalie changed my life. She loved me unconditionally. I know what that feels like, and I've promised myself I wouldn't settle for less. Especially now. I need to know that I can depend on the love and support of my partner. To be honest, Teri, I'm not sure you know what unconditional means." Mia walked past Teri. "Now, if you'll excuse me, I need to shower before my family gets up."

Teri watched Mia walk away. Deep inside, there was a faint nod to the truth of Mia's words. Even her sister and brother had accused her of the same thing.

Teri went back to her room. She might as well finish her e-mails while Mia got dressed. She sat at her laptop but couldn't work. Instead, Teri saw a huge void opening in front of her. It was a world without Mia. Teri bargained with herself. "I'm sure there will be more time after the merger." Yet, she was fairly sure that Mia wasn't going to give her another chance. She was the one who had come to Mia, begging for a chance. The first day she really spent away from work and she was so overwhelmed by all the challenges Mia faced, she was ready to run away.

A sadness seemed to envelop her. The last time she had felt this depth of despair was when her grandmother died. Her parents told her not to cry. She was a Stanton and Stantons didn't cry. Teri felt a tear slip out. She wiped it away.

CHAPTER FORTY-NINE

Mia's father wasn't feeling well. Mia offered to stay and work at home, but Teri promised to stay with them. Mia hoped Teri would keep this promise. After their argument the day before, Teri had been attentive and charming. Mia had no doubt that Teri was still staying up late and getting up early to work, but she saw no sign of the cell phone or iPad during the day. The fear for Mia was that Teri's commitment was to work and not to people. Halloween was just three days away, and her life had been in flux from the first day she had run into Teri. She needed some stability, some routine. She needed to know that her family would be okay. It was time to make a decision.

She would wait until the others were asleep and talk to Teri. She didn't need any more drama and trauma in her life. She needed a commitment.

Michel ran up to her the moment the door was opened. The look on his face banished any morose thoughts. "Mama, come see what I did today?" He pulled her into the kitchen where his backpack and school papers covered the table. Her parents were sitting there admiring his drawings.

"Michel, you are magnifique!" She looked at another picture and then another. Michel smiled and ran to the table.

"I can draw one for you," he said, grabbing another Magic Marker.

Mia smiled at the earnest expression on his face. She could see Natalie in his determined look. Mia felt guilt creeping in. She wished she had told Natalie more often that she loved her. She wished she had more time with Natalie to love her as deeply and unconditionally as she had been loved. Mia looked at her father and wished she had noticed sooner how thin he had become and insisted he do something sooner about his chronic upset stomach. Too many "if onlys" began to weigh her down.

Teri walked into the room. She was actually dressed in jeans, hiking boots, and a silk dress blouse. Mia would have laughed if she hadn't reminded herself that Teri was another of the "if onlys" creating the guilt.

"Sorry about the outfit. It seems that the markers are permanent. My tan trousers are now much more colorful. Michel was trying to teach me to draw, and I was holding the paper on my lap."

Mia couldn't tell if Teri was going to cry or laugh. In either case, Teri was attempting to reassure Michel. Mia was again teetering on indecision.

❖

Both her parents and Michel were asleep by eight thirty. Mia sat in the rocker with her coffee. She waited for Teri to come into the living room. She took a deep breath. "Teri, we need to talk. You've done so much for me and my family. I can't thank you enough."

"You're welcome, but why do I feel like there's a 'but' coming?"

"I have no doubt your intentions were good when you asked me to marry you. I can't."

Teri quickly sat up. "Why not? Mia, I love you."

"Because you and I are too different. We want different things. We have different expectations out of what we want in life. You don't have the time for a family and family responsibilities. You don't have time for me."

"Of course I have time. Why do you think I took time off? I almost have this merger under control, and there have been complications."

"Exactly. You're still working. I bet you were on the phone or on the computer when I got home tonight." The look on Teri's face confirmed Mia's suspicions. "You're finding time for us rather than making time for us."

"Oh, come on. We're parsing words. I'm here, aren't I?"

"The difference is that you're fitting us into your schedule. You're finding a time slot and scheduling us in."

"That's not true. Ever since you arrived here in August I've been making time for you."

This discussion was getting old. "Yes, you've spent time with me and my family, but work has always been minutes or seconds away from whatever we were doing. You were on the phone or your computer or iPad. When you make time, you decide that something is your number one priority and everything else is put on hold. You block out time and you don't allow anything or anyone else to interfere unless it's an emergency."

"Is that what Natalie did? Was she making time when she got herself killed?"

"No fair." Mia felt as if she'd been slugged in the gut. "Yes, that's what Natalie did. It's not any of your business, but she had already told her boss that was her last field assignment." Mia swallowed down the anger, guilt, and sadness. This was about Teri, not her past. "Since I ran into you in August, work has occupied almost everything about you. I never felt like I was the center of your attention."

She stopped. That was not completely true. "Except for the times we kissed. For those few short moments, I felt you were there with me."

"I'm making time for you."

"For too many years, I carried scars, ones from my teen years and you." Teri looked like she was going to interrupt. Mia held up her hand. "No, I need for you to listen. When I was fifteen, you accused me of leading your brother and other boys on. The reason the boys followed me around was because I had this almost obsessive crush on you."

Mia looked down at her jeans and then back up at Teri. "You were my first love. You have no idea how devastated I was that night or how long I carried the humiliation, guilt, and anger." She was staring back down at her pants, picking at imaginary threads. "Natalie helped me to realize that I deserved love and I was a good person. I deserve better, and I demand more. The day I first saw you, I was well on my way to letting go of my past and you. Since then, I've allowed myself to be pulled back into some kind of approach-avoid relationship with you. I've too many other challenges to deal with. I don't need someone in my life who can't decide whether or not she wants me, and all my family, in her life."

Teri sat quietly for a couple of seconds. "Are you done?" Mia nodded. She was sure she was in for a harangue, but Teri hadn't interrupted; she needed to do the same.

"First, you were fifteen and I didn't have a clue that you were gay, much less that you had a crush on me. You were just a kid hanging around my brother. You can't imagine how awful I feel and how much I regret that night."

Teri stood and stuck her hands in her jeans pockets and just as quickly took them out. She sat back down. Mia wondered if Teri was struggling with an apology. *No, won't happen in this lifetime. Or the next.*

"Mia, I haven't done anything but work for at least the last dozen years. I don't have a lot of experience with…with…I don't know how to show what I'm feeling and balance work." Teri sat on the floor by Mia's feet. She rested one hand on Mia's knee. "The reason I'm still working on the merger is because I've been trying to keep Pamela Milton from taking any position of responsibility after the merger." Teri's jaw was tight and anger radiated off her. "When I heard what happened to you that night of the party, and why, I was furious. Once I knew you were okay, I went to the office and started Bren and the rest of our legal staff and our HR people to work to make sure Milton was not part of the deal." Teri took her hand. "I was so frightened that night. I can't remember ever feeling that way, except when my grandmother died." Teri took a deep breath. "I admit being responsible for"—Teri waved her hand to encompass the house and its residents—"all this scares the bejeezus out of me. Not seeing you scares me more. I don't know what the difference is between what you think I'm doing and making time, as you call it, but I'll figure it out."

"You're postponing the merger because of me?"

"It's on indefinite hold, actually. The Miltons are insistent that father, brother, and sister will have some high level position. They want Pamela to actually be vice president for marketing in the western region. I'm now looking at other possibilities."

"Teri, you're throwing away a billion-dollar merger? Why?"

"I don't want you to ever have to deal with Pamela Milton again." Teri's voice was firm.

Mia almost wanted to laugh. "What makes you think I'd ever have cause to see her again?"

"Because that night, I realized that I wanted you in my life, and I wouldn't have Pamela Milton or anyone else hurting you. I couldn't take the chance that, if we became involved, that she would bother you again."

Mia was confused. Teri was blowing a fortune. For her. Yet, except for the proposal, there was little to indicate any real romantic interest. She stopped. No, she had seen desire in Teri's eyes more than once. Was it possible Teri was as emotionally challenged as she claimed? "What's your dad going to say? What about Bren and Jeremy?"

"My siblings are finally proud of me for doing what's right instead of what's most expedient or will make the most money. My father is furious. I have until the middle of November to walk away from the merger without any penalties." Teri reached for her hand. "Mia, you scare me. Being responsible for your folks scares me. Being around a kid scares the hell out of me. Please don't make a decision about us just yet."

A tornado was brewing in the middle of Mia's chest. This was twice that she had resolved to let go of Teri, and now she was again reconsidering. Would she ever get Teri completely out of her life? Or was Teri meant to be a part of her life?

"Please."

Mia leaned her head against the back of the chair. She believed that things happened for a reason. She had to. There had to be a reason Natalie came into her life so suddenly and then left just as suddenly. Maybe there was a reason why Teri had shown up that day in August.

"Mia, I need to ask. Are you still in love with Natalie? The only reason I ask is that twice you've called me Natalie. If you are, tell me and I'll be gone tomorrow."

That was something she didn't expect from Teri, offering to leave if she loved someone else. Could Teri really not be as selfish as Mia once believed? Teri was squeezing her hand so hard it was beginning to hurt.

"I apologize if I called you Natalie. I don't remember that, but I know I will always love Natalie. She's the one who taught me how to love. Her love made me a better person and able to let go of the anger and hurt." Teri withdrew her hand and leaned away. "I often had to apologize to Natalie for calling her Teri. Usually, I was half asleep and so exhausted I couldn't think."

"If it's any consolation, you were drugged the first time and half asleep the second." Teri hesitated. "Should I leave?"

Mia took a deep breath. Her next words would either send Teri away for good or keep them both wondering what was going to happen next. "Stay. I'm not sure of what's going on between us, but there is definitely something going on."

Teri's face lit up. Happiness radiated out and warmed Mia. Whatever happened in the next few weeks, she was glad she had asked Teri to stay. At least for now.

"Thank you." Teri stood and pulled Mia out of a chair. "You said that the only time you felt I was present was when I was kissing you." Teri leaned in and kissed Mia.

This was not a brief kiss. Mia forgot everything but the feel of Teri's lips. When Teri's tongue danced around her lips, Mia opened her mouth and felt Teri's tongue fill her. Mia slipped her arms around Teri's neck and pulled her closer. A moan escaped. Mia had to pull back. "You are definitely here." She sounded breathless. Mia smiled. Teri had taken her breath away.

"What just happened?" Teri's hands were on either side of Mia's face.

"You kissed me."

"You kissed me back."

Everything was forgotten except the warmth and smell of Teri. "Kiss me again." Mia didn't wait. She found Teri's mouth and began to hungrily explore. Teri's hands were sliding up and down her back under her T-shirt. "My mother sometimes gets up in the middle of the night to get something to drink. I think we need to go someplace more private."

"Are you inviting me into your bed?" Teri's breath against her ear sent shivers up and down Mia's body.

Mia could only nod. She was not ready to let go of Teri's mouth. She needed to feel all of Teri. At this moment, she needed Teri as much as she needed air.

"Are you asking me to sleep with you, or do you have any something else in mind?" Teri's hand was now moving around on Mia's hips.

Mia grabbed Teri's exploring hand. "I'll try to let you get some sleep."

Once the door to her bedroom was closed, Mia's reserve disappeared. She had made a decision. She was moving forward. Mia had misjudged Teri. Her own anger and hurt had closed her heart to the one person who could finally heal old wounds. She pulled off her top and was just beginning to pull off her sweatpants when Teri stopped her.

"Mia, I've wanted to make love to you for so long and now..."

Mia placed her arms across her chest. She couldn't believe Teri was having second thoughts. "And now?"

"I want to make sure you are making love with me."

"There are only two people in this room." Mia's arms went around Teri's neck. "I'm well aware that I invited *you* here. I find this a little surreal. I've spent so many years trying to get over you, and now I'm jumping into the deep end. So take me to bed or hand me my shirt."

Teri had already begun pulling Mia's sweatpants off. "You're beautiful." Teri's hands were running up and down her body.

"Why am I the only one without clothes on?" Moments later Teri was undressed and Mia was kissing her way across Teri's chest.

"God, that feels good." Teri pulled Mia's head up. "Come kiss me."

"I want to kiss all of you." Mia started with Teri's eyes, then her chin, and finally landed on her mouth.

CHAPTER FIFTY

Teri couldn't remember ever being as aroused as she was this moment. Mia's mouth was consuming her and Mia's tongue was everywhere. She put her hands on either side of Mia's face and absorbed the feel of Mia's tongue exploring. From the moment she had seen Mia naked, Teri's body began tingling. Mia was gorgeous. Her high, full breasts begged to be tasted. Her rounded hips—Teri couldn't wait to feel them moving against her. Teri had to touch her. Her mind was numb with all the sensory stimulation. It was so easy to let Mia pull her into bed and initiate the lovemaking. Now, however, Teri needed more than just Mia's kisses.

She pushed Mia onto her back. "You're so amazing. I can't get enough of you."

"Show me, then." Mia leaned back against the pillows, a sexy smile on her face. Teri had never known a lover quite like this one.

She nibbled along Mia's chin and down her neck. Mia's moans served as encouragement. Teri's breathing was more ragged. She finally reached Mia's breast. Her tongue danced around the hardened nipple. Teri's hand slid down Mia's stomach, tracing circles until she reached Mia's thigh. She caressed the inner thigh until Mia's legs parted. Teri's fingers teased around Mia's clit, causing it to stiffen.

Mia's hips were moving up and down, seemingly chasing Teri's touch. *God, I want this woman.* Teri kissed down Mia's chest and stomach. Her fingers began to stroke Mia's clit. Mia gasped, her hips began to move faster, and her arms tightened around Teri.

"Teri, I need you to stroke harder and be in me." She pushed Teri's hand harder against her.

Teri's thumb and forefinger pushed harder and gently pulled on Mia's clit. She slid her hand down until she found Mia's center. "Damn, you're so wet. I can't believe how excited you are."

"You've made me this excited. I need you to fuck me." Mia's hips rose to meet her. "Please, I'm getting so close. I need to come." Mia's nails were digging into Teri's back.

"Are you in a hurry?" Teri slid two fingers and then three into Mia. "Is this what you want?" She moved in and out, slowly at first, but soon with increasing speed. "Mia, you feel so good. Let go and let me take you. I need to feel you coming around me."

Just as she was feeling Mia begin to climax, Teri felt Mia's hand slide between her own legs. "No. I can't concentrate." Teri tried to pull away, but Mia was insistent.

"Who needs to, oh, mmm, concent...oh, trate?"

Teri had been so lost in Mia that she wasn't aware how close she was to coming until Mia's hand began to play with her own clit. "Damn." Teri's eyes were closed. Her body was heavy with arousal. Mia beneath her was climaxing, tensing around her fingers. Mia's breathing and soft moans. Everything was driving her over the edge, and there was no way she could hold back. Finally, Mia's climaxing sent her own body flying.

"Ahhhhhhh." Teri let go and road the waves. It had been years since she'd had sex with anyone and never had she experienced anything this consuming. She collapsed on the bed and pulled Mia close. It was several minutes before she could breathe enough to speak and even longer for her to control her emotions. She was raw inside and out.

Feelings long dormant were bubbling up. Memories from her childhood. Times with her grandmother when she laughed a lot. Innocent times when she was happy. Times when she and her brother and sister were close.

Teri wiped a tear from her eye.

"Are you okay?" Mia's voice was soft.

"I'm not sure why, but I was suddenly remembering my childhood."

Mia was now up on one elbow and looking down at her. Teri didn't understand what had just happened, but she knew she needed to get control. "I guess it was the fact that I feel safe with you. Suddenly, I was young again, a time when I felt safe." She took a deep breath, closed her eyes, and forced those memories away.

The best way for Teri to forget was to make love to Mia. She could focus on Mia's body and excitement. Maybe that would put those memories back in the dark recesses.

"I've got other things on my mind right now." She turned onto her side and again began to play Mia's body. She doubted if either of them would get much sleep tonight, but she didn't care. She just wanted to lose herself in pale blue eyes. She wanted to drown herself in the scent of Mia's arousal. She wanted Mia. Nothing mattered but this moment. This woman. Work was a far second, and Teri was happy.

❖

Teri looked at the clock. It was nearly three thirty. She had slept for only forty-five minutes, but she felt completely relaxed. Mia was cuddled by her side. So many emotions were rolling around inside her: safe, confused, scared, incredible, relaxed. One feeling overrode all others: cherished. Teri felt cherished.

She brushed her hand through Mia's hair. It was beginning to grow out. Mia stretched and opened her eyes.

"Good morning," Mia purred. "It's been a while since I've been up that late. What time is it?"

"Three thirty."

Mia brushed Teri's hair back behind her ears. "Any regrets this morning?"

"Why would I have regrets? I've been chasing you lately."

"I'm not remotely related to anything that has to do with your work. Your real work."

"Ouch. You don't forget, do you? When I'm with you, work is the farthest thing from my mind. All I want is to see you smile, to hear your voice."

"You didn't feel that way in Maine."

"You're wrong. You were such a distraction that I had to constantly remind myself I had work to do."

Mia's eyes widened. "Well, you did a good job of hiding it. Most of the time I felt I was a nuisance and you couldn't wait to get away."

"Most of the time?" Teri couldn't resist teasing. "And what about the other times?"

"The other times you had me so confused, I didn't know what to think or expect. Except that I was so determined to forget you that I had to assume you kissing me was an accident."

The laugh was from the bottom of Teri's heart. "You're too much. I can't imagine anyone thinking a kiss was an accident." She kissed Mia's nose and cheeks and finally found her lips. "That morning you dragged to the top of some damn cliff…"

"Mountain," Mia corrected her.

"Mountain. Your face was already glowing with excitement. When the sun came up and you were dusted in the morning light, you were amazing. I couldn't help myself. I needed to kiss you to see if you were real. And you were." She kissed Mia again, this time a long, consuming kiss. "It was the first time in years that I was physically aroused by someone. And it was downhill for me after that."

"Downhill?" Mia may have intended indignation, but a smile quickly crept out.

"I spent more and more of my time thinking of you and not work." Her hand slowly rubbed circles down Mia's body.

"What about the other women in your life?" Teri's hand was slowly moving closer to Mia's crotch. "This feels so good." Mia's eyes closed. "Mmmmm. It has been so long since I've been touched this way."

"I understand completely. It's been a really long time for me."

Mia's eyes widened. "I seem to remember you having a different beautiful woman at every Stanton function. What are they going to think?"

Teri became serious. "Mia, I haven't had sex with another woman in years. Not since the night, I…" All the warm feelings of the previous night were fleeing. She sat up. "I owe you an apology." She felt Mia sitting up next to her, but she couldn't look at her. "That summer night when I said some terrible things to you. I didn't know about you being teased. I didn't know about your friendship with my brother. And I never knew about your crush. It wasn't you. It was me."

"I'm confused. What are you talking about? I don't understand."

Teri regretted that night, more than Mia could imagine. Her nakedness made her feel more vulnerable. She grabbed shirt and put it on then sat back down. "Up until that night, I put my personal life ahead of business, and I was so damn angry because my parents sent me to deal with you.

"It didn't take long for me to figure out that I couldn't combine work and a personal life. At first, I would have sex with women I met in a bar or on a business trip. It wasn't long before even that stopped. I was ashamed of my behavior long before I knew the truth. Bren and Jeremy told me about what was going on. They insisted on keeping their promise to you, but I insisted. I'm so ashamed of my behavior."

"Your parents sent you?" Mia's voice was not as warm.

"They did, and I took my anger out on you."

A myriad of emotions jogged across Mia's face. Teri waited. Would these few hours be all she would ever share with Mia? It would be well meted justice that Teri be given a taste of what Mia could mean in her life and then have it snatched away.

"Twenty-four hours ago, I would have been furious. Tonight, I realized I have misjudged you. When I saw you in August, I wanted nothing but to be as far away from you physically and emotionally as I could possibly be. I was just as guilty as you because I attributed mean-spirited reasons for your behavior, even when you were professing your love for me."

"And now?

"There must be some reason why you keep showing up in my life." Mia patted the bed. "We still have a little bit of time before I need to get up or we have a little visitor."

"Mia, you have no idea how bad I felt that night. That's nothing compared to how I feel now." Teri brushed a tear away. "There are so many things I've screwed up, even with Brenna and Jeremy. Knowing you has helped me to see what I'm missing. I'm sorry, Mia. I'm so sorry." Teri fought the tears. She sat back on the bed. "There's nothing I can do to change what happened. I can promise the future will be better."

"What do you see the future being? What does moving forward mean to you?"

"Without you, I don't see a future. I don't want to continue the way I've been going. I want to be the kind of person that you could love and be proud of. I want you to feel as cherished and loved as you made me feel last night."

Mia finally sat next to her. "Teri, what are we going to do?"

Teri reached for her hand. "Be patient with me?" Mia brushed away a tear. "I'm not very good at this emotion thing. Jer and Bren have already given me the lecture. I'm trying."

"There are definitely times when you are trying." Mia laughed and squeezed Teri's hand. "There are other times when I really like you."

"Then I'm not hopeless?"

"I don't think anyone is hopeless." Mia stroked Teri's hand. It was a tentative link that Teri needed. "I've just realized something. You're right. I was a kid. A young, idealistic, romantic, hopelessly in love teenager. I put you on a pedestal. I knew nothing about you except that you were beautiful and elegant and so much more sophisticated than I could ever be. I was in love with an image. The night you knocked yourself off the pedestal rocked my world and shattered all my illusions. I didn't know how to handle it."

"So what have you decided? Do you hate me?"

"No! Teri, look at me." Teri did, her hands trembling. "I realized that I had to let go of that old Teri to see you for the person you really are."

"And?"

"And I prefer reality to the image."

Teri captured Mia's lips. Her heart was soaring. She finally felt as if there was hope. Teri pulled Mia back down on the bed. "You make me so happy." She nibbled Mia's neck.

"Then show me, because I am getting very excited. You'll quickly find out there are some areas of my life that I have no patience."

CHAPTER FIFTY-ONE

Mia was humming in the shower. She felt light and carefree. It was the first time since before Natalie's death. Teri's lovemaking had been slow and deliberate. Mia could still feel Teri's lips and hands on her body.

She turned the water off and grabbed a towel. "I better get dressed and start breakfast fast." Her knees were barely keeping her upright. Just thinking of Teri had her close to orgasm. Mia dressed quickly and nearly ran to the kitchen.

Coffee on, Mia sat quietly in the sunroom. She was only a few blocks from the train station into the city, yet far enough out to look at trees and yard and sky. The hustle and stress of New York seemed so far away.

"Good morning." Teri leaned over and kissed her. "I'll get coffee and be right back." Teri smelled like shampoo. Mia liked the clean scent.

"I'm beginning to understand why you like to sit quietly in the morning." Teri sat next to her, her face all smiles.

"It's incredibly relaxing. And *you* are certainly smiling." She patted Teri's leg with her left hand while balancing her coffee with the right.

"How's your hand doing?"

"I think I've regained full functioning. What do you think?"

Teri's eyes grew wide. She started to speak several times, but no words came out. Mia couldn't believe the indomitable Theresa Stanton was speechless.

Mia ran her hand up the inside of Teri's thigh. "For once, I have the last word?"

Teri was leaning back against the loveseat with her eyes closed. "If you don't stop, we both may be speechless soon."

Mia put her hands around her coffee cup. She barely suppressed a grin. "I love you."

Teri stared at her in amazement. "I have wanted to hear you say those three words." Teri turned so that she was completely facing Mia. "In the last few months, my life has changed because of you. I dream about you, I think about you, I plan with you. I'm not sure what it means to make time, but I know that I don't want to think of a future without you." Teri reached into her pocket. "Mia Daniels, will you marry me?" She pulled the ring out of the box and held it up.

Mia smiled. "You've already asked me."

'I know, but I really mean it, and you haven't said yes." Teri removed the cup from Mia's hands. She held the ring and Mia's left hand. "I will keep asking you until you give me an answer. If you say no, I won't ask anymore, but I won't go away until you tell me to. So I'll ask again. Mia Daniels, will you marry me?"

"Did you plan on asking me this morning? Is that why you have the ring in your pocket?"

"No. I've had it with me all day, every day, since I asked you. Just in case. You still haven't answered me. Will you marry me, Mia Louisa Daniels?"

"Why are you so determined? Why me?" Mia put her empty cup down.

"Because I am utterly enchanted by you. I'm so in love that I can't think of anything or anyone but you. I've never even considered getting married, but now...now, I want to stand in front of everyone and let them see how lucky I am. That is, if you agree to marry me. We can get married in New York."

Mia was silent and in awe. Finally, she smiled, letting the love she felt show. "In that case, Theresa Marie Stanton, I'll say yes."

"Yes?" Teri seemed surprised.

"Yes." Teri sat staring for several moments. "I think this is where you put the ring on or give me the ring."

Teri reached for Mia's hand and put the ring on. "Thank you," she whispered. She pulled Mia into an embrace. "Thank you," this time louder. "I love you so much." Teri began to laugh. "I can't believe how happy I feel. How happy you make me. When do you want to get married? I would say today so that I could be sure you wouldn't change your mind."

"Slow down." Mia laughed. She kissed Teri on each cheek, then a kiss of promise on the lips.

"How about next month? Before Christmas? Your brother and his wife will be here. Your whole family will be together. I know Brenna will be around, and I know for a fact that Jeremy wouldn't miss this for anything."

"What's all the racket?" Mia's father walked in, his pajamas hanging on a much thinner frame. "Is something wrong?"

"Mia has finally agreed to marry me."

"About damn time."

Mia stood next to her father. "Are you trying to get rid of me?"

His look became solemn. He put his arm around her. "No, my love. I just want to be well enough to walk you down the aisle."

Mia reached for Teri's hand. "Dad, you're going to be around for a long time."

"Mia, no one knows how long I'll be here. I do know that I'm here now and I'm upright." He turned toward Teri. "It would make me very happy to walk you both down the aisle."

"Sir, I would be honored."

Mia's father hugged them both. "Let me go wake up Lisa and tell her the good news. Nothing makes her happier than planning a wedding and interfering in her children's lives."

As soon as her father was out of the room, Mia said, "Now, look what you've started." She was smiling as she kissed Teri.

CHAPTER FIFTY-TWO

I've started the best part of my life, and I agree with your dad. Let's wake up your mom and then go fix breakfast. I'm starving." Teri put an arm around Mia's shoulder and walked with her into the kitchen. "Do you want me to make more coffee? If you show me how, I'm sure I can handle it." Her grin was rewarded with a beautiful smile. Mia was capturing her heart and soul. Teri was in awe of her feelings and how lucky she felt that Mia loved her. There was so much she had learned about Mia, and, yet, so much she had to learn. What she knew now was that Mia was warm, loving, generous, and one of the most caring people. She no longer doubted her depth. Even more, Mia made her happy. Mia might drive her crazy, at times, but she wouldn't want it any other way.

The coffee turned out perfectly, and Teri was almost as proud of her efforts as if she had negotiated a business deal. "That was easy."

"Mmhmm." Mia was grinning. "Good thing it wasn't something difficult like cooking an egg."

She stood behind Mia and pinched her butt. "You may be surprised at how quickly I can learn things."

"That's good to know." Mia's mother walked in. "Now, what is this Tom is telling me about planning a wedding?" She walked up to Mia and lifted up her left hand. "Good heavens! That's one beautiful and expensive ring." She put her arm around Teri. "That must have cost a fortune. No wonder she said yes."

"Mrs. Daniels, you and I both know Mia is too stubborn to allow anything to persuade her to do anything she doesn't want to."

Mia glared at her and then laughed. "I am a woman of principles."

"You are."

Breakfast was chaos. Several conversations seemed to be going on all at the same time. Teri had trouble keeping up. Her own family meals were much more subdued. Her family. Teri felt some of the good mood slip away. Once plans for the wedding were made, she would have to go and talk with her parents. They would have many objections. None of which would make much sense. The sooner she got that over, the sooner she would feel free to move on with her life.

"Teri, are you listening?" Mia's voice was raised. Obviously, Mia had tried more than once to get her attention.

"Sorry, I was thinking about the things I need to take care of before the wedding. I don't want anything to interfere with our plans before and during, and especially after." Mia's blush indicated she had made up for the lapse. "Now, what was it you were saying?" Again, everyone started talking at once.

The raucous noise resulted in a sleepy Michel walking into the kitchen. "Mama, are you mad?"

Mia lifted him on her lap. "No, we're all happy and just talking loud." She looked at her parents and Teri. "Michel thinks loud voices mean people are angry at each other. Natalie and I never yelled at each other, but he heard others using loud voices and, unfortunately, they *were* yelling at each other." Her attention turned back to Michel. "Remember how Maman and I talked about getting married, like your friends' parents?" Michel nodded. "Aunt Teri and I are going to get married and we want you to be part of it. Would you like that?"

"You going to make marriage with Tante? Can I make marriage too?"

Teri laughed. He was just as charming as his mother. "We will make sure you're a big part." His eyes widened and he smiled. Teri was falling in love with the dark-haired, dark eyed youngster. Her heart was exploding with feeling.

"Wanna play now?"

"Hold on," Mia said, "we need to have breakfast first." Mia sat him in the chair and got up to fix breakfast. Teri was quickly by her side.

"Please let me help. Tell me what to do."

Mia stroked the side of her face. "I love you. Now, why don't you get out the baguette on the counter and the yogurt out of the fridge?"

Teri quickly performed these tasks and then helped Mia's mother to set the table. Ten minutes later, they were all eating and talking. It was the most relaxing meal she had ever had and the most enjoyable in years.

❖

Sunday afternoon was interrupted by a call from Bren. Teri couldn't wait to tell her the good news. "Mia has finally agreed to marry me and we're planning on getting married Christmas Eve so keep the date open. Don't tell Jeremy. I want to." Bren was excited and promised to be at the wedding with bells on. "In that case, can you play the 'Wedding March'?"

"I don't believe it. Your sense of humor is back. Whatever you've been doing lately, keep doing it. Mia is a wonderful person. I'm happy for you. And the business is running without you. I'm really quite good at this."

"Why haven't you said something sooner?"

"I've tried, but you didn't see me as anything but a corporate lawyer."

"Bren, I'm so sorry. I've been blind to so many things."

"I'm calling because something serious has come up. Father's called a meeting of all the top execs for ten Tuesday. He's asked them all to fly in from wherever. I'm sure he's planning on announcing a change in leadership. He's been ranting all week because he hasn't been able to find you and he wants the Milton deal completed. He's unreasonable. I've tried to discuss the possible legal ramifications, but he doesn't give a shit. I think he wants to appoint someone who will be a rubber stamp. He's doing this out of spite."

"What about you?"

"I told you. He's doing this out of spite. You appointed me and he's ignoring anything associated with you. Teri, we need to talk."

Teri paced. Mia stopped her, a questioning look on her face. "Hold on, Bren." Teri covered the speaker on the cell. She quickly explained what was going on.

"What do you want to do? I know how important all this is to you."

"I don't know. I can't believe my father is being so vindictive. If I oppose him, it may tear my family apart. If I don't, it may tear my family apart. If I do, I may get pulled back into the life I had before. Then I risk losing you. I don't know what to do. I don't want to lose you."

Mia linked her arms around her neck. "If I wasn't around, you wouldn't hesitate. In fact, you would have prevented this from happening. The fact that you are hesitating tells me how much you do love me." Mia placed a kiss on each cheek. "Let's talk to my dad. I know he thinks highly of you. He's always given me good advice."

Teri picked up her cell. "Bren, can I call you back? Maybe twenty or thirty minutes." Teri turned off the phone. "Mia, I'll talk to your dad, but I doubt there's anything he can do." She grabbed Mia's hand and went in search of Tom Daniels. Her dream all of her adult life had been to be chief executive officer of the company and be able to run it the way she wanted. While Mia had initially been a distraction, now she was the most important person in Teri's life. She had worked so hard to make the company successful and now had to watch Pamela Milton become a part of the company and someone else take control. It hurt.

Tom Daniels was in the study listening to music and reading. He was relaxing and Teri felt bad interrupting. "Mia, we can come back later," she whispered.

Mia walked past her and sat on the couch next to her dad. "Dad, Teri's father wants to fire her. There are some other problems, too. You're the smartest man I know. I told her you may be able to help."

"Honey, you're a flatterer. I'll be glad to listen and help if I can. So, Teri, tell me what's going on."

She tried to be concise, but still it took at least ten minutes to explain the situation. She carefully edited the problem with Pamela and Mia, saying only that Pamela Milton had been observed sexually harassing a female guest.

"My daughter already explained why she came home with her arm in a cast. This woman is definitely a legal and financial liability. Do you think your aunt and uncle would vote with you if a shareholders' meeting was called?"

"My sister thinks so."

"Let me make a quick telephone call." Tom Daniels got the house phone and dialed a number. Teri was not expecting that. The conversation on this side was vague. She kept looking at her watch, knowing that her sister was expecting a call any minute. Finally, he put down the phone. "I think I've got a solution for part of your problem. There's a French company that's selling off some of its subsidiaries. One is an American company that has been providing similar kinds of products and services in Asia and South America. They have excellent leadership and good profitability. The French company is unloading their non-European holdings because they're looking to expand in Europe. The company is available and looking for an American buyer. They're in Boston, and the president of that company can be here at nine in the morning. I think you can get the company for less than what you're paying for Milton." He scratched his head. "Teri, your father is a great poker player. His bottom line is making money, no matter how. If you bring this deal to him and threaten to take his position to the shareholders if he tries to remove you, and you have proxies from your aunt and uncle, I think he'll back down. It's worth the try."

She was unsure if her father was that much of a gambler, but it seemed the only course. Teri thanked him and then walked with Mia back to living room. "I'll call Bren and ask her to meet me here in the morning."

Mia left to check on Michel while Teri called her sister. Brenna was excited about the new company, but she wondered if their father could be bluffed. "I can call our aunt and uncle and see if they're willing to overnight the proxies. I think Father will be madder than hell if we threaten to bring in the shareholders. He'll also realize I made this possible."

"I'll take the lead in this. He doesn't need to know. He's already angry with me. Call Jeremy and ask him if he can be back here tomorrow. I'd like you to come out here tonight if you can. We can get ready for our meeting in the morning. I'm sending a driver out to pick up the representatives from the new company and bring them here. I don't want anyone to know about this until after we meet and this is a done deal."

"Let me make some calls and I can be there in about ninety minutes. You two still going to be awake?" By Bren's tone of voice there was no doubt she wasn't really hinting at Mia and Teri being asleep.

"Just get here as soon as you can and bring clothes to stay over. We seem to have a spare bedroom right now." Teri hung up before Bren could make another comment. She realized that she had been in bed no later than ten and up no earlier than six each day for the last few days. With Mia cuddled next to her, Teri didn't want to get out of bed.

Teri looked at her watch. Maybe they could take a nap before Bren got there.

Chapter Fifty-three

Mia had just finished reading another book to Michel when Teri walked in. "How's it going?"

Teri sat on the floor next to them. "Bren is coming out to spend the night. We need to talk with your dad for a little while and get ready for tomorrow." She stroked Mia's back. "I'm so sorry. I feel as if I've let you down. I promised to take time off from work, and it hasn't even been a whole week."

"Is this really important to you?"

"Of course! I've worked so hard over the last eight years, since I became C.O.O. to make the company successful. And I'm pissed Father is ignoring Bren and threatening to bring someone else on board just because I'm not there and I don't want the Miltons active in the company."

She pulled Michel onto her lap and then reached for Teri's hand. "Then I'll support you." The look of confusion on Teri's face brought a grin to Mia's. "Not that long ago, I think you would have said, 'It's my damn company and I'll do what I want.' But now you're angry because your sister isn't given a chance to prove herself and you find your father's actions unfair." Mia rubbed her thumb over Teri's hand. "You're not the same person who came to Maine. You're definitely different now."

"What do you mean by that cryptic comment?"

"For one, you're usually in bed by the time I am and I'm usually up before you."

"Mmmm. That's because you put me to sleep and I don't want to get out of a warm bed."

"Mama, can you put me to sleep?" Michel's lids were heavy.

Teri stood and lifted Michel into his bed, then she put out her hand to help Mia. "I can't tell you enough how happy I am and how much I love you."

"You can show me later," she whispered. "Now go get ready for your meeting." She kissed Michel and they walked out of the room. "I'll find my mom and we'll let you plot and scheme."

CHAPTER FIFTY-FOUR

The breakfast meeting had gone so well Teri had the limo drive them into the city to the Stanton offices. Bren would have the contracts written up and signed by the end of the day. That also meant the letter to terminate the Milton offer would go out that afternoon.

Teri arranged for lunch to be catered and she spent the afternoon talking with her new business associate while Bren took care of the legal work. By four o'clock, they were signing the papers. "I'm so excited by this opportunity. I like your company and I think we're a perfect fit."

"We've got a great company. We just needed the cash infusion. This is a win-win for both of us."

Teri nodded. She had her assistant call her father and ask him to come to her office.

"Well, it's about time…." Her father stopped at the door. Mia's dad was right. Her father hated public scenes.

"Father, let me make introductions. This is Fred Abbott. He is C.E.O and sole owner of Abbott Corporation, our latest acquisition. Fred, this is my father. I'll leave you two to chat. I'll be right back."

She walked to Bren's office and signed the termination letter and had it sent overnight to the Miltons. "I'm sure Father is bullshitting Abbott. As soon as Abbott is gone, he'll want to know what the hell is going on." Teri stopped and briefly hugged her. "Thanks, Brenna, for everything."

"It's good to have you back. I've missed my older sister. Hopefully, you won't get lost again."

"What are you talking about? You've known every single day where I was."

Brenna clasped Teri's arm. "Teri, I knew where you were physically, but mentally and emotionally, you were gone. And have been for as long as I can remember. I can't remember the last time you smiled, and lately, you've been smiling more. You're an attractive woman, but you're beautiful when you smile." Bren lightly pushed Teri. "The advantage for me was that, with your constant scowl, I was the more attractive Stanton daughter."

How many times had Mia complimented her when she smiled? Hearing Bren's words embarrassed her. Had she been that much of ogre? She doubted it. She just did what it took to make the company successful. Teri also felt there was a kernel, a large kernel, of truth in her words. The last few months had brought a change in her life. Even she was aware that she felt different.

"Bren, you're beautiful, both inside and out. Thank you. I never felt lost, but I definitely feel different."

"Well, I hope this is a permanent change."

Teri hoped so, too, but she knew how easily she got wrapped up in work. Today, she felt the familiar adrenaline rush of closing a deal. Not just any deal: one that would keep Pamela Milton out of her company and still achieve the expansion she wanted. She loved that feeling of power and infallibility that went along with closing a deal. She would celebrate tonight. Suddenly, an image of Mia naked flashed in her mind and she was almost painfully aroused. She still needed to deal with her father first.

As expected, her father was acting like Fred Abbott was an old friend. She sat next to the two of them. "I think Fred is going to be a real asset to Stanton Enterprises."

"Obviously." Her father's comment was probably the most committal he was willing to make. He stood and shook Abbott's hand. "Good to have you aboard." He smiled and turned toward Teri. "We'll chat after you're finished with Fred."

He left quickly. The smile was for Fred Abbott's benefit. To Teri, it was an indication he still wasn't happy. She didn't care. She got what she wanted. A great acquisition and no Pamela Milton.

She chatted briefly with Abbott and then walked with him to the Human Resources office. "They'll talk with you about transitioning your folks over. If you've got any questions, you've got my number. Look forward to working with you."

Teri was feeling smug. She knew the Miltons would be calling tomorrow. She'd deal with them when the time was right. Now, her father.

"What the hell is going on?"

"I bought Abbott."

"Obviously. Are we still going on with the Miltons?"

"Father, Brenna told you they were a liability. This company is much stronger and a better fit."

"Is that why you haven't been in the office? You were chasing this?"

She knew what he was asking. *Hope you weren't spending time with Mia Daniels.* "No, Father. Mia's father actually arranged this deal for us. I've been spending time with Mia and her family. I promised Mia I would take some time off."

"For what? What about work? If Daniels was arranging this deal, why weren't you in the office? I tried calling you. I've even resorted to having my secretary text you. Your place is here. This girl is a distraction. You need to get your head back in the game and stop chasing any attractive piece of tail that comes along. I thought you were past that."

Teri was blind with anger. Her father had never talked to her like this. Even worse, he was talking about the woman she loved.

"I'll ignore your comments because you're surprised by the decisions I've made and because I refused to proceed with the merger. I won't forget, however. Mia Daniels is intelligent, talented, and well respected. She saved our butts when the French showed up. Her only concern was for the success of our merger while Pamela Milton behaved abominably." She paused, forcing some semblance of control back in her voice. She took a deep breath. "Mia finally agreed to marry me, and we're getting married Christmas Eve."

"Theresa, you've done a great job with this company. I won't deny that, but now, I don't know what's gotten into you. With all the right families you've grown up with and the proper girlfriends you've dated, your mother and I expected more from you. Now you want to marry this Mia Daniels? What kind of hold does she have on you? You're neglecting your family and work responsibilities. You're definitely not showing any respect to me or your mother. You dare choose this—"

"Father!"

"You dare choose this person over your family."

She could no longer hold back the anger. Mia was being dismissed, even after all Mia and her father had done. "What the hell is a proper girlfriend? Let me make this perfectly clear. Mia is more than a proper girlfriend. She is the woman I love and will spend the rest of my life with. Brenna, Jeremy, and I will choose whom we will love and whom and when we will marry. And I will continue to run this business and Brenna will become C.O.O. when I become C.E.O."

"What makes you think you'll even continue to be C.O.O? I still lead this company." He crossed his arms over his chest.

Teri handed over the copies of the proxies. "I still have more to learn from you, Father. I'm not anxious to have a stockholders' meeting and fight. I hope we can move forward."

"Forward!" She could see his jaw muscles clinch and release. "I don't believe you have the votes to unseat me, but you know how much I detest public scenes. Especially now with this merger." He stopped and stared at her. "Well done. You've earned the job of C.E.O. I was afraid you weren't ruthless enough. You've proven me wrong. I just didn't expect you to use that skill against me."

He dropped the copies on the floor. At the door he stopped and looked at her. "I hope to hell you've chosen wisely, Theresa." *What the hell did he mean by choose wisely and I am not like you.* Her recent past, however, indicated she was. Teri knew it was time for change. She wasn't sure she could…without Mia.

"What's up with Father?" Teri hadn't noticed Bren walking up behind her. "I've never seen him so angry. He also demanded that all three of us be at the family holiday party. I was hoping to be in Colorado skiing."

Teri had to take several deep breaths before she could answer. "He's not happy, and I showed him that I had the proxies to take control of the business."

Bren's eyes widened. "I thought that was only to be used as a last resort."

She glared at Brenna. "It *was* a last resort." She picked the papers off the floor. "I need a fucking drink." Teri stopped what she was doing. "Bren, sorry. The meeting with Father didn't go well, and I realized that this is the first time I've ever stood up to him and refused to do what he wanted."

Bren gave her a brief hug. "I'm sorry, too. I've wondered what would happen if you ever said no to him. Come on; let's call it a day and I'll buy. Then you can tell me what happened."

Bren had only once asked her to have a drink. It was the night after Bren graduated from law school. Teri had said she was too busy. How many more mistakes had she made in her life?

CHAPTER FIFTY-FIVE

Mia grabbed her cell phone. She couldn't believe how much she was missing Teri. "I hope you're telling me you've left the office."

"I am, but I'm staying in the city tonight with Bren. We're going to get something to eat and drink and then head to her place."

She was disappointed but she wanted to give Teri space. Mia knew all too well how relationships could feel entrapping if you weren't completely committed. As soon as she had felt that, in the past, she began the sabotage process. "I'm glad you're spending some time with her. I'll miss you."

"I'm already missing you. By the way, my parents are having their annual holiday party on Friday. My father has made it a command performance for the three of us. I'm sure Alan and Elaine will be there. Is it okay if I confirm for the two of us?"

Mia was touched that Teri would think of asking. "Sweetheart, I would love to go but an old friend is in New York for the weekend and she wants me to accompany her at some party?"

"You are some other woman's date? Should I be jealous?"

Laughter was Mia's first response. "No. By accompany, I mean, play the piano. Her regular accompanist has a family emergency and had to fly to Oregon. May be gone two days or two weeks."

"You play the piano? I'd forgotten you took lessons with Jeremy. What other hidden talents do you have? Why don't you have a piano?"

Mia was reluctant to answer, but, she was learning to trust Teri. "I had one in Paris and I sold it to a friend. I needed the money. I've got a keyboard I get out and play. My skills are a little rusty but not completely gone."

"Not in your small apartment in Paris? There's hardly room for a full-size couch."

"No, Teri. I lived in a much larger apartment until my mother got sick. My dad's company was very understanding but still he wasn't paid for all the days he was off. I sold the piano and moved to the smaller apartment. I rented out the larger apartment and it paid for itself and I still had money to send to my parents as well as the money from the piano."

"Mia, you are a saint. That must have been hard."

"Yes and no. Natalie, Michel and I had lived at the other apartment with Natalie and the place reminded me too much of her. We bought it together. The smaller place was perfect for just two."

"I hope someday I can be the kind of woman you will be proud to love because I am in awe of you. Now, I'm more determined than ever to marry you. I love you."

"I love you, too. Will you be…." She almost said home but wondered if Teri thought of this place as her home. "Will you be back tomorrow?"

"I'll try. So much is happening right now. I just need to take care of a few things so I can dedicate my time to you and rediscovering your body."

The call only lasted a few seconds longer and Mia hung up. She wondered how she would sleep tonight, alone in the bed that stilled smelled of Teri's scent.

❖

The next night was the same story only she was spending the evening with Jeremy and Elaine. The good news was that the shareholders meeting had been cancelled. Mia could hear the excitement in Teri's voice. And authority. Teri was extolling her victory. Mia was happy for her but would have preferred knowing Teri was on her way to their home.

Wednesday and Thursday Teri again begged off. Mia could hear increasing stress in her voice. She was becoming fearful that Teri was falling back into her work mode. There was an underlying tension that Mia couldn't identify. She needed to talk with her.

Meanwhile, Mia practiced every night. She was familiar with three of the pieces but the fourth provided some challenge. It kept her mind off her other trials. Thursday afternoon she met with her friend, Annamarie Christie, at the hotel to rehearse.

"Mia, you look thin. How are your parents? Michel?"

Annamarie had lived in Europe long enough that she had adopted much of European customs and speech and kissed Mia on both cheeks. She was one of Mia's closest friends and a former lover. The affair had lasted three months. In spite of Mia's obnoxious behavior, she had retained Anna's friendship.

"Anna, you're still as beautiful as ever. Dad's been diagnosed with a serious form of cancer. Prognosis is not that great. Mom's getting better but she has some mild permanent damage. Michel has started school in the U.S. and his English is a challenge. Other than that, life is great."

"My friend, you always had the gift of understatement. Come, let us practice, then we will have wine and whine."

"Your humor hasn't changed." She nodded and followed her friend. Mia couldn't help herself. The Steinway was beautiful and keys responsive. She played some scales and then random passages from the music."

"Stop!" Annamarie's voice had reached the high octaves her soprano voice was noted for. "What is that?" She lifted Mia's hand and pointed to the large diamond ring.

"You wouldn't believe it. It's a long story." Mia knew Annamarie would give her grief, not as much for being engaged, but for whom.

"Give the ten second version. Who? When did you get engaged? And have you set a wedding date? Okay fifteen seconds. Will Liesle and I be invited?"

She took a deep breath and would try to rush through the responses quickly, hoping the name would not draw attention.

"Teri, I finally agreed about a week ago, Christmas Eve and yes, the invitations went out yesterday."

"Non? Teri the Terror Teri?"

No luck. "Yes."

"This will require a whole bottle of wine. Practice first."

For the next two hours, they rehearsed. Sometimes they talked about nuances in tempo or volume marking. They rehearsed individual sections until the voice and the piano were one. Mia was completely absorbed by the practice. Her other life was left behind and she and the music were indistinguishable.

"Enough. You have not lost your touch." Annamarie kissed her on the cheek. "It's one of the reasons I fell in love with you. Now, if you have time, let's eat and drink and tell this story."

Mia looked at her watch. A nurse was supposed to come in check on her father and then a respite care worker was staying until seven. It was only three. "I have time. Who are you performing for? You haven't given me any details."

"Tomorrow night at eight-thirty, I will sing for about fifteen minutes. We can stay for dinner or perform and leave. They will have a small string orchestra performing until then. After I finish, they will set up for some contemporary singer and then dancing at nine. Some rich art patrons. Gott im Himmel. Mia, their last name is Stanton."

"No! Teri invited me to the party but I had already accepted your invitation. This could be complicated. Let's sit down." They quickly placed their food orders with Annamarie on insisting on a bottle of wine. "I keep forgetting how quickly you switch languages. You were in a German opera when we were together and you insisted we speak German. Because of you I became quite fluent. Now, tell me about this invitation from the Stantons."

"A friend called and asked me if I would be willing to sing for fifteen minutes. The fee was outrageous. I usually get that amount for an entire evening. I asked what the catch was. She said it was some wealthy art patrons with too much money and not enough good taste. I reluctantly said yes. The rest I told you. Now, speak."

Mia recounted the unexpected adventure since August and her coming to New York. The time in Maine, the meeting in New York. Even the reaction of Teri's parents to their relationship. She tried to be brief but Annamarie knew her too well.

"This woman must be really good in bed. I have never known you to truly dislike anyone but Teri Stanton could only be described in the most vituperative terms."

She tried to hide her embarrassment. Annamarie was direct and insightful. "It's not just about sex. You know how long it took Natalie to convince me I was worth loving and that I'm a good person. Underneath Teri Stanton's bluster is someone afraid to love and be loved. Just this week she said she hoped she could one day deserve me."

Annamarie's hand was warm to the touch and felt so comforting. "This must be very difficult time for you. If there is anything Liesle and I can do, don't hesitate to ask."

"Merci. Danke. Thank you. I love you, my friend."

"And we love you. I'm so glad you finally let Natalie into your heart." Annamarie again held up Mia's left hand. "And now you have the crown jewel, in more ways than one."

Mia laughed. "Let's say the stone is getting polished and she's beginning to shine."

"Do we stay for dinner then and embarrass the hell out of everybody? We certainly can teach them to do a very sensuous tango."

"That could be a problem. We seem to be asked to leave wherever we tango. Let me talk to Teri. I'll call later tonight and we'll decide whether to come early and be outrageous or come later and be outrageous."

"Ah, that's my Mia. Glad you haven't completely changed."

❖

Once she got home Mia tried calling Teri but she got her voicemail. She left a message and waited. By nine-thirty, her parents and Michel were asleep and Teri hadn't returned her call. Two more times she left messages. The last time she indicated it was urgent. She gave up and went to bed. Tears threatened. This wasn't like Teri to not return her calls. Doubt was finding a pinhole in her heart and pushing itself in. "Can she really change?"

She pushed away the tears and tried to go to sleep. Instead she tossed and turned and wondered if she had said "yes" too soon.

Mia woke to the phone ringing and the morning sun shining in the windows. *Teri!* It was Annamarie.

"You're not old enough to be getting senile. You were supposed to call me last night. Well, are things settled with the Terror?"

"I'm so sorry. I didn't get a chance to talk to Teri and then I fell asleep. And, please don't call her a Terror."

"My dear, you sound perfectly depressive."

Once again, she was on target. "No, I just woke up. What would you like to do?"

"My preference is to spend the evening with you, do our breva performance and then go drink ourselves silly. Liesle is flying in tonight and I plan on ravishing her body. So, I will definitely need distraction until around ten."

Mia was finally smiling. "I will look forward to it. I'll meet you early and we will warm up. I'm looking forward to seeing your better half, so I will limit your drinking so that the poor thing will get some sleep."

It wasn't the evening she had hoped for but her good friends would be great substitutes. Something was going on with Teri. She was fervently praying that this was an aberration rather than a return to previous behavior. Had she made a mistake in falling in love with Teri Stanton?

Chapter Fifty-six

Teri tried to make sense of the pounding on the door, but the pounding in her head was greater. She looked at the clock. "Shit. It's nine. Hold on, I'm coming."

She pulled the sheet off the bed and wrapped it around her. She needed to get some clean clothes. Most of her clothes had gradually ended up at Mia's. She couldn't wait for this day to be over.

"Well," Elaine said, "you certainly don't look as good as you did earlier. Jeremy wanted me to tell you breakfast is here. So hurry."

She nodded and ran into shower. A memory of Mia stepping out of this shower suddenly appeared. Teri felt a tear threaten. "Stantons don't cry, and you're a Stanton." Her father's voice wiped away the brief feeling of emotion. That was quickly followed by the argument she had with him yesterday. "Fuck him!"

Ten minutes later, she was dressed in the outfit she had worn yesterday. She would be forced to go up to the penthouse and find appropriate clothes for the evening. She missed Mia. She needed Mia. The thought of being with Mia had kept her moving forward this week. She would get a few things from her apartment and then have the rest of her stuff sent. She didn't care if she ever went back there.

"That was quite a bender last night." Jeremy poured her some coffee. "You shouldn't let Mother and Father get to you."

"If I remember, you were the one who got angry first." His hand turned into a fist but relaxed as soon as Elaine touched it.

"I hoped their offer for the three of us to have dinner with them was a peace offering. Instead he was in rare form and more obnoxious than ever. Mother was certainly keeping up her end, explaining our lineage and their expectations of each of us. Bren was the only one who wasn't a total waste since she had captured a trauma surgeon."

"True, but that's only because they don't know he worked his way through school."

Teri pushed her plate away. She was no longer hungry. "I'm sorry for being such an ass. As much as I hate it, I now know they're not willing to change. We either force Father to step down or I'm done." She saw the way her brother was looking at Elaine. "What's going on? Have you changed your mind?" Teri couldn't believe her brother would take her parents' side.

"I've accepted a teaching job in California and I'm applying to graduate school to study anthropology."

She hugged him. "Jeremy, I'm so proud of you. You've always loved anthropology. When do you start?" Even as she said this, she felt sadness. She would not be seeing her brother as much and they were just getting close again. Breakfast was more lighthearted as they discussed his future and his plans for a wedding in June. "We'll be there."

❖

By seven-thirty, they were all dressed and having a drink while waiting for the limo. Teri had again forgotten to call Mia. Now, she was in a panic mode, wondering if Mia could or would forgive her. She should have left dinner and rushed to Mia's arms. She would as soon as this dinner was over. She would plead and beg, if needed.

"Limo's here," Bren announced. "Let's put on our Stanton faces and get the evening over."

❖

No matter how much she dreaded the evening, she almost walked out when she realized Shayla Carter was her dinner partner.

The Carter's were old friends of her parents and she had been lovers with Shayla when they were in college. Neither of them were exclusive since permanent partners were the farthest thing from their minds. Shayla had become a wealthy Wall Street trader, bought some top properties in New York, invested in some start-ups. From what little she knew about her at present, Shayla was very wealthy from her diverse adventures.

This was her parents' doing. That she had no doubt.

"Theresa, how good to see you." Shayla kissed her on the cheek. "I was delighted when I received your invitation. It's funny, I was thinking about you recently and was going to call you."

"My invitation?"

"Of course, my dear. To be your guest tonight." Shayla slid her hand up and down Teri's bare arm. "I hope we can make it a long evening."

I just have to survive tonight! "I'll need to leave right after dinner. This has been a long week."

"Of course," Shayla purred. "We've got plenty of time to become reacquainted."

Teri was tempted to say she was taken but, somehow, mentioning Mia to Shayla would be degrading to Mia and what she felt for Mia. She doubted Shayla would understand.

Once they sat down, Shayla tried to play with her thigh, rub her foot, and just be overtly abhorrent. Even Alan, Bren's date, commented. He even asked Shayla to go to the bar with him and get drinks.

"What the hell is going on?" Bren was furious.

"Mother and Father invited her and signed my name. Now she thinks the two of us would make the perfect power couple."

"Why didn't you tell her you're engaged?"

"I finally did, but she didn't believe me. She sees this as the ideal business deal." Teri looked at Bren and then Jeremy. "Please tell me I never acted so demeaning." The silence was all the answer she needed. "I'm not that person anymore."

"We know," her siblings echoed.

Conversation stopped as Shayla returned to the table. Teri sighed and prayed that she could be pleasant. Her father stopping by and speaking warmly to Shayla only made matters worse.

"I look forward to having dinner with all of you soon." Shayla may have been looking at Teri's father but her hand was in Teri's lap. For once, Teri was glad she had on an evening dress. She didn't want to think about that hand trying to slide between her legs.

Someone behind her was making announcements and welcoming the guests. At nine thirty, dancing would commence. She would leave before the dancing started and pray that Mia could forgive her one more time. The appetizers were being served. She would count down the courses until she could leave.

"Who's that gorgeous blonde? I wouldn't mind having a night with her."

Teri shook her head. First, Shayla is propositioning her and then salivating after some stranger. She turned her head to see who the unfortunate recipient of Shayla's attention was. The tall blond woman standing next to the piano began to sing. Teri was impressed with her rich soprano voice. "I don't think the soprano is your style."

"Silly. I'm talking about the one at the piano. She has a huge ring on her finger, but I don't care. Do you think the two of them are lovers? It's obvious they are close. Wonder if the singer shares?"

She didn't know what to react to first. The pleasure of seeing Mia or the anger at the salacious way Shayla was speaking about her lover.

"Mia!" Jeremy whispered. "Did you know that she was going to be here?"

Teri shook her head. Then she remembered her phone. She hadn't looked at it since yesterday. She pulled her phone out of her bag. There were several calls from Mia with the last two marked urgent. She felt like a shit. How could Mia depend on her if she couldn't even take the time to return urgent calls? She turned her chair around. Mia now had her rapt attention. At the next table, her parents were barely maintaining a façade of calm. Obviously, they didn't expect to see her tonight, either. Good!

Suddenly, her father was at her side. "What is *that* woman doing here tonight?" he hissed.

"I believe your staff arranged the entertainment for tonight."

"Just make sure she leaves as soon as she's done." He was just as suddenly gone and back in his seat.

Teri could barely control her temper.

When the music was done, the soprano introduced her accompanist. "I want to thank my dear friend, Mia Daniels, for stepping in at the last moment to accompany me."

"Is there anyone that woman doesn't know?" Teri felt another chunk of her heart lost. Mia stood and bowed, accepting the excited applause. She was wearing the blue dress Teri had bought months ago. *She still loves me.*

Teri turned back to the table. "If you'll excuse me, I have a previous engagement. Good-bye, Shayla. I need to catch up with my fiancé." As she walked past her parents' table, her father grabbed her hand. "Don't you dare leave. You're expected to stay until this is over." His voice was commanding and harsh. "Don't you dare embarrass me and your family and ruin your future by chasing after a piece of tail."

"Good night, Father. I have someone more important to be with. By the way, you'll have my resignation on your desk Monday. Brenna has already stepped into my position." She heard some whispered comments as she rushed out of the room. She didn't care. Fortunately, Mia was standing outside the ballroom talking to the soprano.

❖

"I'm sorry I didn't ask if you wanted to stay. I noticed Teri seated not far from us."

Mia's pace wasn't fast enough for her. She needed to get away from the ballroom and the image of the attractive woman with her hands on Teri. *What was I thinking? Teri could be faithful to anyone or anything not related to work.*

"Liebchen, what's the matter? You're upset. Did you want to stay?"

"No!" Mia stopped. No need to bark at her friend. "No. I'm sure Teri has too many distractions already."

"Well, it appears they're not that important because she is trying to run after you in that lovely dress."

Mia was stunned when she turned around and saw the huge grin on Teri's face.

❖

"It's about damn time you wore that dress. Do you have any idea how many miles I've carried that around?" Teri pulled Mia close to her. She needed to feel Mia's love and strength, to absorb it and to make it part of her.

"I assume this rude interruption must be the infamous Theresa Stanton." Annemarie introduced herself. "I love this woman and if you ever hurt her, you *will* have my German wife to deal with."

Teri stood back to see if Annemarie was teasing. The look on her face indicated it was a promise. "I can't promise to be perfect. In fact, the harder I try, the more I seem to screw up. I'm not the person Mia is, but I hope I can learn to be as loving and strong. So, I hope I can make a few mistakes and still have my life while I'm learning." She turned to Mia. "I'm so sorry I didn't answer your calls. I love you. Let's go home."

Mia hesitated. A seed of doubt had been planted, but it hadn't taken root. Yet.

"Oh, go on," Annamarie said. "I can crawl into bed and wait for that beautiful German and fantasize. Let's make plans for tomorrow. Late tomorrow. Teri, I look forward to knowing you better." She hugged Teri and headed for the elevator.

"Interesting friend."

"Where's home, Teri?"

"With you. Always. The only time I'm really at home is when I'm spending time with you.

"What about your parents? Won't they be upset?"

Teri laughed. A deep, soul-freeing laugh. "No, they won't be upset. They will be furious. That's what this week has been about. And frankly, I don't care anymore. I just told my father that I'm resigning and Brenna is the new C.O.O. and there's nothing he can do about it. But that's not what I want to talk about now. I just want to go home."

"You quit?"

"I quit. I have no doubt that my running out of that place after you will set the tongues wagging. I don't think either one of my parents will ever speak to me again. Jeremy quit and is going to graduate school in California. Bren is doing what she wanted. Tonight, as I watched Jeremy and Brenna and my parents, I realized I never wanted to major in business. I just did what I always thought was expected of me. I don't want to do that anymore. And I'm going to spend my life with you."

"Teri, that has been the only place you've worked since your senior year in college. I don't want you to regret this later and blame me. What are you going to do?"

Teri pulled Mia close. "Mia, I'll thank you for this. I can't tell you how relieved I feel. When I saw you tonight and then discovered that I missed several calls from you, I knew I had let you down. Again. The only light in that darkness was the blue dress you're wearing. That's when I made my decision. If you will still have me, I choose you." She held her breath and prayed. She hoped Mia would choose her.

"What are you going to do then?"

"Once upon a time, when I was very young, I wanted to be a teacher. I may go and get my teaching credentials. I could stay at home and take care of your parents. I can do anything as long as I know you love me."

"I don't know what to say."

"There's only one thing I want you to say. Please tell me that you still want to marry me

CHAPTER FIFTY-SEVEN

December 24

They had spent a whole day doing nothing but shopping for their wedding outfits. Now Mia was finally putting the dress on. Her mother, her sister-in-law, Brenna, and Elaine were all fussing around her.

"You're beautiful, honey. Your father is so excited to walk you down the aisle." Her mother began to cry again. "I'm so happy for both of you."

Words would not come out. Mia grabbed a tissue and handed it to her mother. Finally, she was able to speak. "I love you. Thank you for all you and Dad have done. Now, why don't you go sit down while I talk to my bridesmaids for a moment and then we'll be out."

Once her mother was gone, Mia felt freer to speak. "I can't tell you how much you three mean to me and my family. Especially helping me with my folks and Michel this week."

Nora, her sister-in-law, hugged her. "Mia, we thank you for all you've done. Bless you. Now let's get this show on the road before Tom falls asleep."

Because of her father's illness, it had been decided that Michel and the bridesmaids would go first, then Mia and her father, then Jeremy and Teri. Teri hadn't heard from her parents since the night of the party. Teri had sent her father an invitation, but her parents hadn't responded. She had watched Teri check the mail every day and seen the hope fade with each passing day.

Teri was now resolved to not expect anything more from them, but Mia saw how much it was costing. "Let's just enjoy this time and give them time."

"Yes, as you reminded me. There's a difference between finding time and making time. If I give them time, they might find the time. Eventually, they may make the time. I figured it out, but I'm not putting any hopes on them figuring it out."

"Look at what's in your favor. You're the oldest, you're the first to marry, and you already have a son, or will soon."

That conversation had taken place last night. Teri seemed happier afterward. Mia was determined to keep her smiling. She stepped into the small chapel at the Unitarian Church, following her son and friends, her father at her side.

"I love you, honey, and I'm so proud of you. Always remember that."

Mia felt the tears threaten. She wanted her father to live forever, but she had already learned of the fragility of life. She wasn't planning on wasting one day of his, hers, or Teri's life in regrets.

"I love you too. Always."

Her father walked her to the front of the chapel and sat down. Mia turned to see Teri only a few feet behind her. She was grinning from ear to ear. Happiness was written in her expression, her movements, the way she strode down the aisle. She was wearing a pastel yellow floor-length off the shoulder gown. Mia was stunned. They had argued for nearly thirty minutes about that dress. Teri was determined to get something white, gray, or black. Mia had vetoed the black and Teri had refused the yellow. Now, here she was looking elegant in a color other than black, white, or gray.

"When did you get that?" Mia whispered when Teri stood beside her.

Teri's grin was infectious. "Oh, I found a little time to take the other one back. You're right. When you want something bad enough, you make time. You're also right. It's time to add a little color in my life. And you have."

Mia's heart was full. She could almost hear Natalie whispering in her ear. "Okay, she's not a bad second choice."

"I love you, Teri Stanton."

The End

About the Author

C. J. Harte has lived in many places while growing up, mostly military towns. She was born in New York and still has family there. She completed her undergraduate and graduate degrees in Florida with her family cheering when she graduated with her doctoral degree. They suspected she was a perpetual student and were finally able to breathe a sigh of relief.

The college years were the years of civil rights and anti-war protests. She dipped a toe in activism and was soon immersed in women's and human rights issues: organizing, campaigning, and marching. She developed a passion for equality that drives her today. She discovered there are many ways to share that activism. When she moved out to Wyoming she joined a GALA Chorus and let music speak for her. She is the co-lyricist for the musical "Am I Blue" written especially for The Rainbow Chorus, Ft. Collins, Co.

Words have always held a special magic for C.J. Her parents were great storytellers and she quickly learned the importance of a well-told tale. C.J. now lives and writes from her Wyoming home where she lives with her four-footed friends, looking out at the mountains and blue sky. Each day is an adventure and provides fodder for another story.

Books Available from Bold Strokes Books

Because of You by Julie Cannon. What would you do for the woman you were forced to leave behind? (978-1-62639-199-4)

The Job by Jove Belle. Sera always dreamed that she would one day reunite with Tor. She just didn't think it would involve terrorists, firearms, and hostages. (978-1-62639-200-7)

Making Time by C.J. Harte. Two women going in different directions meet after fifteen years and struggle to reconnect in spite of the past that separated them. (978-1-62639-201-4)

Once The Clouds Have Gone by KE Payne. Overwhelmed by the dark clouds of her past, Tag Grainger is lost until the intriguing and spirited Freddie Metcalfe unexpectedly forces her to reevaluate her life. (978-1-62639-202-1)

The Acquittal by Anne Laughlin. Chicago private investigator Josie Harper searches for the real killer of a woman whose lover has been acquitted of the crime. (978-1-62639-203-8)

An American Queer: The Amazon Trail by Lee Lynch. Lee Lynch's heartening and heart-rending history of gay life from the turbulence of the late 1900s to the triumphs of the early 2000s are recorded in this selection of her columns. (978-1-62639-204-5)

Stick McLaughlin : The Prohibition Years by CF Frizzell. Corruption in 1918 cost Stick her lover, her freedom, and her identity, but a very special flapper and the family bond of her own gang could help win them back—even if it means outwitting the Boston Mob. (978-1-62639-205-2)

Edge of Awareness by C.A. Popovich. When Maria, a woman in the middle of her third divorce, meets Dana, an out lesbian, awareness of her feelings bring up reservations about the teachings of her church. (978-1-62639-188-8)

Taken by Storm by Kim Baldwin. Lives depend on two women when a train derails high in the remote Alps, but an unforgiving mountain, avalanches, crevasses, and other perils stand between them and safety. (978-1-62639-189-5)

The Common Thread by Jaime Maddox. Dr. Nicole Coussart's life is falling apart, but fortunately, DEA Attorney Rae Rhodes is there to pick up the pieces and help Nic put them back together. (978-1-62639-190-1)

Jolt by Kris Bryant. Mystery writer Bethany Lange wasn't prepared for the twisting emotions that left her breathless the moment she laid eyes on folk singer sensation Ali Hart. (978-1-62639-191-8)

Searching For Forever by Emily Smith. Dr. Natalie Jenner's life has always been about saving others, until young paramedic Charlie Thompson comes along and shows her maybe she's the one who needs saving. (978-1-62639-186-4)

A Queer Sort of Justice: Prison Tales Across Time by Rebecca S. Buck. When liberty is only a memory, and all seems lost, what freedoms and hopes can be found within us? (978-1-62639-195-6E)

Blue Water Dreams by Dena Hankins. Lania Marchiol keeps her wary sailor's gaze trained on the horizon until Oly Rassmussen, a wickedly handsome trans man, sends her trusty compass spinning off course. (978-1-62639-192-5)

Rest Home Runaways by Clifford Henderson. Baby boomer Morgan Ronzio's troubled marriage is the least of her worries when she gets the call that her addled, eighty-six-year-old, half-blind dad has escaped the rest home. (978-1-62639-169-7)

Charm City by Mason Dixon. Raq Overstreet's loyalty to her drug kingpin boss is put to the test when she begins to fall for Bathsheba Morris, the undercover cop assigned to bring him down. (978-1-62639-198-7)

Let the Lover Be by Sheree Greer. Kiana Lewis, a functional alcoholic on the verge of destruction, finally faces the demons of her past while finding love and earning redemption in New Orleans. (978-1-62639-077-5)

Blindsided by Karis Walsh. Blindsided by love, guide dog trainer Lenae McIntyre and media personality Cara Bradley learn to trust what they see with their hearts. (978-1-62639-078-2)

About Face by VK Powell. Forensic artist Macy Sheridan and Detective Leigh Monroe work on a case that has troubled them both for years, but they're hampered by the past and their unlikely yet undeniable attraction. (978-1-62639-079-9)

Blackstone by Shea Godfrey. For Darry and Jessa, their chance at a life of freedom is stolen by the arrival of war and an ancient prophecy that just might destroy their love. (978-1-62639-080-5)

Out of This World by Maggie Morton. Iris decided to cross an ocean to get over her ex. But instead, she ends up traveling much farther, all the way to another world. Once there, only a mysterious, sexy, and magical woman can help her return home. (978-1-62639-083-6)

Kiss The Girl by Melissa Brayden. Sleeping with the enemy has never been so complicated. Brooklyn Campbell and Jessica Lennox face off in love and advertising in fast-paced New York City. (978-1-62639-071-3)

Taking Fire: A First Responders Novel by Radclyffe. Hunted by extremists and under siege by nature's most virulent weapons, Navy medic Max de Milles and Red Cross worker Rachel Winslow join forces to survive and discover something far more lasting. (978-1-62639-072-0)

First Tango in Paris by Shelley Thrasher. When French law student Eva Laroche meets American call girl Brigitte Green in 1970s Paris, they have no idea how their pasts and futures will intersect. (978-1-62639-073-7)

The War Within by Yolanda Wallace. Army nurse Meredith Moser went to Vietnam in 1967 looking to help those in need; she didn't expect to meet the love of her life along the way. (978-1-62639-074-4)

Escapades by MJ Williamz. Two women, afraid to love again, must overcome their fears to find the happiness that awaits them. (978-1-62639-182-6)

Desire at Dawn by Fiona Zedde. For Kylie, love had always come armed with sharp teeth and claws. But with the human, Olivia, she bares her vampire heart for the very first time, sharing passion, lust, and a tenderness she'd never dared dream of before. (978-1-62639-064-5)

Visions by Larkin Rose. Sometimes the mysteries of love reveal themselves when you least expect it. Other times they hide behind a black satin mask. Can Paige unveil her masked stranger this time? (978-1-62639-065-2)

All In by Nell Stark. Internet poker champion Annie Navarro loses everything when the Feds shut down online gambling, and she turns to experienced casino host Vesper Blake for advice—but can Nova convince Vesper to take a gamble on romance? (978-1-62639-066-9)

Vermilion Justice by Sheri Lewis Wohl. What's a vampire to do when Dracula is no longer just a character in a novel? (978-1-62639-067-6)

Switchblade by Carsen Taite. Lines were meant to be crossed. Third in the Luca Bennett Bounty Hunter Series. (978-1-62639-058-4)

Nightingale by Andrea Bramhall. Culture, faith, and duty conspire to tear two young lovers apart, yet fate seems to have different plans for them both. (978-1-62639-059-1)

No Boundaries by Donna K. Ford. A chance meeting and a nightmare from the past threaten more than Andi Massey's solitude as she and Gwen Palmer struggle to understand the complexity of love without boundaries. (978-1-62639-060-7)

Timeless by Rachel Spangler. When Stevie Geller returns to her hometown, will she do things differently the second time around or will she be in such a hurry to leave her past that she misses out on a better future? (978-1-62639-050-8)

Second to None by L.T. Marie. Can a physical therapist and a custom motorcycle designer conquer their pasts and build a future with one another? (978-1-62639-051-5)

Seneca Falls by Jesse Thoma. Together, two women discover love truly can conquer all evil. (978-1-62639-052-2)

A Kingdom Lost by Barbara Ann Wright. Without knowing each other's fates, Princess Katya and her consort Starbride seek to reclaim their kingdom from the magic-wielding madman who seized the throne and is murdering their people. (978-1-62639-053-9)

Season of the Wolf by Robin Summers. Two women running from their pasts are thrust together by an unimaginable evil. Can they overcome the horrors that haunt them in time to save each other? (978-1-62639-043-0)

The Heat of Angels by Lisa Girolami. Fires burn in more than one place in Los Angeles. (978-1-62639-042-3)

Desperate Measures by P. J. Trebelhorn. Homicide detective Kay Griffith and contractor Brenda Jansen meet amidst turmoil neither of them is aware of until murder suspect Tommy Rayne makes his move to exact revenge on Kay. (978-1-62639-044-7)

The Magic Hunt by L.L. Raand. With her Pack being hunted by human extremists and beset by enemies masquerading as friends, can Sylvan protect them and her mate, or will she succumb to the feral rage that threatens to turn her rogue, destroying them all? A Midnight Hunters novel. (978-1-62639-045-4)